Praise for *Fin*

With grace and poetic insight, *Finding the Daydreamer* explores the power of imagination and the prescience of the heart. It is a page turner, a love story, a profoundly affecting book.

—Donna Kane, author of *Summer of the Horse*

This beautiful and poetic story is a quick wind moving through the imagination. It arises out of the memory and dream of the obligations to life in right relationship. Its insights both color and cut through the layers of forgetting brought upon this continent, the forgetting brought by control of women, water, land and sky, all the doorways to life. Its clear and vivid images of people moving in the surrounding world of Nature reveal the layers of that obsession, and at the same time they lead the way to the necessity of remembering a better, truer way to be. The brilliant young mother at the heart of the story, the storyteller herself, gives testimony to the insistence and courage it takes to find and live a life of dignity, trust, and respect. In this, she keeps the dream alive of what it means to be truly human, which is to love.

—Stan Rushworth, Citizen of the Chiricahua Apache Nation, author of *Going to Water: The Journal of Beginning Rain.*

The poetic imagery invites the reader to savor every sensory experience as if it were her own. When I find a book I enjoy, I will read it several times, like visiting with an old friend. *Finding the Daydreamer* will become one of those books.

—Laura Emerson, author of *The Delegates of 1849*

Exquisite imagery drew me in, words painted on a canvas captivated me, and the unexpected turns in the story had me on the edge of my seat!

—T.L. Fladager, *Peerless, Montana*

Finding the Daydreamer

by Estella Kuchta

ELM BOOKS, 2020
Laramie, Wyoming

Finding the Daydreamer by Estella Kuchta (aka Carolye Kuchta)
Copyright © 2020 by Elm Books

Paperback ISBN: 978-1-941614-32-7
E-Format ISBN: 978-1-941614-33-4
Print Edition

Elm Books
1175 State Highway 130 Laramie, WY 82070 (http://elm-books.com)

Cover illustration by Irene Suchocki
Cover design by Lottie Patterson
Copy editing by Alison Quaggin Harkin

To Maxwell and Celia

1

NIGHT BLURS THE edges of things, like cold and fear. Blankets and air. Thought and premonition. The ghosts of glaciers came down from the mountains. They drifted into the valley, rippling over the wild grass and fiddling with skeleton leaves in the moonlight. They slit through pine trees, cold as blades, and into the wool blankets where I lay curled around my sleeping daughter. I tried not to wake her by trembling too violently.

I could hear my husband's mood. Though he was a fair horse ride away from me, I could feel his disposition, his temper. The sound of teeth grinding upon teeth is the same as glacier against rock. I listen real close. Northern explorers know the sound of ice can foretell disaster. Perhaps all wives can hear their husbands in this way. It's a great discomfort to know so much, but an even greater one to know too little.

With my cheek on Katie's nest of curls and my eyes wide in the moony dark, his face flashed before me like lightning. Some folks know hatred. Hugh is one of them. They drink it down like some fortifying medicine and check their muscles in the mirror. I could see him devising plans in his head—mapping out the whole Cariboo-Chilcotin region, mulling over the valleys, trails, and mountains, talking to townsfolk, ranchers, and cowhands. He was making a great wide net to catch me up and haul me home. But we'd gone north of Williams Lake—and he'd be sure we were heading south. We'd passed Soda Creek in early evening, eerily close to the ranch.

Now we were camped out in a small wood in an unnamed valley, right where the cowboy had left us. We simply hadn't enough bedding for the lot of us to sleep out. He said he'd return first thing in the morning. We didn't have to say it. We both knew good and well we had detoured around Hugh's ranch a ways back.

I ached with the hope that Hugh wouldn't tell the neighboring ranchers about a reward. It was just the cowboy's luck to get burdened with a runaway woman and a three-year-old girl. The poor Joe. But you can count on the kindness of many to make up for the cruelty of a few. Even if Hugh did put up a reward, he wouldn't be done hashing out the details yet. I imagined him, elbows framing his head on the pillow, having a ripe fit about the poster he'd make. *Humble reward for missing wife and girl. The one's an airhead. Off her nut. The other's a finicky crier. More trouble than they're worth. But they're mine and should be rightfully returned.* He would be thrifty with calculations. He would wait until he was sure of the amount. I'd only left the ranch that very morning.

Night was in motion. Pine branches swatted the stars. Trees wrenched up their roots and tiptoed about in the dark. Stars rolled over and swapped places with the mountains. Clouds set upon the moon. My thoughts drifted. He cannot see us. Not even in his mind. He cannot register my mood. If he could sense things, he might catch our scent in daylight. But night penned him in with his thoughts. Come morning, we'd be moving along.

I slipped an arm behind me to check for the rifle. It was still there. I had tried to sleep with one hand on it. There were grizzlies and black bears waking up from starvation sleeps, one-ton moose ambling along, and all manifestations of cowboys loping about in the Cariboo. But who can sleep with one hand on death? I suppose if you're a cowboy and used to pine needle beds and a roof of wind, you can get a night's sleep snug up against metal, but I had never slept outdoors a day in my life—and I'd never touched a gun. I turned my back on the thing, but only after tucking it real close to the bedroll.

Night folded itself this way and that like an origami creation made of wind and wood and worry. Was I still myself now that everything was gone? The future disappears with the past. I still had Katie. Her breath made small white puffs in the moonlight. I pushed my nose into her curls to smell her apple scent. She was my smallest, dearest friend. Now, we were a team of two.

Finally, a blue-grey dawn unfolded. I leaned up on my elbows to watch. Chickadees dotted the morning with high-pitched incantations. Ghosts of glaciers rose up and faded away, called home to the mountains. Something was calling me too, pulling me to an unknown home. Salmon know this feeling, I thought. This instinct to swim hundreds of miles to something faint and far away and indefinable. That's what I was doing.

The blue spark of Venus pierced the horizon. If I were still at the ranch, I'd be sifting through the stove, hoping to find one red ember so I could start the day's fire. Instead, I stared up at the dented-tin sky and let myself dream about another cowboy. The one who was the only ember in all the ash I'd made of my life.

2

I'VE NOT STARTED at the beginning. Time ties itself in knots.
The middles of stories lead to beginnings. Beginnings loop
through to ends. One can lose their way in remembering.
Months before that night in the forest, a seed was planted. Brush
against the dandelion puff, twirl some helicopter seeds from
maples, add water and sunshine, and up pops a miracle. Seeds fall
inside us, too. Usually, we don't even know it. Only later, when
yearning elbows us do we see that something has taken root.

It began when the beef drive was in full swing. The beds of
our stopping house sank with the weight of a new cowboy every
night. It wasn't a real boarding house. Stopping houses were just
ranches with a few extra rooms for cowboys, a spiffed up barn for
men. Our pens swelled with hearty, cud-chewing cattle en route
down to Vancouver for slaughter. They stood there blinking fat
flies from their eyes, shifting their hooves over clouds of dirt. The
most contented death march you ever saw.

It was a dry October, so the men arrived with dust on bristly
cheeks and a glassy hunger in their eyes. Sometimes they arrived
eager for meager civilization. They sat at the dining table bench
while I poured tea into their cups, and they sighed long with
contentment. Some never fully arrived at all. Those ones fidgeted
like children, ill at ease walled up in a house. They looked out the
windows, listening to something the rest of us couldn't hear. One
thing they all had in common was a shortness of words.

The Cariboo region was chock full with somethings. After so

much beef—roast beef, cold roast, stewed beef—I rather craved a bit of fish. And I rather longed for the company of women. In town, there were always cowboys leaning on fences, tying up horses, scraping mud from horse hooves. Out at our ranch, they were strolling to and from the cattle pens, hoofing a saddle toward a barn or toward a horse. Or smiling weakly, awkwardly, or gregariously at me from the kitchen doorframe with dust, straw, or wind in their hair, and hunger in their eyes.

I was used to the comings and goings of cowboys, so I hardly looked up from the garden patch when three more men rode into the yard with a couple of dozen slow-moving Herefords. I only counted them, and made the culinary calculation as I pitchforked more hay onto the potato plants. Three more men plus Hugh, our ranch hands—Will and Peter—and the five cowboys already staying over. So six more potatoes, a double batch of biscuits, and no leftover roast for tomorrow. Better open a jar of pickles, too. I brushed a sleeve over my sweaty brow.

There was no danger of overfeeding them. Cowboys ate everything put before them. Many of the cowboys who stopped at our ranch were starved half to death. They hadn't eaten anything but a bit of dry bread all day. But my hope of satisfying their hunger was always futile. During the beef drive, I wouldn't even have time to fasten their buttons or sew torn cuffs of shirts. The beds we offered were thin as pancakes. The outhouse was four holes in a board. The shower was a pitcher of water they poured over their own heads after hauling water from the well themselves. And all this was luxury compared to the trail.

As the new arrivals closed the corral gate on their herd, I heard Hugh greet the new men. I recognized the voices of two. They'd stayed over before. Teddy and Louie were born cowboys. Raised cowboys. Their fathers were cowboys. The saddle fit them like a home. They knew nothing else except the weight of hay and sound of padding hooves, the cool white breath from the cows at dawn. Some of our guest cowboys were the ones who simply came upon the cowboy life. They might have come from other countries—like Hugh, from Ireland, the sixth son in a family of eight. They might have arrived in Canada penniless and followed a trail of fleeting jobs across the country until they reached the Cariboo. Poor luckless souls. With hard times hitting everyone, I'm sure they were happy for any work at all. The born cowboys were nice enough, solid folk. But I couldn't chat much with them. Many had never seen a newspaper and still believed the earth was flat.

"Any goddamn fool knows the earth is flat. Can see it with yer own damn eyes. Don't need no book to know that. Books full of stuff that's not sensical. People go believe it because it's written!" That's what Teddy told me when I first arrived on the ranch. Like most born cowboys, he was illiterate. I'd laughed when he said it, then blushed when I saw he was earnest. One might imagine it was the 1530s, not the 1930s. Canada is a strange country. So big and wide that time can't reach all of it at the same pace. Some parts remain humbly left behind. Back in Vancouver, I knew of people who had fancy radios in living rooms with great chandeliers, people who had traveled to many faraway countries and spoke several languages. People who had studied Buddhism, Kant, tea ceremonies, the Moroccan kings, and Arctic explorations. But up in the Cariboo, cowboys collected around the dining table under a single twenty-watt bulb and talked about whether it was possible that Natives spoke a real language.

"I swear sometimes Natives is saying real things."

"Course they's saying real things. But only they knows what they's saying. It's not like real talk. It's just grunts and hiccups that they can understand. Like how birds talk."

Hugh added, "No, that's real talk there. That's their own language. You just don't have the ear for it."

"Hugh's making like he knows something!" The cowboy snickered.

Hugh looked over at Will, our Native farmhand, for confirmation, and so did everyone else. These ask-the-Native moments came around infrequently, but Will was inclined to simply wait them out like bad weather. He filled his mouth with a forkful of mashed potatoes and shimmied the rest on the plate while he chewed. He'd been with Hugh longer than me, and not once had I known him to talk about anything Native. He drifted off to visit relatives on Christmas and other holidays, but those relatives might as well have been on the moon. We knew nothing about his family, his past, or his life outside the ranch. He wasn't inclined to talk and we didn't think to ask.

I left the pitchfork stuck in the hay and went to grab the laundry. By the corral, the newly arrived cowboys were a familiar sight of jeans and scruff. Katie sat near the barn feeding twigs to Chester, our floppy-eared hound, who entertained her greatly by chewing them and then wriggling his large tongue to spit them out. I lugged the washtub outside to do the laundry while the roast cooked and the water boiled for the potatoes. Laundry was my most dreaded chore. The soap was so coarse and hard that my hands often turned red for the rest of the day.

Sunlight glared off the dull metal sides of the tub. I dashed the soap flakes over the water and they melted away like murky snow. The basket beside me overflowed with Hugh's shirts, grey flannel sheets, and Katie's dirt-kneed dresses. I tossed a few items into the tub, pushing down billows of trapped air. I twisted Hugh's shirts until they rained. I pushed bedsheets beneath the surface, my hands disappearing beneath the glare of sunlight. People don't pay enough attention to the stories hidden beneath shiny surfaces. The ocean is like that. I'd spent childhood mere feet away from the ocean in West Vancouver. A great undulating mirror shines back at us when we peer at the sea. Some people are like that too.

That's how the laundry got done. I only half did things in those days. The other half was always somewhere else. That suited me just fine. Hands can scrub clothes, iron sheets, and peel potatoes by themselves. They don't need watching over. Put food in the mouth and the teeth know to chew. The mouth can swallow, and if necessary, can comment politely. Sometimes Katie pierced my reverie with her rolling tears or a firm yank on my hand. But in the five years I'd lived in the Cariboo, I'd hardly touched a toe to the ground. It's a bit of luck. When the beef is tasteless, the feet are achy, and the ill mood of a husband sends a chill, I simply drift away.

So I wasn't watching Katie put Chester's sticks into her own mouth and spit them out. I wasn't paying attention to the cowboys. I had my hand on the rubbery side of the whale in the wash bin, watching its slow rotating eye. That's why I didn't hear the approaching footsteps. *What would a whale say to me, if it could speak? It would impart the secrets of my future with an eye the size of a fist.*

"Drinking water?" said a voice as a pair of boots appeared beside me. I contemplated their pointed tips. The question was difficult. Was the *washing water* drinking water? Did I *need* any drinking water? Did I *use up* all the drinking water for washing? I shielded my eyes with a dripping hand and looked up, squinting at the silhouette standing above me. Did he *want* drinking water?

"Do you *want* a glass of water?" I questioned. I'd never seen him before. His flannel shirt was steel blue—just like a whale. I didn't know his name. Handsome fella, I thought. He smirked sideways, bemused. The question had been obvious after all, but he'd watched me working it over like a dog with a bone. Embarrassment fired up my cheeks. He settled into his stance, fingers in pockets, and basked in the glow of it.

"Yup. If you've got such luxuries."

"Of course," I said. Then to give it more authority, I repeated it. "Of *course.*" I shook the water from my hands and stood.

As a peace offering, he intoned with a smile, "Didn't mean to wake you up."

"You didn't wake me," I retorted. We both frowned at the lie. "Well . . . it's no bother, in any case." Before I could redden further, I turned on my heel toward the rickety door of our lean-to kitchen, extra mindful of the lumps of dirt ready to trip me.

I've talked to women who claim they can read their future with a man the first moment they meet him. One friend professed, "Why, I knew in the first few blinks that he could be my husband because he had dignity and cleverness and he was just my kind of fellow." Another friend reported, "From the moment I saw him, I wanted to say 'yes' to everything!" But I only have curiosity. If I have none of it, then that's that. But if he makes me curious, I'm like a moth moving toward some undetermined source of light. No plan. Just blindly drifting forward.

As if performing a dull magic trick, I reappeared a moment later with a glass of water. The sun was on his face now, turning his bristled sailor's chin to copper. He had an elegant mouth and a charming way of taming his smile. God makes some faces out of dough, but his was carved. He stared at me with sea-grey eyes. Sunlight shone like a medallion on water's surface as I passed it to him. I smoothed my skirt as he gulped it down. I thought to pin down the moment with some charming or witty comment. My head was blank. So I fiddled with the cuff of my sleeve instead.

"Thank you, ma'am," he said, looking rather long into my eyes, which are as pretty and colorful as damp dirt. I simply nodded and hurried the empty glass away. *Magic trick over. Please hold the applause.*

Water, sunlight, and a seed of curiosity. That was the start.

Later that evening, I was splashing milk into the potato mash when he entered the room. Katie wiggled off my hip to hide in my skirt when his tall frame filled the doorway. I still succumbed to holding her though she was over three and plenty big enough to stand. For my part, I placed two fingers on the stove's edge and thus succeeded in not teetering over with sudden unsteadiness.

"I was wondering if you might spare another glass of water, ma'am." It was an ordinary question, but we both knew he had a pitcher of water in his room, too. I dressed up muteness as self-respect and nodded. The water sloshed into the glass. His cool, grey eyes sought answers over my arms and blouse to unarticulated questions. Sensing competition for attention, Katie knocked the back of my leg with a fist.

"Harvey," he said. "Walcott." It sounded like a magic spell. I considered it accordingly. Its enchantments and potentials.

"Annabelle." The name blurted out of me with a silly air of surprise—as if I were hearing it for the first time. I turned toward the potatoes quickly before the pink spawned in my cheeks. Katie looked up at me with a scowl, but I ignored her.

A problem with the cattle came up that night, so Hugh and the cowboys supped late, a common occurrence. I left pot roast in the wood oven and damp clouds of potatoes in the pot while I hurried Katie to bed. She was fretting about sleeping on account of all her nightmares, so I curled up beside her in the narrow bed until her shut eyelids twitched in the lamplight.

Downstairs, a shuffle of work boots and muffled men's voices entered the kitchen. I caught none of the words, but the tone imparted neither disaster nor relief. Chair legs slid over the hard floor. Hugh's curt voice was tense with hunger and exhaustion. Which voice was Harvey's? I strained to listen. *That* one might be his. Softer, slower than the rest, a low purr. I stared up at the slanted ceiling. On the other side, distant white pearls seared through the sharp night air, pinpricks of light drifting from millions of miles away. We understand so little about the science of light, the great reach of luminosity across the heavens. The illumination we seek in another's eyes. The sense of being lit up from within.

The kitchen was dark and empty when I finally descended the stairs. I straightened up and climbed the stairs. A different kind of darkness filled our bedroom. I eased into the bed and urged a corner of sheet away from the shadow beside me.

The next morning when I pushed the lacy curtain aside, I saw only Hugh and our farmhands in the dawn-lit yard. Sometimes cowboys leave at the first peek of daybreak, old biscuits in pockets, smudges of night still denting the sky. Not always, but when it matters, they do.

"How many are breakfasting, Hugh?" I called from the kitchen door to confirm my fears.

The barn door was open, and he was carrying the saddle blanket over to his horse. "Just the regulars," he called back. I creaked the door closed. Fewer mouths to feed. Fewer interruptions to my reveries. I should be delighted. Instead, I folded my arms and stared down at the ugly shape of my disappointment. I arranged the breakfast. By the time the tea kettle was wobbling and whistling on the stove, I'd recovered myself. He would come back. From here to Vancouver was about a two-week journey with cattle. The men had to walk the cattle slowly to keep the fat on them. But the return—with the cattle gone—would only be five days. Of course, other stopping houses dotted the long trail, so there was no guarantee he would return to our ranch. Indeed, I'd never seen him before, though I could tell by his manner that he'd been cowboying a while. I traded disappointment for a wishbone of hope, but it wasn't a clean trade.

When the stove was lit and breakfast ready, I set the porridge bowl on the table and hollered to the men. They came in with a rustle of boots and jackets and the usual rubbing and blowing on fingers. I ladled the porridge, poured the Red Rose tea, snapped kindling into the stove, and set a big pot on it to warm for dishwashing. I bit down on my tongue. I'd forgotten to save a bit of water for the rest of the porridge, the bit I'd saved for Katie and me which was getting rather stiff and thick on the back burner. I made a scene of hefting the empty water pail over to the door while I fished through their jackets for my own.

"You need water, Annabelle?" Will asked, rising courteously from his chair. Peter kept Hugh occupied with descriptions of cow diseases. Sometimes he offered too, but mostly he was too wrapped in conversation to notice.

"Oh." I feigned the usual surprise at Will's offer. "That'd be lovely. Thank you, Will." He smiled; Hugh frowned. Will strolled out the door with the pail.

I suspected Will fetched the water as much to annoy Hugh as

to help me. Hugh thought wives should fetch their own. He took my complaint about the steep slope to the well as a personal insult. "This ranch not satisfying your expectations?" he once interrogated. I shrank a little and said nothing, my usual response to his gibes. Will got gibed at, too, but you couldn't tell from his demeanor. He would keep eating, keep picking at the dirt specks on his shirt, keep smiling at Katie like he hadn't even heard Hugh. Will knew even Hugh wasn't going to scold him for being courteous to me.

When Will returned, I ladled a few teaspoons of water into the pot and began daydreaming about bumping into Harvey in the big city. We were on a crowded bus, and I was holding the leather strap above for balance. A voice from behind me called my name. Before looking, I knew it was him. Sunlight sank into his grey wool jacket as he smiled at me.

A cry ripped open the thought. Katie thumped down on the bottom stair. Her hair ribboned one way and her white night dress another. Morning arrived too abruptly for her. She needed Mother to make it all better. "Mummy," she whined, raising her arms out toward me. She was warm and smelled of sweet caramel and freshly washed sheets. I stepped onto the staircase intending to dress her upstairs before the two of us ate.

"Annabelle," called Hugh, my name cracking like a horse-whip. "I'm culling the big pig today. So ham hock tonight." He spoke with an efficiency of words. It was tiresome for him to communicate with me. He wished I just understood his needs. Sometimes I wished he didn't need to talk to me too. The sound of my name in his mouth was all horsewhips and hammers.

"All right," I confirmed. "Ham hock." I rocked Katie up the stairs, already sorry for the doomed pig. I disliked culling days. Even with the kitchen door closed I could always hear the squealing and screaming as the men dragged it into the slaughter room. I don't suppose Hugh, Will, or Peter were terribly fond of the killings either, but that's ranch life.

When I was little, I imagined I might be a schoolteacher and marry a wealthy sea merchant. But when I was twenty-one, work was scarce, and I was lucky to find any job at all, even if it was teaching for pennies way up in the Cariboo. Perhaps I should have hesitated when Hugh asked me to marry him a year later. But unlike the other two men who'd proposed that year, he owned a ranch. I knew little about him, but Mrs. Adams said he was "good and respectable." In those days, we didn't expect glorious marriages. Hugh was enough. And I was delighted that he thought I was enough for him, too. And screaming pigs could be tolerated when many were eating nothing but stringy raccoon.

3

M ONTHS FOLDED UP weeks, pressing down on days, and making indistinguishable the hours that passed by while I waited for Harvey to return. Either he had remained in the city or, more likely, stayed at a different stopping house on the way back. Meeting him was going to be one of the short-lived pleasures in my life. Like the time I was seven and Father came home to England during the war. I had not seen him in a year, and he embraced me into his onion-scented uniform and told me that when the war was over, we would move out to the countryside, and he would buy me a pony. Six months later his ship was sunk. A year later, Mother moved us to Vancouver instead. No pony. But a bit of beach by the ocean where I could sit and throw stones into the cold grey ripples, daydreaming of a life with Father and a pony. Perhaps I would see Harvey again, but it's foolhardy to wish for luxury in times of scarcity.

It seemed that nothing in the world would ever change. Cattle were corraled, herded, tended to, and butchered. Cowboys came and went. Peter went to Windemere for his father's funeral, and returned with his fourteen-year-old brother, Edwin. Will vanished for two months and then showed up again, casual as day. "Grandfather was ill," he said, while Hugh stared disbelievingly, hands on hips.

Meanwhile, I paced the circles of wifehood. Stove, garden, wash bin, clothesline, back to stove. Katie made her own usual tracks. She pampered Chester with crowns of leaves and scolded him when he ate bugs. She filled her basket with make-believe eggs and made stews of dirt and grass. She fed her doll by the little bench I set up for her in one corner of the kitchen. One afternoon, she became quiet—completely silent—while playing under the kitchen table. When I peered underneath, I saw that she'd fallen asleep on the splintering floorboards.

I scooped her carefully into my arms. She smelled of warm petals and sweet wood. My chest ached with love when I held her. Times like that, I didn't know if she pulled me out of my daydreams or let me pull her inside them. I laid her like a stolen angel upon her bed, pulled a blanket over her, and creaked down the weathered stairs. A small ray of sunlight broke through the clouds and landed on the dusty floorboards. I walked through it, my mind empty, but for the light. Those were the good moments. At the end of my life, they would have counted as the high points, if I hadn't altered the course of everything.

Hugh came in the door with his usual tight, darting movements. He was all coiled springs. "More men came," he announced without glancing at me. "Make enough for two more."

"I'll take out the cold roast, and we can have it on bread before the meal," I answered. He nodded and the rusty spring snapped the door shut behind him. Although the main beef drive would not be starting for several months, habit had taught me to always have extra food on hand. Now, only moments until dinner, I suddenly had two more guests to feed. Could it be Harvey? I blew out that puny hope before it lit a fire.

I rushed the leftover roast to a plate and clunked the tin water pail onto the stove. The men liked to have the chill out of their water when they washed up for dinner. I pummeled the masher into an army-sized pot of potatoes. I extracted two ham hocks from the oven and poured melted butter down their sides. I set the glasses, silverware, and chipped white plates out on the checkered tablecloth.

With a scuffing of boots and a tipping of hats, the men began to shuffle in, our usual three leading the way with the new hired hands and stopovers trailing behind. They were not unlike cattle entering a corral: dusty, uncertain, casual. On the stairway opposite, Katie appeared, sour faced and puffy eyed. Children have the strangest clocks.

"Mummy!" she demanded, holding out her hand. Obligingly, I took her hand to lead her into the kitchen.

And when I turned back—there was Harvey. Sitting at the table with a cat's smile. His eyes fell across my face, but I was an ice block.

My feet marched me over to Katie's bench, where I sat her down with a plate of ham hock, carrots, and bread. A lot of nerve he has, I thought, showing up after I chewed through the leash he had around me. Katie took less effort to disguise her feeling. She was scowling sleepily at the strangers around the table. They would have to do a lot more than slop food on plates to impress her. I smiled tightly at each man as I circled the table with napkins.

When I came to Harvey, I avoided his eyes. He was clear out of luck if he thought I'd muster a smile after his long absence. I turned with haughty indifference back to the stove to clean up. I never ate at the same time as the men. Katie sat on her bench, rubbing the grump off her face. I scraped aggressively at the roast bits stuck in crockery. Chester—with exemplary politeness—lay on the floor and patiently licked his jowls with anticipation.

I wiped the counter and readied the dessert plates. Harvey's eyes were just as I remembered them, like twilight sky with stars. By then, I was certain I'd made them up. I pulled baked apples from the oven and drizzled melted butter over them. My back felt warm. He's staring at me. I scooped the steaming, soft globes onto a white serving plate, and pretended not to notice. And then, as if he was leaning right over my shoulder and into my heart, I knew he could see my disappointment, too. The yearning, the months of frustrated waiting, of wearing the ill-fitting garment of rejection. I set the large serving spoon soundlessly onto the plate.

I smoothed the blue cotton of my dress and turned to face him. He was at the far end of the table. And, yes, he had been watching me, waiting for me to turn. I aimed for dignity and indifference. I aimed not to be swept off the ground by his gaze. He smiled that subdued smile. Perhaps I should have treated him like all the other dusty cowboys. That would have been the good and proper thing to do. The logical thing for a married woman. But I was so hungry for that message in his eyes. Many kinds of logic exist in the world. My logic would never survive practical scrutiny, but it made perfect sense for the soul. The men's conversation was an ordinary, humdrum noise, a muffled quilt of sound. I heard not a word. A blue silence passed between Harvey and me that said everything.

4

THE NEXT MORNING, I awoke when Hugh slid off the bed and stretched in the cloudy light. All our mornings were like this. A downy-blue light on the comforter. Hugh pulling a dark sweater over silhouette-blue arms. And me lying far away in the warmth of whale-blue dreams, watching him from a great distance. How far apart can two people be while in the same room? I watched him without seeing. He kept me in his periphery. There are clues left in absences. Wide-open spaces that speak. An imprint on a bed. The distance between us where our eyes might have met. These things should have sparked my curiosity, but my dial was not tuned to the world. I failed to register grave pauses in the music of mundanity.

Of course, I was thinking of Harvey. Bristled chin. Tiny stars in eyes. That voice like a purring cat. A kaleidoscope of images falling across my imagination. I tried to reconcile myself to the possibility that he might be gone again. And if not gone yet, then immediately after breakfast.

After Hugh left, I put on my most flattering ranch dress— which is like washing up in the cleanest puddle. I peered out the window for signs of the cowboys, but saw none. Downstairs, I yanked the chain on the kitchen bulb. Weak yellow light shooed shadows to their corners. The windows were our wall art, and they framed a blue-grey scene: barn and beasts, grass and garden. I shuffled the stove ashes to uncover some embers and stuffed in straw and kindling. I shut the door and listened to the purr of the fire take hold inside. What did he look like sleeping? Was he right now in the cowboy quarters, warmed in wool blankets and dreams? The door creaked. Where was his dream's gate? I'd walk right on through if I found it.

"Don't mean to disturb you. Listening to that stove song."

I turned abruptly, staring wide-eyed at Harvey. "Oh! I was just . . . daydreaming."

His eyes fixed on me. "Must be a nice place to be. In your daydreams, that is."

I nodded. *Did he know? Could he read my mind?* I shooed the thoughts away and clutched the pleats of my skirt.

He eased his long giraffe legs under the table to sit at the bench. I found occupation by paring apples onto a plate. He didn't shift his gaze off me. I was all fits and starts. My smile was minced with sobriety. My graceful arrangement of apple slices dropped with a clunk on the table before him. And when I was done, I finally remembered to tie on the apron. I wanted him to leave. I wanted him to stay. I wanted to sign over the deed to my desire with a pen dipped in ink made of light. I wanted to speak, but words cinched up good and tight in my throat. I tipped the flour bin and a cloud of white rose from the bowl. Biscuits too begin as puffs of daydream.

"You don't look like you belong here," he offered, still studying me. "Seems like you're owned by another place."

I flinched at his insight. Deflecting the arrow of his question, I suggested, "Perhaps none of us know where we belong until we arrive there." The pastry knife wedged through the butter.

"Could be," he mused. "But some of us belong every place we go. Or else," he scratched his chin, "no place."

Sensing that the arrow was moving too far away, I added, "Well, I do hope you feel at home here." I exhaled, "And I hope you return soon."

With a creak and a wince, the kitchen door announced Hugh. He strode in with a perfunctory "Hello!" and a jolly grin for his guest. Will and Peter followed, unsaddling hats from their heads. Trailing after came the silent and skittish teen, Edwin. A man herd gathered for the feeding—oats, leaves, and wheat. It was horse food, but to prove our civility, I fashioned it into porridge and biscuits.

The conversation was mostly sound and gesture. A ruminating on the crunch of apples, clink of jammed-up butter knife, slurp of hot tea. Then after, a thin crescendo of sighs and muffled belching. Peter and Harvey tipped their head to Hugh to thank him for the meal. As if he'd done real good in acquiring a cook who, incidentally, didn't need acknowledgment of her own. Edwin appeared to be counting dust motes. The day's first rays of sunlight slivered in through the window, setting pale fires to plates, plaid shirts, and chin stubble.

A palpable feeling passed between Harvey and me. How could the others not stop and stare? Hugh was not a jealous man, even when the occasional cowboy looked me over right in front of him, rubbing the sticks of hunger and heat right before his eyes. His provocations to anger were unpredictable, though. He kicked a barn cat who got underfoot in a moment of tension. And once, he broke Will's pipe. Just up and snapped it in half, the context for which I couldn't discern from the filmy kitchen window. I kept caution on my side. I stepped deeper into distraction so Harvey's fire wouldn't redden me.

They left right after breakfast. I did not feel sad when the men funneled out of the kitchen, even when sorrow wilted Harvey's lingering gaze, a flicker about his mouth where he might have spoken if we'd been alone. The sharp edge of loss did not cut me because the space inside me was filled up with dandelion puff, a pretty drift through the sunlight. How could I mourn the loss of him—in that moment—when he was everywhere?

He stepped out with the others and the door squealed shut behind them. For a few moments, I observed them untether their white-breathed horses, let loose the cattle. They mounted and touched their hats at Hugh. Then the morning took them away and turned them into sound. Hoof falls. A trampling and stamping out. The moment froze me in place with a headful of light and legs full of lead. Now, he was gone. I turned to gather up the chinked porcelain, the last pages in the story of a meal. Something sharp and unexpected cast a shadow over me.

5

A GOOD HOUSEWIFE is industrious, resourceful. She can assemble dinner with an absence of food and stitch a quilt without cloth. My skill was with words. His words. I returned to them again and again, fashioning and refashioning them for comfort or beauty or salve for loneliness. I rubbed his words together and made fire. Effervescent sparks riding up and up to the cave of night. From that height, I was poised at the threshold of *was* and *could be*, overlooking the unimaginable, heady with vertigo.

One day scientists will discover that love is measurable and quantifiable, and can be dripped into the body over decades or flatten a person like a tidal wave, knocking them over and tumbling them away from their life. Here it is, the most important element in our existence, and scientists can't press a ruler against it or weigh it on a scale. We know everything there is to know about a lowly stone—its age, the condition of the earth when it was born, the particles it contains. What scientists have learned about love—all added up—amounts to a scant shot of whiskey at a bar.

I ought to describe my long wait for him to return, but it's hardly a compelling story. They say if you wake the sleepwalker, he might go into shock. Picture a woman stopping before a window, wiping dry hands on a dishrag. One day I found my sewing needles in the icebox. Another time, I was wiping Katie's face when she questioned, "Why does the facecloth make you sad?"

One night, I rediscovered the softness of my own hair while unwinding the chestnut braid like a satin stream. Hugh slept with his back to me, sawing into his sleep. Another evening, I wandered out into the twilight. Our mare strolled over to the edge of the corral, snorting steam and nodding. I ran a hand down her nose. We could leave right now. Ride over the hills together to some other place, sharp white wind on our faces. The rhythm of escape generated in hoof falls and panting.

More than ever, I began to dread the moments when Hugh appeared in the kitchen. Had his mood switched? Become more sullen? Or was I just less tolerant? Hugh's not much entertainment for conversation, but at least he's quiet. I'm ill at ease with jarring voices and rowdy leers. Hugh hardly glanced in my direction. If I required a husband's attention to be happy, I would have languished in misery. But as it was, I preferred the privacy of my own world. At least, that's what I told myself. And since he seemed often troubled, I was relieved he didn't unload his worries on me.

Lately the clouds around him had become more electric. And was it my imagination, or did they darken most when he saw me? Outside he still joked with the new cowhands, performing the role of the charming and gracious rancher that I recognized from our courtship. Alone with me or Will, his mood was cold as metal. He passed a lot of time in the barn. I did notice that. It crossed my mind that Edwin, Peter's young brother, might be slowing the work. The boy was willowy like a colt. He should have been in some dusty schoolhouse, but with his father dead and mother long gone, he had to work.

"That new boy slacking off?" I inquired one day when Hugh came into the kitchen.

He visibly jolted. He looked at me like I'd thrown something. "Mind your business," he quipped and exited.

Cleverer wives might have registered something amiss, but noticing requires interest. I followed his advice and attended to my own business. Hugh and I slept in the same bed every night, and every day he became more faded and tattered about the edges. He was hard to recognize. It didn't matter. Did it?

6

A COUPLE OF weeks later, I was slopping a half-hearted dishrag over the breakfast plates. Out the window, clouds unrolled a thin mat before the sun, dimming the keenness of barn, fences, and fields. The cowboy's horses were gone from the corral. Beside me, Katie chattered in sing-song, herding an unlucky spider into a jam jar. Confinement and containment. The jar atop me was not visible, but in that moment I sensed it.

Hugh's container was opaque. Did anyone peek inside and know his mysteries? Not Will. To Hugh, Will was a mild irritant. An agreeable but unloved receptacle for instructions. Not Peter. He'd been treated to the same good-old-boy camaraderie and charm that all the cowboys and cowhands experienced when he first arrived. Hugh jostled him with good-natured ribbings and clapped a hand affectionately on his shoulder. Edwin, the boy, received the gentler, more playful version of these antics. Will smiled on cue for the retelling of Hugh's famous stories, but perhaps for his own reasons. Sometimes he was distracted with scratching Chester's ears or watching the hillside belch out a cloud.

In any case, that was six weeks ago. The fires of charm demanded constantly stoking. I was too much work for Hugh. Will and I had seen this before. When Hugh abandoned the charm, he didn't let the coal burn down slow. He doused the whole flame in one go. One lunchtime, sobriety, abrasion, and distance characterized his mood. He spoke when required. He provided curt direction. His tone was spent. And that's how he remained. He felt no apology for this change, either. If anything, he blamed Peter and Edwin for wearing him down.

In my distraction, I chipped a plate against the metal drying tub. Most of our plates had been damaged—not by rough cowboys used to roping calves and cinching knots, men with hands the size of bear paws—but my own featherweight fingers. A sharp chinking at the edges. A swift severing in the wholeness.

Hugh's mood was different this time. The edges were acrid. It was a faint fishhook, barely perceptible. Something about it. It snagged. I whipped my hands across the apron, front and back, to dry them.

"Katie, wait here," I mumbled to the window.

She slapped a jar onto some eight-legged victim. "Gotcha now!" she sang.

I coaxed my feet into rubber galoshes and slipped out the kitchen door. The spring won't squeal if you only open the door a body width. Clouds like bloated ghosts in petticoats were drifting in from the south, hurrying for higher ground. Despite the galoshes, my feet padded soft as a deer toward the barn. I'm famous for my light step. That's what happens when you've got a head in the clouds. Cowboys remember you for scaring the bejesus out of them when all you do is wander up behind. I touched the lead-grey handle of the barn, and in one swift motion, slid open the door.

Light shocked across Hugh. He let go of Edwin. He let go of Edwin—whose face was a mess of fear. Edwin, who is a boy—a boy, warped with anguish. *Why are their pants down*, I thought or said. Jeans crumpled around their ankles. Edwin's hand moved in front of his groin. Covering it. Hugh wrenched up his long johns and jeans, muttering cusses, laboring over the refastening of his pants. The ground grew weak. My legs wouldn't walk away, even when Edwin, fumbling, gathered up his pants and dashed past me out the door, knocking into me so that I turned and swayed with cold facts, even as the sound of his footfalls running away died off, indistinguishable from bilious wind. Hugh bent over, bracing his arms on his knees to steady reality. Something reached up and touched my temple. My own hand. *Don't believe in this.*

But Hugh found a foothold in the world. He got himself a plan. I saw it land in his eyes. He would erase it—not the mistake, but the witness. His elbow lifted, and he lunged forward with a square-shaped fist. My legs hurtling me toward the house—the thunk-thunk of galoshes propelling me forward. Chester dashed past, barking anxiously. I slapped open the kitchen door and hauled Katie up by her middle, kicking over the jar on my lunge to the stairs. She squirmed but my arms were abundantly strong.

In her bedroom, I closed the door, pulled her onto my lap, wrapped my body around her, listening. Breath throbbed and wheezed in my chest. On the way up, she fought me, but now, with my panting pressed against her, she froze. The arms wrapped around Katie were mine, I saw. There were new rules to the world. Bones and flesh no longer owned me. I could stay perched on that bed, wrapping Katie, and go look out the window. Drift down the stairs, listening. Witness the barn again. And again. Shadows and manure. They were inside me, too. My skin trembled with queasiness. The boy's footfalls fell inside me too.

"What's Father doing?" Katie whispered barely audibly. I had a rough go making sense of the question.

I shook my head. *No, don't ask.*

Outside, a crow blared. Wind snuck up and rattled the tops of the alders. The mare called out. I wished we could get to her and break a full gallop over the hillside. I listened. Minutes ticked on. The kitchen door didn't creak. He had not followed me. What had he done instead? Grabbed the boy? Hauled him back? Edwin, the delicate, skittish. Red stuck in his cheeks like youthful apples. Edwin, just trying to be one of the men. *Run*, I thought to Edwin. *Run!*

I wanted to move closer to the window to look below, but

thought couldn't spur the body. When Katie tried to slide out of my lap, my arms opened like leaves parting in a wind. No resistance. She went to the window and smeared a finger down the pane. Perhaps she was checking that it was still real. In the old world, she wasn't allowed to do that. How could it matter now?

Parts of things stuck out of the mud like landslide victims. Blue jeans wrinkled over work boots. The squareness of a fist. Hugh's one leg lunging forward. The touch of wind as Edwin passed. White skin. When it was safe, I would collect up all the parts and make sense of them. Later, I'd tack the lot of this to the ground. Fix it down.

The kitchen door groaned and snapped. Katie flinched. Yanking her dress sleeve, I got her next to me. We looked at the closed bedroom door together.

Silence called out first.

And then, "Annabelle?" Will inquired. Will. *Not* Hugh. He was staring down at the hole in the floorboards, waiting for our reply, respecting the privacy of the upstairs so much that he averted his eyes. Answering was the good and right thing. But no sound came from me.

"Annabelle?" he inquired again more slowly.

With sizable effort, I stood, moved in front of Katie, and cracked the knob. I was required to speak. I couldn't locate any words. Useless things. I tried to remember the shape of them. The weight in one's mouth. Or was it the throat that felt them first?

"Annabelle? You up there?" he asked, knowing the answer now. He drew the words out, stretching the length to give me a moment.

"I'm here." Deception lives in language. Another moment passed. He was listening to the queerness of my voice, playing it again to find sense in it.

"Have you seen Edwin? Peter saw him run west from the barn. We don't know where he went."

I hesitated. Truth roared through me like a river, and again words were swept away. My fingers gripped the doorframe. "He ran past," I blurted, nonsensically.

Will listened long after the words fell. Finally, he answered, "That's okay. We'll go look."

7

I LOOKED THROUGH the haze of Katie's window until the men were only sporadic, invisible hollers and shouts. My mind went after them, imagining all the places the boy could hide. Inside the hollow of a burned-out tree. Tucked up in the tree roots under a creek overhang. Stumbling through the wild grass. I willed him on.

They didn't return for lunch. Katie nibbled bread with jam and silence. I did not want food, but I ate for Katie's sake. Her eyes were sharp as a hawk's, and she trained them on me. We were not so separate, she and I. Hardly three years earlier we had been one body, moving about the earth with shared emotions. With some fumbling, I managed to thread a needle for some stitching, a good way to avoid her inspecting eyes. Wise children can become dumb adults. Events of the world are idiotic and can't be explained. So we lie. *Mummy's not upset. Mummy and Daddy aren't fighting. There's nothing to worry about.* Children's inborn wisdom cannot survive it.

The rest of the afternoon, I tried to hold the world together. He made a mistake. That's all. That wasn't all. Perhaps I'd gotten it wrong, misunderstood the situation. But the facts were evident. He wouldn't hurt Katie. He wouldn't hurt me. Could I really know for certain what happened out there? I knew men could be attracted to other men. My friend's uncle and his "living companion" shared a quaint cottage stuffed with books on the Sunshine Coast. Everyone in Vancouver knew about the secretive, men-only dance club in the basement of the Sunset Bar. But this was different. Edwin was a boy. An unwilling participant. If I could be reasonable, act reasonably, everything would make sense. Everyone else would act reasonably. Both feet touching soil. Both feet.

The sun was nearing the horizon by the time the men returned, unsaddled their horses, and entered the kitchen with heavy boots, first Peter, then Hugh, last Will. Hugh's movements were slow, heavy. He had other things on his mind now. I was pressed against the dish shelves, blending in with its colors. Katie's hunger-induced tantrum puttered out at the distraction of arriving men. Hugh didn't look at either of us. They hadn't found him. The weight of their limbs told me so. Their silence confirmed it. Will distinctly avoided eye contact. He felt he'd failed. Chester, who'd accompanied them on the search, now took uncharacteristic solace by staying outdoors during our meal. He'd had enough of men for one day.

I set the carving knife, roast, and boiled cabbage before them. An ugly scent. Peter, Edwin's older brother, raised the knife to the meat. He was a taut stockpile of angles—chin and elbows, shoulders and knuckles. He took it all out on the poor roast beef, hacking and sawing away at it with a disturbed dullness in his eye. Hugh glanced sideways at me, keeping me in check, making sure I was doing what was expected. My whitened hands fluttered about the potatoes.

Tantrum extinguished, Katie slumped on her bench, trails of tears streaming like warrior marks down her cheeks. She mouthed the thin strips of beef between cry hiccups. That sound always irritated Hugh. On another night, he might have snapped, "Think you can oil that squeaking already?" And then I would have tsk-tsked her and mopped her face. Tonight, neither Hugh nor I spoke. Katie sniffled and surveyed the world with grief.

But Peter ate heartily. Ripping bread, stabbing beef, thrusting potatoes in his mouth. At the end of the meal, he yanked a handkerchief from his pocket. Then, he picked up the entire half a roast remaining on the table, gave it a few good shakes to shed the drippings, and wrapped it up in the cloth with the remaining bread. When he stood, he knocked over his bench. Katie jolted at the noise. I was plumb out of nerves to shock. He left the bench lying on the floor, hardly noticing the mishap. We all watched as he stood there, glaring at the table. His eyes met Hugh's. Hugh was stiff as steel. No one knew what would happen next, not even Peter. His mouth turned like he was going to growl, then he snatched his coat and hat from the rack. He nodded once in my direction and left. We never saw him again.

And that was the closest anyone came to talking about what happened.

Soon after, I perched on Katie's bed, gently patting her back as sleep overcame her. I did not want to leave her. I lost track of time. The sun fell into the earth's edge, scattered its blood across the bellies of clouds. The kerosene lamp remained unlit. I couldn't pull myself from Katie.

Daydreamers appear harmless. Therein lies the danger. The house may be on fire while the daydreamer bathes in bright blue pools in the mind. The sideboards can crack with flame, the ceiling shriek and collapse, but the daydreamer imagines someone else will intervene. She shrugs at responsibility. She holds contempt for the real world—the mud and manure, the tombstone sky, the shattered dreams of youth. The real world is reprehensible. A brutish tedium. Let mundanity be handled by others. But in failing to partake, her world becomes a true monster.

I didn't know who Hugh was anymore. He had committed a crime, a horrifying and incomprehensible error that drained him of dignity. And the boy—Edwin. Well, he was stuck out in the wild now, surely humiliated to the point of recklessness. I winced when his anguished face flashed before me. But if I'd paid attention to the clues—Hugh's tightening mood, the excessive, affectionate charm he doled on Edwin, the way he snapped when I asked about the barn—I could have intervened earlier. I'd seen the clues but looked away. Why? Because I was a coward, that's why. Because I was afraid to open my eyes and touch the monstrous world with my bare hands.

To avoid provoking Hugh's ire, I eventually returned to our bedroom. Hugh was still doing evening chores. The quilt was heavy as graveyard dirt. Sometime later, the oily light of the kerosene lamp swung into the room. I feigned sleep and watched through narrowly opened eyes. With a solid hand, he closed the door behind him and placed the lamp beside the washbasin. He unbuttoned his shirt and, with punctuation, tossed it onto the chair. A waft of whiskey pierced the room. Then he stood at the foot of the bed, looking at me, hands on hips, like he was undertaking a project and needed time to contemplate its execution. The sudden stamping of my heartbeat overrode the sound of his breath. I dared not move.

He was not sorry. Not sorry at all. Only regretful that he'd been caught.

Do something! I told myself. *Get up!* My ears throbbed. I was dizzy with fear. The bedsheets rustled violently, and before realizing what I'd done, I was up. Terror stood me before him. His eyes were cold, unsurprised. I opened my mouth to tell him that I would sleep with Katie that night—that in fact, maybe I would not sleep next to him again. *I know who you are now*, I wanted to say. But before a word could come out, he seized me by the wrist and bent my arm behind my back. I bit down on the small cry that escaped me so I wouldn't wake Katie. I turned, wrenched, and pulled, but he held me like a steel trap. I pulled and pulled to try to free myself.

In one deft motion, he threw me against the door.

Shocked, slumped on the floor with white pain in my head and ringing in my eardrums, I listened for Katie. There was silence. He stood over me, tightening curled fingers. I glimpsed something in him that I hadn't noticed before. Violence was foundational. This wasn't a lapse in reason. He simply hadn't needed to hurt me before. Now he did. And he would again. I grasped the knob and half crawled, half ran out the door.

I burst into Katie's room, shut her door, and pressed my hands against it, listening. He wasn't following. Moonlight lit the room. Katie lay curled in dream. My skin twitched involuntarily. I strained to hear him. A shuffle of bedsheet from down the hall. My arm ached, my heart slowed its sprint. Maybe an hour or more later, I sat down and leaned against the door.

All night, I watched Katie and tried to understand. It came to me eventually, in the dark hours before dawn. This is an old story. Its tattered pages lay scattered all across the country. Perhaps across all countries. Tucked under mattresses. Patched over ripped nightgowns. Folded like bandage under a scarf where no one can see. This old story says truth doesn't matter. In the wake of abuse, silence becomes the new language. Many are forced to speak it. This old story says there is no story. This old story says forgive and forget. Other women do it. They're doing it right now. So can you.

8

I spent my nights in Katie's bed now. To my relief, she simply accepted my presence without question. The reddened marks on my wrist turned purple then blue. In that short season, I thought hard about my future. Hugh had come undone. I didn't know what he would do next. He was not speaking to me, but now I turned toward his silence, not away. I kept Katie close to me. Sometimes she whimpered in her sleep.

Because work was scarce, Hugh was able to hire new farm-hands within days. The new hire was twenty years old and had the blank and shiny pupils of hunger. He was the son of a rancher whose herd was depleted by wolves and poor grazing grounds. He was taller than Edwin. He was gruff as a war dog, but naive as a duckling. Not inclined to speak. When I asked if he wanted more mashed potatoes or tea, his head simply wagged in a nod. There was an older new hire, too. His nose was rough and red like a bruised apple. Probably a boozer. His unsmiling face and folded arms gave the impression that he was quite done with the world and simply hanging around until his ticket ran out. Hugh typically tried to avoid hiring men like him. Probably he'd up and leave a few weeks from now, when the hankering for booze overcame him.

Two days after they arrived, Will said he needed to head back to the reserve to care for an elderly uncle. He addressed the table when he spoke. My shoulders sank. Will knew. He didn't want to be employed for a man like Hugh now. Hugh sucked the meat out of his teeth, fingers clenched around his knife and fork.

"Well, bloody hell," he murmured, rocking his upright fork on the table. "You'll stay till I find new help to replace you," he commanded, and stabbed the mash.

Will nodded, long and slow, like he was pondering some solid new theory about the world. But the next morning, he drifted away right after breakfast. Gone, without a goodbye. Hugh didn't even realize he wasn't with the cattle until lunchtime. None of us noticed him leave.

A few days later, Hugh went to town and put out word for a new hire. People would say it was bad luck that Hugh was losing three of his crew just when the heifers were starting to calve. Bad luck that some kid up and shot off into the wilds. *Bad luck hitting lots of folks*, they said. *Lady Luck's got a bone to pick with us*, they said. *Well,* they said, squinting in the cool glare of sun, *She's picking the wrong bone!*

My entire life was contained within Hugh's. Our marriage tethered me to the Cariboo. His ranch bought the food I ate and the clothes I wore. His cattle and horses and cowboys delineated the hours and minutes of my days. His reputation, by default, was my reputation. I wore his name. Our child wore his name. If people knew what had happened, they would level half the blame on me. Why hadn't I satisfied him? Why hadn't I known and prevented it? But if the situation were reversed—if it was me who abused a child—they would say, poor Hugh. A good guy, but that no-good wife should be shot and put down. Poor fella.

There was no way to untangle myself from Hugh and his wrongs. This creaking shack of a house was his ship, and if it sank, so did I. I also knew this: I was incidental. Hugh's acquisition of me came with as much commitment and practicality as the purchase of a tractor. A wife was a necessary feature of his ranch. Half a bed and three meals were all she needed, and in exchange, she'd work dawn till dusk every day of the year. And what alternative would she have? The convent? Spinsterhood in her parents' home with disappointment settling like dust? If times weren't so lean, perhaps she could eke out a living of her own and afford a shoebox home, chilled with loneliness. That had been Mother's life with me.

These dilemmas churned inside. Other questions lurked farther below, but I wouldn't look at them. Uttering some questions, even to ourselves, will beckon the most malevolent answers. By asking myself the hard questions, I could avoid the impossible ones: *What else was Hugh capable of? Had he done this to others? What would stop him from doing this again? And Harvey. Where was he when I needed him? Could a man like him hide monstrous secrets, too? How could I be certain of any man? Could Hugh hurt our daughter the way he hurt Edwin? Could he murder?*

Stoicism, I considered, one sleepless night in Katie's bed. *That would be Mother's priority.* I'm expected to continue onward, bearing the weight of the family like a great marble pillar, not collapse into grief, self-pity, and anxiety. I should rise up to the challenge like Mother's friends. Like Ethel—who worked as a seamstress and a maid to care for her seven children when her husband returned from war, eating dirt and chattering to himself in the rain ditch. Or like Martha—who carefully glued and reglued the broken vases and plates when her drunkard husband returned in a rage. Or Mother—who at fourteen years old assumed all the duties of her mother when the latter took to her bed with terminal grief about the condition of life.

But I am not stoic. God makes stoics out of river stones, but I'm made of dandelion puff and May breeze. I couldn't continue on in this life. But what choice did I have? My throat tightened when I imagined revealing the truth to someone—anyone. And who would I tell? Hugh was well-known and liked around these parts, while I was still a newcomer. People would laugh ridiculously or shake their heads in distaste at my sordid tale.

The boy wouldn't go to the constables. The two of them roamed the region in Stetson hats and broad belts, concerning themselves more with trapping licenses and pocket crimes. A murder would whip them into a froth of excitement, but a tale of this sort turned men cold. I'd seen it before. A year prior, a boxer stayed over with us for a week while on tour of the rings from Vancouver to Barkerville. Unlike the cowhands, he could yackety-yak till the moon rose and cows started snoring. Well, one dinner he started on about a conversation he'd had in a bar with a Native man.

"No joke, this fella starts spilling stories faster than the bartender can pour. Says first his niece and then his nephew were taken away to the Indian School. He says pupils get summoned to the priest's private quarters every week, and he lays down with them like they're wives. Says he'll off and kill their families if they speak of it. Reckon it! A white collar and some poor sap Native kid!" The boxer, full of wonder, slapped his knee and laughed over the crackling silence of the others.

"That sort of yarn has no business at the dinner table," said Hugh, steady as steel.

The others, Will included, mumbled or nodded in assent. Some things were too unfathomable, too distasteful, even for yarn weaving. It's no wonder that evil takes hold of the world. The rest of us shrug it off as tall tales.

The Royal Canadian Mounted Police served as a useful secondary plan if self-styled law proved insufficient. Citizens' primary security came from the confines of expectation—from appearances and cordiality, the pressure to act like the rest of the Joes. That meant a whole lot of tipping of hats and not stepping on toes. That's why a man with a black eye "stepped on a rake," and a runaway child always "went bonkers." Easy answers covered hard truths, like broken glass beneath a layer of freshly fallen snow. And Hugh—if he hurt a boy like that again—would be more careful not to get caught.

I rolled over, tightening the crisscross of nightgown, sheets, and quilt, cheek tickled by Katie's curls. Soapy moonlight cut silver squares on the floorboards. I remembered waking in the early light of morning when I was a little girl. My father said goodbye to me the night before because he would be off to war before the crack of day. But I awoke anyway. I heard the front door open, and rushed to the window to watch. Mother stood on the step below me, waving brightly. He turned back to wave several times as he sauntered down the dark, cobbled road. I pressed myself onto the steamed-up window, aching to go with him—my chest near bursting with yearning. When he rounded the corner out of sight, sobs huffed in my throat.

I couldn't bear it. I slipped back into my bed and forced the gasping away. *I will go with him*, I promised myself. I closed my eyes and made it so. I ran behind him. He was aghast to see me on the lamplit street. But surprise slipped into sweet joy as I slipped my hand into his. The youngest child ever to go off to war. He used to carry me on his shoulders when I tired of guns and bombing. We played games together and laughed in the trenches.

Outside Katie's window, clouds migrated over the moon, blotting out the light. Thunder boomed in the distance. The house was quiet, but for the creaking of cold. For days, I'd prevented myself from thinking of Harvey. Now the thought of him overwhelmed me. I blurred over with tears. Where *was* he? Where was anyone to help me? To protect Katie and me? Why could no one hear the plea in my heart? It was so urgent, I grew weary from the sound.

My grandmother, a bitter Catholic, used to say when women complained of their husbands, "Better the devil you know than the devil you don't." I hated those words. I hated the smallness of that thinking. If I'd had any money at all, I could have gone somewhere—Vancouver or Kamloops, or booked a passage back to London. Damn our reputations. I could live with the tarnish of "divorcee." Mother was in London. I wished she were still in our cottage in West Vancouver. Although she wouldn't understand or forgive me for abandoning a husband, at least she wouldn't turn me away. But she moved back to England three years ago to live with her ailing sister.

If I left, a cloud of rumors would kick up in my wake. *Must be chasing a man. Too frail for the Cariboo life, anyway. Stole that poor girl right out from under her father.* Leaving would mean the very real risk of hunger and homelessness. That's why women don't leave. Our vows said forever. Forever is an eternity in some marriages, but might be a few short weeks sleeping on the cold streets.

Outside, lightning's flashbulb whited the room. Thunder's feet stomped the earth. Wasn't hunger in the belly better than emptiness in the heart? A life drained of life? Constant vigilance to protect daughter and self? The false judgment of others instead of the moral decay of one's actual life? And perhaps—if fate or God willed it—I would even find Harvey. Surely, if he knew, he would come rescue us. Surely. One last snap of lightning shattered the rain from the clouds. The chattering drops fell over the dark earth. *Why couldn't Harvey hear me?*

9

WHILE HUGH AND the new hires were soberly chewing breakfast biscuits the next morning, I mentioned to my husband that I was fresh out of laundry flakes and salt.

"I will need to go to town today to buy more," I said, while busying myself with a tub of dirty potatoes. Custom demanded that I ask permission. Since the incident, I'd been overly occupied when he was around, snapping the knife through radishes, snapping the dried sheets to straighten them, snapping at Katie to stop sitting in mud. I did this to avoid his watchful eye. He was checking me. What would I do next? Would I reveal him? Ironically, his nervousness was reassuring. *If no one would believe my story anyway, he wouldn't care who I told*, I reasoned. His vigilance was slackening. If I hadn't run to town to expose him immediately, perhaps I never would.

He finished chewing before speaking. "Road is slick as a pigsty," he uttered.

"Yes, it's just I should have gone yesterday, or the day before. I'm completely out and Katie has not a shred of clean clothing."

"Well," he acquiesced, glancing up at me, "then go to town." His tone said what the words could not: *Watch yourself.*

"I'll go after Katie eats." Unlike most children, Katie slept late and awoke blurry-eyed. On this particular morning, I was relieved she was still in bed. Children often notice what husbands miss. By the time my trembling hands scrubbed off the last of the potato dirt, the men were finished eating and heading out to their morning chores. I poured the last of the tea for myself, first spilling on the counter, then bumping the cup against my tooth.

I had a plan. By temperament, I'm about as organized as an April wind. But this time I had a plan. Hugh kept all his savings in a pouch in the wooden chest in our bedroom. It wasn't much, but I'd already counted and it could buy train tickets to Vancouver for Katie and me. By the time we arrived, I'd have three cents to my name. Not enough to use a phone booth or take a bus. As a last-ditch effort to save money, I'd swing past Edison's Market and ask Ed if he knew anyone driving south that day. If not, we would use up the money for tickets, spend a night in the Vancouver train station, and the next day make our way—with a kindly truck or ferry driver—to West Vancouver. I could knock on the door of our old widowed neighbor. Or the family home of my childhood friend, Betsy. And then, with a heap of luck, perhaps a job and a place of our own. New life. And if not . . . well, it was better not to think about if-nots.

Vancouver was a good three hundred and seventy or more miles away. Impossibly far. But people made their way by train or truck every day. It was a full day and night of travel. My thoughts of Vancouver kept slipping back to the Cariboo, like magnets repelling each other. "Start with one foot," my mother used to tease me when I was slow to go out the door as a girl. "Just start with one foot. Left or right. No need to consult the premier of the province about which one. Just put it down, and then the other." Katie came down the stairs looking like she'd survived a hard wrestling match with sleep. I scooped her up and marched straight back up the stairs.

"Today we're going to town." I pitched a cheery voice over my nerves.

"I want a lollipop," she announced.

I rifled through her chest of clothes for something warm, presentable. I pulled the strings at the nape of her night dress and plucked it over her head. While she ate, I would have to grab some of her clothing and stuff it in a sack. The difficult part would be getting the sack of our belongings out to the truck without anyone noticing. Where would Hugh and the farmhands be by midmorning?

Katie's voice sounded like a meowing cat. She folded inconveniently into a crumple of complaint. I pulled the dress over her mop of curls. Pink arms poked out, followed by worried face. What would I tell her? How would I explain? When she was grown, would she understand and forgive me for leaving? The enormity of the question made me light-headed. I buttoned her up.

Once she was fully outfitted, in a yellow cotton dress and robin-blue pullover, I popped her onto my hip and hurried toward the stairs. Was it truly best for her? To escape from her own father? Her face sank into my shoulder with great weight and a long cat's cry came out.

"Mummy! You're not listening to me!"

Perplexed, I tilted my head to scan her face, searching for clues. What need had I not heard? Her need for her father? For this home? Could she read my mind? "What do you want?"

"A LOLLIPOP!"

She had been repeating the request while I dressed her, but only now did it take shape in my mind—a flat, lemon-yellow candy on a stick. "Right. Right. A lollipop. Yes, you can." Then to reassert my motherhood, I added, "But do not forget your manners."

Downstairs, I slopped sugared porridge into a bowl for Katie, rifled the breakfast dishes through clouds of steaming dishwater, slapped together some sandwiches for the men and for us, and then ran upstairs to stuff our clothes into a canvas sack. The bag was tight with clothing, but I managed to squish in my prettiest scarf and hairpins, in case. A few hours into the morning, Hugh stuck his head through the door to say they'd be out in the west pen for their lunches.

This meant—luckily—no one was around when I carried our sack to the truck. But—unluckily—I'd have to drive right up to the men in the truck with my hidden sack stuffed behind my seat. If Hugh needed to tell me anything, he would come right up to the driver door and I'd risk him noticing.

I thought of this when I tried to push and cajole the sack as far as I could behind my seat. Luckily it was the color of dirty hay and blended in with the grubby floor of the truck. How foolish to leave my suitcases behind—one of the only valuable things I owned—a gift from my mother when I'd left for the Cariboo. But they couldn't be hidden behind the seat backs.

Finally, it was time. We stepped into the yard muck in our galoshes. I lifted Katie onto the passenger seat. She liked trips in the truck and trips to town all the more so. The men's cold roast sandwiches sat on a plate between us on the vinyl seat. Ours were wrapped in a linen. With a formidable clunking of metal, I pushed Katie's door closed and skipped around to mine.

I did not glance back at the ranch's sag of wooden bones, asphalt cap, and flecking green paint. I'm not nostalgic for houses. But Chester came up to the truck with a lazy wag and an eager query. Sometimes I let him come to town for the ride. I bent to pet his auburn fur, but when my fingers touched the softness, a gasp of grief tightened in my throat. I stood up quickly. "Shoo now!" I told him. He looked at me like I was making a joke and he was waiting for the punch line. Tongue out, smiling. "Shoo!" From sheer politeness, he took two steps to the side, half standing in a puddle. He didn't believe me, wasn't convinced that I really wanted him to go.

"Sorry, Chester," I whispered, and heaved myself up into the truck.

A moment later, the engine roared with promise, and Katie and I were bumping down the road to a humble orchestra of seat springs and crunching rocks. Katie looked out the back window. Involuntarily, I glanced in the rear view mirror. Chester, still bewildered by my strange goodbye, was resigned to his station beside the house.

"Bye-bye, Chester," Katie called forlornly.

The great machine bumped and swayed beneath us as we bounced along. Wheels and road spoke a loud and garbled language. A wacky babble of progress. Its omens incoherent. My foot was heavy on the gas pedal despite my better judgment to slow down. The passing forests gave way to the hay-green meadows, and I cut off the main road onto an even lumpier one. By the time we rolled to a stop on a slight rise in the meadow, I was shaken good and through like soda in a bottle. Twenty feet away, one of the hires hunched over a coil of barbed wire. The other held it to the post, and Hugh pecked a determined hammer against it.

In the pocket of my brown wool coat was the three dollars for laundry soap and other groceries. In the bottom of my boot was thirty-five dollars I'd stolen from Hugh's tin box. I left fifty dollars for him. His only savings. I needed to leave him, but I couldn't bring myself to hurt him. Indeed, anguish and fear were laced with guilt. It wasn't exactly stealing, since we were married. But the pit of my stomach knotted all the same. After all, if I'd been enough for Hugh, maybe . . . Maybe I wouldn't need to run away now.

He set his hammer atop a post and made toward the truck, wearing a workaday face. *I'll just quit thinking,* I figured. *Can't read my mind if it's blank. Blank. Blank.* The hires stood in their layers of jean and flannel, surveying me with dim interest. Not much happened in these parts. The arrival of a deer would have compelled their attention for a good many minutes. But I made myself dull as stone. An empty tin.

I winched down the window, pried Katie's hands off the tray. She flopped aggressively against her seat, grumbling over the injustice of handing it over. A perfect distraction. I admonished her and passed the tray to Hugh.

"What'd you bring?" he questioned.

"Roast sandwiches." Of course it was roast. What else would it be? All we ate was beef. He was checking my temperament. "With Jim's mustard." His favorite.

He lifted the cloth to verify it, then lowered it. His mouth tilted down, approvingly.

Katie thumped dramatically against the seat back. A child's way of dispelling tension is to provoke it. Hugh looked away, making space between him and his daughter. His eyebrows peaked in worry then flattened again. He didn't like what he couldn't control, and that included Katie.

After I handed over the teapot, he returned to the men. The young one perched on a stone nearby, staring hungrily at the tray. The older one raised a palm in thanks. Then they both tipped their hats. I saw my hand wave back at them.

The engine rumbled alive. I looked over my shoulder to back up, as Hugh had taught me. We pulled away, leaving the men on their rocks, chewing away at their own private thoughts. Ahead of us, the wet road bent into the forest beneath a tin-grey sky.

That was that.

10

HUGH WAS RIGHT about the road. It was dented with puddles and littered with broken branches. Conifers leaned over top as the wheels squelched and slipped on the greasy mud. A doe and two spotted fawns stared at the absurd metal animal clambering toward them. Their wide ears twitched as we sloshed and skidded nearer. With elegant heads held high, they sprung into the woods. Even in fear and flight, they were graceful, composed. My damp hands gripped the steering wheel.

Much later, the noon sun defeated the morning's clouds. We winced at the glinting light on puddles. Halos of steam rose off cattle in the holding corrals. Finally, the trees opened up to a smattering of civilization: the Williams Lake bank, hardware store, courthouse, and train station. Never mind that the bank hadn't enough cash to fill a potato pot. Never mind that the courthouse only saw hat-ringing drunks and permit-violating trappers. But the hardware store was something every man in the region came to admire. All the latest in tractor ploughs, saddles, winches, axes, potato seed varieties, and other widgets of metal and leather. Past those structures sat Edison's Market, its red clapboard aglow with sunlight. Before cashing my bootful of cash for train tickets, I'd go inside and talk to Ed.

The truck grumbled to a halt in front. I left the key in the ignition. No one was daft enough to steal a truck. Everyone knew it was Hugh's. No one even stole milk from doorsteps, though many were hungry. Katie pranced along the wooden sidewalk. Smallest feet make the loudest sounds. We stepped out of the glaring sunlight into the cool, dark shade of Ed's store. It smelled of molasses, spice, and wet floorboards. Ed was wearily slumped over on his elbows, eyeing the newspaper. He unlooped the glasses from long ears.

"Mrs. Darcy!" he announced brightly. He liked me. And he was an observer of life, not a judiciary. He had a wife once, so I heard. But she died many years ago when her horse reared at a bear and flipped her onto Heaven's doorstep. Bears seldom attack horses or people. "But the *fear* of the bear," Ed told me one day, "that's killed many a man."

Ed pulled up the paper and began caressing it into folds. "How wonderful to see you! And you, too, little Miss Darcy." He leaned over the counter and gave Katie a wink. Her pretty rose lips wilted in a frown.

"Good afternoon, Ed. Don't pay any mind to Katie." I wouldn't tolerate her rudeness when I was about to ask a favor. I felt a knock on the back of my leg where Katie's small fist rapped me. For a three-year-old, she packed a lot of pride.

"Real shame about Hugh's team. Will mentioned it." He shook his head glumly. I held my breath. "All those heifers ready to calve just when he's lost his boys. A shame it is. A devil's ride. You don't want the ticket, but now you owe the fare."

I exhaled, "Indeed." A pregnant pause followed. Katie had a hold of the folds of my skirt with both fists.

Ed was rolling now. "Old Jameson's on that bad luck train, too. Went to Vancouver last month to find a wife. Came back reeking of hooch. Vapors coming off him strong enough to tip a bull. 'Whiskey don't work like cologne,' I told him. 'Can't attract a wife like that.' Anyways, while he was gone, his brainless brother left his only heifer in an open pen. She went and fell in the creek. Drowned. Couldn't get her hooves out of the mud."

Katie's fist knocked me again, impatient for her lollipop.

Ed mused, "I guess ranching life ain't all the glory and fame it's cracked up to be." The arrow shot toward humor—and he chuckled to prove it—but landed in resignation. "Even the toughest among us need a bit of the spirits to soften up."

This old conversation again, I thought. I must have been the only citizen who didn't have a shred of care about prohibition. Everyone else seemed ever poised to debate the nation's dryness, ever hunting for an opportunity to win support for their view. Ed, however, used the topic as a conversation starter. Get someone riled about prohibition and soon they were passing an hour in the store. He already knew my views on the subject—perfect indifference. The province had long since voted against it but maintained the rules against selling hard alcohol in public. Yet he broached the subject every time I stepped inside. In past times, those exchanges had been a welcome distraction from the chortling of truck engines and farting cattle. But time was urgent today.

Katie gave three hard tugs on my sleeve, a child's Morse code. I lifted her onto the stool. Ed, registering her intent, lifted the lid of a great glass jar. After performing a most sober selection, he handed her a lemon lollipop—her favorite—as if it were delicate as a glass slipper. I sent her outside to sit on the steps.

I looked at my folded hands. The words blundered out all at once: "I'm leaving Hugh. The ranch. I'm leaving today for good. He doesn't know. I have to go, Ed. I have to go." My bluntness surprised us both. Pain pressed the back of my eyes. I swallowed it. "I need help, Ed. I need *help*."

Ed's face contorted with bewilderment. He scanned the counter, the store for reason, before his eyes settled back on my face. He couldn't figure it. How could I leave my life? That's like saying I'm all done with my skin or going nameless. Life narrows in on us, creating a tighter and tighter maze. Many folk, like Ed, just adjust to the smallness. They just move less and less. And one day, they move no more. Even the heart is too squished to sound.

He gulped audibly and cleared his throat. "But—*where* will you go?" he asked. As if leaving meant strolling right over the brim of the earth into a cavern of stars. I cringed.

"The train. Taking the train. Unless—I can—I can find another way." *Slow down and make some sense*, I warned myself. "Ed, you've always shown me kindness. I only have enough money for a train ride, no more. So I thought, that is, I thought . . ." The words didn't want to come out. I had to push them and they fell over each other in a mess. "If you know someone. A driver. Someone who could give me a hand. A ride. To go south. Perhaps."

A puzzle of wrinkles wove between his eyebrows. "But, Hugh—" he began.

I shook my head stubbornly, and we both stared at the counter.

Ed ran a worried hand down hollowed cheeks. "No, ma'am. No." He tapped the counter with his fingers to emphasize. "No train today. No drivers. There's a slide on the road. Road and rail—wiped out."

"No," I blurted. "We're leaving. I have to leave." I felt it—I was going today. Ed was wrong.

"I was going to say it next," he continued. "Tell you about the slide. Felled half the mountain near Runner Creek. No trains, no cars, no buses. Mayor Bradley was out this morning rounding up men to shovel it clear. But," he pursed his lips, "maybe you could go north. You have a truck, no?" The rain the night before cracked open the sky with a biblical drenching. I should have considered a slide.

"It's Hugh's, of course. I can't take it. And north is the wrong way."

"Nope," he continued. "Only way out of here is to head north to Barkerville. But—mail truck and merchants all stuck on the other side of the slide. Only people I know going that way are a couple of cowboys." He was thrumming his fingers on the countertop. "Probably already gone."

"Please—we'll go with the cowboys then. We will!" I could contemplate the wisdom of that choice when I was safely out of town.

"But they're just dusty roughnecks on horseback. I couldn't see you and the girl bumping along the cattle trails like that."

"Please, Ed. Please see if they're still here." I was sure I could find my way back to Vancouver, even if it took a couple of weeks. And besides, one of those dusty roughnecks might even be Harvey.

He looked at me like a remorseful father. I hoped he wouldn't scold me. I couldn't bear it. "Well, I'll see if they're still at the bar. It's an awfully big risk you'll take." He paused and a puff of breath escaped him. "I hope you know what you're getting into."

"Well, I don't. But I know what I'm getting out of, and that's more important right now." A horse, some cattle, and a trail. That's about all I could imagine. "I'll be forever grateful, Ed. I won't forget your kindness."

His shoulders softened with pride, and he sighed like an old horse. "Okay. Okay. Wait here. I'll see what I can do."

I heard someone greet Katie out in front of the store. What if she was speaking to Harvey? I held my breath. Strange things happen when daily life breaks open. Destiny rushes in. I set a hand against the counter to steady the dizzying. If it was him, everything would make sense—the long lonely wait, the ruins of my marriage.

But outside, the face that greeted me was just a cowhand from Moose Head Ranch. His sloping eyes settled on me with thirsty interest. The voice of imagination likes to imitate the voice of intuition.

"Ma'am," he said crisply, rocking forward on his toes.

"Oh, hello." Disappointment caught hold of my voice. Therein began one of those long rambling talks about nothing. Bird speak and chattering. Up in the heady blue sky, my thoughts reached out for Ed. Katie tucked a pudgy hand in mine, an anchor.

A lifetime later, the cowhand sauntered off to buy fish tackle. I sank down onto the step with Katie. She unplugged the frayed and soggy lollipop from her mouth. We were hungry. My bones were too heavy and my head too light to fetch the sandwiches from the truck. I removed my jacket, and the sunlight fell inside me.

11

I N ABOUT AN hour, Hugh would expect me to bring a pot of Red Rose tea to the field. If I didn't show, he would believe I'd been held up in town. *Too much gossiping around,* he might tell the others. But a while after that, the men would arrive at the house, worn out and weak with hunger, expecting a steamed-up kitchen and hot supper. I wasn't fretting over Hugh's hunger, though. There was cold roast and mash in the icebox. I was fretting over his wrath.

If the local priest wasn't quaking with morality and finger shaking, I might have gone to confession before leaving town. Probably not. Mother and I had been Protestant before we left England, but religion washed off with the salt air when we crossed the Atlantic. Back in London, one stepped off the cold cobble streets into the kaleidoscope of stained glass and celestial archways of a church—and just like that—they believed in God.

But up in the Cariboo, churches were clapboard boxes smaller than barns, and not much prettier. The real cathedrals were outdoors: forests nestled between mountains so tall, they ripped holes into Heaven. Gold light spilled down from formidable clouds onto the shiny-backed crows. Awe and glory. Even Hugh didn't bother with church in this country. But I'd seen him stop in the middle of chopping wood to admire a raven gliding overhead.

Time is an unequal thing. I lived whole lives waiting for Ed to return. Then what happened next—flashed—and was done. Ed appeared in the door behind us. I grabbed our things from the truck. He told us to take the trail behind the store heading north. A little ways up, we'd meet a cowboy with an extra horse.

"Oh, you'll get me in some royal trouble, if anyone finds out that I helped you." He pressed his lips to prevent his other thoughts from spilling out. "Better hurry now. And take good care of that little miss."

"Thank you, Ed—" I began, resisting the urge to hug him.

"All right, all right. Just get on your way." He waved us off.

The mucky trail ran clear down to the railroad tracks and up into the conifer forest. Why any horse rider would choose the trail over the road, I don't know. Maybe cowboys used it for making a quick getaway from town, which fit our bill quite right.

"Where are we going, Mummy?" Katie brimmed with enthusiasm.

"For a horse ride," I said plainly, as if it were ordinary to sit around in town half the day and suddenly hop on a horse. Other children of her age might have pummeled me with *why* questions. Katie had had a brief stint of asking *why* questions just before she turned two, and ever since, she preferred to wait for life to unfold. Probably our answers had too often disappointed. In my periphery, I saw her widened and curious smile. She was imagining. I shifted our sack over my shoulder and pressed her small, warm hand tightly in mine.

Our feet moved swiftly over the path but my mind waited up ahead. I knew that this time it could not be Harvey. I reminded myself with every other step. The flame of hope burned hard despite my efforts to blow it out. Hope is a tiresome thing.

Soon, the trail sloped up into the trees and met the road. The broad-faced cowboy waiting for us was not Harvey at all. This one had hawkish eyes and the same ease and toughness of his sorrel quarter horse. The two shuffled from one leg to the other, looking like the same creature. They didn't like to stand still. He said nothing.

"Ed sent me," I began.

He nodded slightly and helped me onto a palomino tied to a nearby tree. While his mare impatiently nudged his back, ours raised her nose, flared her nostrils and looked haughtily at us with sideways eyes. I gave her a couple of pats on the neck. She could feel as much contempt as she fancied as long as she carried us away from here. Katie came next. Huge cowboy hands under her arms settled her onto a rolled blanket between me and the horn. He cinched our canvas sack to the back of the saddle.

We rode on the main road before cutting down to the lake to the cattle trail. And here it fit. The puzzle piece. It slipped right into place: Vancouver felt so very far because I wasn't going there. Not yet. The way out was to go around. Katie chit-chatted to herself, while the scuff and clap of horse hoofs lulled us onward.

I didn't ask where we were going. Maybe that's nuts. It felt taboo to crack open his clean silence with questions. Or maybe I didn't want him to pronounce our future yet. Right then, it didn't matter. We'd made it out. An unexpected turn to the north. Any stop we made—even if it lasted a week or two—was just a stopover on our way home to Vancouver.

Stupidly, I'd forgotten the cowboy's name as soon as Ed told me. Over the many hours that came next, I rode behind him and fitted him with various names. None rang the right bell. Had I asked Ed if he was trustworthy? He leaned down and patted his horse on the neck now and again. I supposed his ears told him that we were still trailing behind him. After a few cursory glances to ensure the palomino was behaving—she was—he left Katie and me to ourselves. Sometimes the trail widened out so we could walk side by side, but even then, he had eyes only for the trail.

Katie had decided she and the palomino were the best of friends. She leaned over often to chat her up and paw her long neck to prove it. The horse scuffed and clapped hooves behind the sorrel and occasionally pinned its ears back at Katie's chirping. Katie surprised and relieved me by asking me very little. Some time later, she leaned against the nest of my chest and fell asleep.

Several hours into the journey, I was surprised to realize a faint smile lit my face. Katie was warm in my arms, the mare swayed soothingly beneath me, and the forest spread over the distant hills like the fur of a beautiful beast. Ahead, the bowl of northern mountains cradled a bright blue freedom. Just for a moment, I'd spent all my anguish. The crisp pine breeze and gentle sun washed clean the soul. Just a woman on a horse with her girl. Not moving away or moving toward. Just moving. For a brief moment, the world made a kind of sense, a rhythm that fit with the horse hooves and heartbeats.

The peace broke when I began to dwell on the trail of rumor and disbelief that would surely kicking up behind me. "Mrs. Darcy up and left? I doubt that," a rancher would say, giving the bank teller a coarse look. Women didn't leave. Kind, well-behaved women especially stayed tethered close to their husbands. There would be quiet disagreement, and then shaking heads and sighs. Our familiar cowboys would chuckle about it over whiskey. The merchants who stopped off for tea on their way past the ranch would offer Hugh wide-eyed condolences. And, perhaps, other, faraway wives in the region would bow their heads and wonder. All this time, I'd felt like an outsider, a new and little-known arrival in the Cariboo. But I would pull many threads when I left, loosening the fabric of community. Cowboys and ranchers are none too keen on gossip, but when gossip saunters up plain as the daily news, the talk will spread far and fast.

When the sky turned jewel blue, Katie awoke, grumpy and hungry. At the cowboy's gesture, we steered the horses toward a creek that churned sapphire water over black stones. My legs were so accustomed to riding that my first step off the horse nearly spilled me onto the rocks. We sat on a bed of dry stones, passing a cold can of Spam and some biscuits. The cowboy ate quickly and leaned back on his elbow, gazing north. His pockets might have contained the maps to the Northwest Passage, such a traveler was he. With a gesture, he offered us some smoked salmon jerky. Katie and I reached for it eagerly. The sweet, dry flavor was worth the effort of ripping and chewing the tough flesh.

"You have sleeping gear?" The sudden sound of his voice was startling. I roughly swallowed my bite.

"I'm afraid we haven't anything."

The cowboy looked away down the creek, poker-faced.

"You have a canvas?"

I shook my head, not comprehending the question.

With square fingers, he tore off a piece of smoked salmon and chewed for a long while.

"How much food you have?"

By way of answer, I opened the sack beside me. He leaned over to examine the darkened contents. A can of beans, a brown bag of oats, an old spice pouch that I'd filled with cinnamon and sugar, and a jar of my own peaches. He sat back. The creek chortled and gurgled beside us. The horses slurped and snorted the wet from their noses. He said nothing. Katie leaned her head on me and began squirming in my lap, trying to make herself comfortable. She'd had enough of riding for one day. The cowboy seemed to be working something through. Perhaps my answers unsettled him. Perhaps Katie and I were a perplexing problem that he'd become responsible for sorting out. Hoping to assist, I asked, "Where are we heading to tonight?"

He studied the jerky in his hands as if it would answer for him. "I'm taking you two into that patch of fir over the next hillside." He tipped a finger toward north. "You'll sleep with my gear." He folded the piece of jerky into his mouth, chewing slowly, ceremoniously. "I'll leave you there. Can't all sleep in the same bag." A spark of the setting sun flickered in his eyes.

Heat rose in my cheeks as I stared down at my jerky.

"I'll go up to Gain House Ranch. 'Bout four miles on. See if Oakley can loan more stuff."

"Oh," I said. Then because that sounded impolite, I added, "I see." How ridiculous to spend our first night mere miles from

Hugh's ranch. I smoothed the hair on Katie's head.

"Mummy, I want to go home." Katie arched back in my arms, with a horseshoe frown.

"You'll have a forest bed. Like an adventure." But it didn't sound like adventure to me. The idea of spending the night alone in the woods sounded downright stupid. Katie grumbled but curled up against me, reluctant but curious. I had pictured that I might be in someone's ranch, or sneakily sleeping in their barn. I'd thought I could be asleep in the back of a car with Katie in my arms winding slowly toward Vancouver. Now the cold and loneliness of the past months amassed in the night ahead of me.

12

S HARP WIND AND pine needles brushed against my face as I clutched the reins and pulled Katie closer. Tree branches laced over the twilight above as the horses stepped gingerly into the dark wood. When the cowboy moved a few steps ahead, the tan collar on his jacket was all I could make out of him. In the blurry dark, the wood filled with sound: horse clops, heartbeats, and imagined rustlings. If the cowboy knew precisely where we'd end up, he didn't say.

I've never done well in cold. Mother says it's because I slipped into an icy creek as a toddler and have never shaken the chill. I was too little to remember that, but I will forever remember the ghostly breeze needling me through the rough blankets that night. Anger runs hot but fear is cold as ice.

On the horse, I wrapped an arm around Katie to assure her. In truth, she was braver than I. If the cowboy's mission was to keep us hidden in the center of the wood, he wholly succeeded. We didn't even know where we were. I hopped down on weary, bowing legs, and pulled Katie into my arms. Before he left us, he checked the knotting on our canvas tarp roof and hung our food sack. I was fully clothed and curled around Katie in his sleeping sack which smelled of sharp wool and onions.

"Be back before daybreak." He glanced at us again, then went to his horse and unfastened the rifle. For one terrifying moment, I thought he might aim at us and shoot. My mouth fell open, but he only brought it over and set it on the ground next to me. "In case of trouble," he said softly.

He lingered strangely, squatting next to me. My heart thumped too loudly for me to imagine why. *Was he going to lay a kiss on me?* My whole body was stiff as ice. But a moment later, he rose and moved toward the horses. Whatever temptation, whatever vague hope, extinguished. He left with them both and not another word.

As the sound of horse footfalls faded to memory, I told Katie a story about two birds flying north toward a star. It calmed us both. Soon her restlessness gave way to heavy slumber. I stayed awake listening to the faint din of night sounds, the elbows of trees aching in the cold, pine needles breaking under imagined paws. The what-if moths landed all around me as I shivered and fretted through the long turn of darkness.

Morning unfurled in a miracle of light. Katie opened her eyes with a cry. "There, there," I soothed. No sign of the cowboy. The rifle was still lying prone beside the bedroll. Our food sack still hung in the tree like a sagging moon, out of the reach of bears.

"It's all right, Katie," I said again, the voice of motherly instinct, not reason. She tightened grief into a stoic pout and rubbed her nose with a round hand.

"I want biscuits," she moaned.

"I know." I kissed her forehead. "I know you do." I left her to cry while I pulled and let the rope on our food sack slip, sinking it to the ground. I unfolded the linen and revealed the biscuits. Calmed, Katie chewed in silence, looking out at the trees, hair a tangle of curls. A pattern of crumbs gathered down the front of her dress. Through the trees, the low flame of sun brightened the sky's lamp.

"When are we going home?" Katie mewled. Of course that question was coming. Only a matter of time. I'd considered it regularly on the horse ride but hadn't managed an answer. I listened to the words that arrived in my voice.

"We're not. We're on a journey now."

She considered it. "Is it a good journey or a bad one? Peter Rabbit took a bad journey and ended up sick in bed."

"It's a good one." I hoped.

"But why?" she added thoughtfully. Tough question.

"Because," I began slowly, "it's time to go. It's like cooking a cake in the oven. If we don't take it out at the right time, it's ruined. It's no good. That's like us. We're like cake." I smiled. "It was time for us to go."

A grave look crossed her face. "I'm glad we won't be burned up."

"No, it's not like that. We wouldn't burn. Maybe—maybe it's more like a chick. You know that chicks grow in eggs. But what happens when the chick gets too big for the egg?"

"It breaks free!" Her fingers splayed in demonstration.

"Yes. We are like the chick. We've grown and now we must leave." Next, I thought, she'll ask about her papa. What will I say then?

"So, the ranch was our egg," she reasoned.

"Something like that, yes."

"That's why we have to sleep outside now. We're too big for a ranch."

"Well, sort of."

"And what about Chester? He needs to come for a journey, too."

I smiled at the thought of dear Chester. "He's all right. He'll stay there for now. To keep Papa company."

She weighed the answer, then nodded, satisfied. She stood and set her hands on her hips. "I'm getting bigger every day!"

"Yes, you are," I assured her. "But the kind of bigger I'm talking about happens on the inside, where you can't even see it."

She leveled her gaze at me, but since I'd been truthful—in a sense—I could face her. We looked long into each other's eyes. "I'm going to be really, really big inside one day," she decided.

"Yes, probably you are!" I agreed.

We finished washing down the biscuits with water when I

heard horse hooves. A few minutes later they produced a worn and wearied-looking cowboy and a pinned-ear horse. He got down and stood there, waiting for the words to come. I waited.

"Borrowed you a bedroll." Motioning to the bedding beneath me, he asked, "Mind if I catch some shut-eye on mine?"

"Course not." I rose and joined Katie. "Generous of you to share it. I hope you haven't worn yourself out too much on our account. It was fine of you to let us use your bedding."

He grunted softly, waited till we were clear away from the bed, then flopped belly down and fell asleep.

13

FOR THE NEXT two days, I learned much about a cowboy's life. You eat slowly because eating comes only twice a day. Make it last. Appreciate it. The Queen's cake would not fill you with as much gratitude as a hunk of dry bread on the trail under a sky crowded with starlight. Put no effort into the riding. Let the riding do itself. On the trail, the land does the talking, not the people. Horse hooves skim over stones and shift through grass. Birds trill for a mate. Breezes ruffle against horse manes. Parades of clouds take all day to pass by, heading east while the horses head north. If Katie is quiet, don't interrupt her with words, even the pretty ones she likes.

Often, I looked over at the cowboy beside me and wondered. He wasn't all filled up with words the way I am. I envied that. I'm silent inside only when sleeping. Perhaps not even then. But he brimmed with silence, like still water in a lake. And he was separate. Whatever family he came from, whatever people he had known, fell away from him on the trail. He left no nagging threads dangling behind. The ultimate freedom: a man and a horse in a country of wilderness.

I, on the other hand, would have been a rotten cowboy. The grief of loneliness would gnaw me through. Loneliness lived in him, too, but his was the beauty of a sorrowful song. A man could find comfort in the steadiness of being solitary. Loneliness was a familiar and comforting companion. If I wanted to know him, I would have to lay a hand on his loneliness first. He wouldn't recognize you otherwise. Loneliness stood in the way of real people, like Katie and me. We interrupted his isolated peace.

At night, he slowly chewed his jerky and biscuits, leaning back on one arm and staring into the red bellies of coals. I trusted him now. If he were planning to hurt me, he would have done it already. Catching a glimpse of his tanned face over the tangle of flames, I couldn't tell what he was thinking. I stroked Katie's bronze-lit hair and imagined. *He had a sweetheart once. He danced with her to the thump and whistle of music. He had kissed her and thought often since of her ruby lips. The last notes of music faded, but the echo lingered a long while. And after the echo, the silence that rings on and on.*

When he thought of her now, he saw her long hair looping over her shoulder. He caught whiffs of her almond scent. He saw the eager blue of her eyes and gently dimpled smile. He would be weakened by her. A man who traveled for days on horseback in all weather and slept outdoors with the howls of wolves and cracking of twigs—a man who ate near nothing and would shoot a charging bear without flinching—would be utterly weakened by those blue eyes. Love and yearning made him ridiculous. Unsettled and clumsy with want.

I didn't mean to pry, but his memories were plain. If he knew I could read him like this, surely he'd tell me off. The fire hummed and crackled between us, and Katie curled sleepily on my lap. Above the flames, where the sparks turned into stars, his thoughts hung ripe. Did mine, too? Probably, but not a soul could see them. Not the cowboy, not Harvey, not Hugh. *What would it be like to be truly known?* I couldn't imagine.

The cowboy yawned and nodded good night to me, signing off from our long shared silence. He stretched on his bedroll and slept. Could a man stay strong and be in love at the same time? With some, perhaps it wasn't possible. This cowboy had turned away from love. His choice, not hers. He couldn't overcome the discomfort it caused. Vulnerability was intolerable.

I turned my gaze on myself. In daydream, I tried on many

lives, spinning in a mirror to catch the full effect. In one life, we rode across the meadow of stately ranch home with lace curtains and a hedgerow of roses full of new buds. The owner was Harvey. He bought the place himself. That's why he hadn't been out cowboying on the trail. He promised to protect me and keep me safe. He looked in my eyes and knew—*truly knew*—me. He proposed and I married him many times. In another life, I awoke one morning and the cowboy was gone. I didn't know where to take Katie. How to find food. I wandered the hills for days, and when I came to cabins in the woods, people turned us away because I'd abandoned my husband. In yet another life, we happened upon a merchant on the road who knew someone taking the train to Vancouver, and I could certainly come along if I liked. So we rushed to make it on time and sometimes we did, and sometimes we arrived to the churning of steel wheels on rail, and Katie would slump against my panting chest in despair.

Over the days, my prayers and hopes—*Please Lord, let me see Harvey once again; please Lord, let me find my way to Vancouver; please Lord, let Katie and me make a new life for ourselves*—all whittled down to one: *Please Lord, do not make me go back to Hugh.* That direction loomed with a storm front and pulled with guilt. Not just guilt. Practicality, moral expectations, and Mother's voice inside me. I could not go back. But the future was little more than elusive shadows flitting between trees.

I discreetly wiggled my wedding ring off. I looked down at the shadowed dirt. I held the gold loop in one hand, feeling the weight. Hugh had looked earnest and steady when he put it on my finger. At the very least, it *is* gold. I dropped it into my coat pocket, touching the outside to make sure of its shape.

It was day three of the journey before I asked where we were headed. I must have been rattled in the head from all the bumping along because the question leapt out of its own accord.

"Shuswap." He leaned his gaze toward me and nodded in the direction of the trail. "Xat'sull."

"Cat's skull?"

He smirked, suppressing his full amusement. "*Xat'sull.* Shus-wap folk."

"Is that the reserve?" I asked dimly. Anyone else in these parts would know, but I was new and didn't pay attention.

"Yup," he agreed, further amused.

"Is that where you live?" I asked, incredulous. He studied the distress bending my expression.

"Nope." His mirth could not be contained, and he chuckled softly. "Can't take you where I'm going. Get us both in a heap of trouble."

Most white women in my situation would have sooner slept in the mud with the pigs, believing that the safer, cleaner option. My high school friend, Betsy, would tsk-tsk. *And what next? Join the circus and prop Katie on the tightrope?* Our old farmhand Teddy had told tales of the reserve—hunchbacked men and women with no teeth, a perpetual stench of smoke and fish, houses so slovenly and ramshackle that even stray dogs turned their noses. But with Teddy, a glass of spilled milk was an avalanche.

Yet reserves were mysterious places. Governments thought of them with perpetual worry, but ordinary white folk rarely considered them. That was the Canadian way. The whole topic of Natives was shadowed in avoidance, polite aversion. Will never spoke of his reserve, which sat farther south than this one. But he left it to hunker in our meager and drafty cowboy quarters, where winter's long fingers cracked open the clapboards and summer's mosquitoes came to feast.

Mother was different in this way. She had often told me that the Native folk were a misunderstood people. A few times a year, Native women paddled up the shore to our West Vancouver cottage and traded woven baskets for our old dresses. Mother brought them tea and sat with them on a log by the shore. I hadn't paid much attention to their talk. The exchanges had seemed mostly silent to me. Mother told me on a few memorable occasions, "The white man has done the Native people no favors. They lived fine enough lives before our lot showed up and started telling them what to eat, how to talk, and who to pray to." As a teenager, I wondered if Mother hadn't just projected her own feelings of suffering and injustice onto them.

I looked off to the mountains, hoping for a distraction from the unsettled feeling taking over. "They ain't going to hurt you, just so you know," the cowboy offered, still amused. I hadn't even thought of that. I just couldn't fathom why they would take me in. And if they didn't—what then?

Katie whispered to me, "Does Hat Shell have food?"

I looked at her blankly, then pleaded with the cowboy. "Is there no other place?"

"If there is, I can't help you find it," he said, not unkindly.

My fingers tightened around the horse's reins. Mother once said it's the mark of the ignorant to fear other cultures, but she was speaking of the French then.

Finally, I mustered my courage and blurted, "Quite probably, they'll turn me out."

"Nope," he said confidently. "I'll pay them to take you."

"Oh?" I felt like cattle. "I couldn't allow you to part with your own money on my account."

He chewed at the dry skin of his lip. "Not my money. Ed's."

"Ed?" I tried to piece it together.

"Don't take this wrong, ma'am, but I don't usually take women and children on beef trail tours." He smiled to soften the gibe.

"Dear Ed," I whispered. Here we were: a sack of stones being burdened from one shoulder to another. Now we'd be dumped on the Xat'sull people.

So this is what happens to women who leave their marriages. The hand of fate—of God or of guilt—presses them down. Hugh would laugh. Hugh would say that those who try to run from their cross only drag it farther.

"And then what? I mean, where do I go after that?"

"God knows. But that's as far as I can take you."

Cloud shadows patterned the earth like puzzle pieces loosening apart. Our trail-weary palomino scuffled over the stones. I sighed heavily, and she with me.

Soon enough, we stopped for lunch on a hillslope overlooking the thick knots of forest. The cowboy chuckled again to himself. I flashed him a look of tangled worry. He turned back to his sandwich.

"They ain't animals," he said. "Just so you know." I wasn't sure whether he was being obscure on purpose or whether too much breeze had gotten into his head.

"Pardon me?"

"Shuswap." I watched him try to contain his smile amidst my obvious displeasure. "They ain't gonna *eat* you, you know." He chuckled and got up to remount his horse. *Ridiculous,* I thought. *Of course they won't eat me.* But I felt a burning pain that I couldn't name, the future seeping into the present. I shook my head. At the very least, I would be an unwanted visitor. But at least Hugh would lose my trail.

A few hours later, we eased the horses to the edge of a well-worn switchback. Through the fir and cedar boughs, I caught the first glimpses of a half dozen shed cabins. A rushing river chattered on the far side, but I couldn't see a soul.

"Wait here," he instructed me, pointing to a spot near a fir tree where I couldn't see the reserve; nor could anyone see me. I felt wholly uneasy. Below me, the palomino shuffled from foot to foot. We waited so long, the palomino fell asleep, my rear end went numb, and Katie had three temper tantrums. She was loud, but the cowboy didn't return. I truly wondered if we would ever see him again. Yet I didn't dare descend the trail to the reserve uninvited. It seemed the Xat'sull people were as reluctant about me as I feared.

I had nearly given up hope when he and his horse rounded the bend below us. As he sauntered up, he said nothing but waved his arm for us to follow him. He didn't lead us down the trail to the reserve. Instead, we wound all the way up a small hill, to a clearing among the trees. Across the clearing, an old Native man fed the licking flames of a fire and woodsmoke clung to the birch boughs like thick fog. Behind him sat a small government-issue shack, the kind designed to house traveling mailmen, government census takers, and the like. But perhaps these were the same shacks built for reserves.

The cowboy looked at Katie and me expectantly. Not sure what I was supposed to do, I simply sat there until he dismounted, moseyed over, and lifted Katie off the saddle. She smiled and blushed shyly at the attention. With aching legs, I thunked down to the ground myself. I went to smooth down my skirt, but my hands touched jeans. Awkwardly, I pushed my hands in the pockets.

I spotted a woman around my age, a toddler, and a boy not much older than Katie, standing in the shade of the shack. The woman's buckled frown and sideways glances seemed plenty clear. The boy walked across the clearing straight up to Katie with a poker face and extended hand. Gingerly, Katie put her hand in his and followed him toward the shack as if she belonged to him. I followed behind, belonging to no one.

The cowboy went to the woman. I couldn't hear everything he said, but I caught the words "runaway" and "Vancouver." She glanced me over and gave a brief nod. So it was decided. Cowboys often stopped to trade things or buy smoked salmon. One of them could take me. If no cowboy came, someone else would ride me south to 108 Mile House.

The cowboy explained this to me as he roped the palomino to his sorrel.

"Why aren't these people living on the lower reserve with the others?" I asked.

"They're collecting food up here. And they're not Xat'sull, anyway. Just passing through."

I turned to ask more, but he had already mounted and merely touched his brim in goodbye. He and the horses were eager for the trail, for the earth gleaming beneath their feet. I saw my arm rise to wave goodbye.

14

I CROSSED THE clearing. Katie and I seemed to inspire an eerie calm. They were Native, but visitors, like us. Why weren't we staying with the Xat'sull as planned? Perhaps the cowboy thought it safer here? Likely the Xat'sull were unwilling to accept the burden. Well, if these folk wanted to fetch their hunting knives, to drown us in the roar of the river, or shoo us off the hill—this was their moment. Of course, they did none of those things.

The woman had joined the old man next to the fire. Her pretty mouth curled slightly up, as if under ordinary circumstances, she spent a good deal of time laughing. They spoke in low tones in a language that sounded like shushes and soft clicks. A toddler in a wool sweater and moccasins stood nearby with wide, curious eyes. I pressed my lips. Shame and neediness competed for heat in my cheeks. Hot pink spread over the rippled-sand clouds above us. Weariness and awkwardness eased me down onto a log by the fire.

The boy motioned to Katie to hold out her hands. Katie spread her pudgy palms open like a book. He dipped his hand in a basket nearby and dropped a handful of thimbleberries into her palms. Katie gasped, beamed, and savored several before pausing to admire the beauty of the rest. The boy's poker face broke, revealing gleeful pride. The smile that broke on my face wouldn't have convinced anyone.

I punctuated the silence with pointless questions.

"What food are you collecting up here?"

"Where are you coming from?"

"Do you want me to do something? To help out?"

No one seemed to speak English. I was embarrassed, ashamed to feel like an outsider among outsiders, and annoyed with my shame. I stabbed a stick at the coals. I sank into the silence and my own self-pity.

At last, the woman motioned us into a kerosene-lit cabin. She wore no expression and uttered only one word, pointing to herself: "Mary." Inside, two other women and a man reclined on their elbows on grey blankets. Mary began to cook over a tiny woodstove. My stomach quaked with hunger at the scent of stew. She served us boiled potatoes and cod stew in enamel bowls, and we ate heartily. After, the boy and Katie sang nonsensically and pretended to smoke a stick.

I listened to the conversation around me. Their language sounded like Russian, but softer, more careful. Like cracking open soft nuts. Like dry leaves blowing in a breeze. Lulled by the sound and the satisfying meal, I wondered if it were possible for a woman to simply disappear. I had come from Vancouver—a city that people in Paris, Moscow, and Jerusalem had scarcely heard of—to Williams Lake—a remote village in a remote province of a little-known country. And now to the very edge of the world: a solitary cabin on a hill with Natives who were visitors here themselves.

Mary announced, "Fried bread," and passed me a greasy, dense pancake.

"Thank you!" It was hearty and filling. I broke off pieces with my fingers and stuffed them in my mouth.

The old man was saying something to me. He wanted Mary to translate, but she shook her head and scolded him. With a lift of his chin, he pressured her. Finally, she said, "He says you're not as dumb as you look." The old man cracked up with laughter. I smiled so I could feel in on the joke. *Yes*, I thought, shrinking a little. *Perhaps even dumber.*

What would it be like to call this place home? I imagined

living on the reserve below. The raised-shoulder hills, those cables of crashing waters. The gush of spring salmon, valleys thick with pine. Those people were born from this place. Even these visitors seemed to fit in a way I never had. They were natural here whereas I felt juxtaposed upon a landscape. If the white man had never come, the Natives would have continued living the way they always had. Or at least changed according to their own needs and schedule. What would it be like to belong to *a place*? I couldn't imagine. Maybe I didn't belong to anything.

I brushed some crumbs into my bowl. If someone asked me just then where I was from, what would I say? *England? Vancouver? The Cariboo, Williams Lake, Soft Creek?* I skittered up the hillside just there, and now I'm here. But I was less than *here*. Hiding from Hugh, I shrank my edges, cringing at the thought of what the next day might bring.

It wasn't just the placelessness that bothered me. I didn't belong to anyone. Just Katie. Mother was far away over the sea. At that moment, her love for me felt light as imagination. I was unmoored on the open seas of life, without tribe or community or family or friend. I looked hard at my bowl and winced back tears.

After the meal, Mary asked the boy something. He sat against the wall and began chanting a song. Though he sang in another language, he seemed to know many words. The tune was flat, but he never strayed from the rhythm. Charmed, I felt, or imagined, the words. It was a song about being on the trail, about keeping going despite the troubles. *Your many disappointments lead to the greatest gifts.* When it ended, he put a stone in his hands and, holding out two fists, waited for Katie to guess.

"I have three other children," Mary said, surprising me with her English. But the words were weights. "The others. All gone."

For a moment, I didn't understand English myself. "Gone?" My eyes went wide. I believed she must mean deceased. "I'm so sorry," I gasped. I'd heard tale of diseases on reserves, of frostbite and losing one's way, of gushing rivers doubling in volume in minutes.

"The oldest one, gone four years in school already. The others, they followed her."

"Oh," I was putting the pieces together. "You mean . . . they're in *school?*"

She nodded gravely.

"But—" I peered at her, not comprehending the deep sorrow in her eyes, "You can still see them, can't you? They'll come home soon for summer."

"They don't come home. When they come home, they are different. Like frightened rabbits." Her open palm lay upturned and empty on her lap. My gaze fell to the floor. Katie and the boy were lost in their game of play. What good was a place, if you couldn't keep your children in it? That's not a home, as I well knew.

The air pricked with tension, as if she had said something unkind. Of course she hadn't. But I came from the world that stole her children away. I felt complicit. The thought of someone taking Katie away made me catch my breath. Leaning over, I scooped her into my arms. Sleepily, she leaned against my breast. My white hands circled her bright sweater.

The boy crawled up onto Mary's knee. She set a hand on his back, patting him instinctively. Numbness seemed to fall over her like an invisible avalanche. She was already anticipating this next separation. Although the unease lingered, I couldn't find the words to make things right. I suppose I believed words *could* make things right, and maybe that was part of the problem.

I rocked Katie in my arms, gazing at her pretty hands. We had lost so much. But we could retain our way of life, our language. That, I supposed, was another kind of belonging. One that Mary and her family didn't have. I glanced up at her in time to see her look away from me.

That night, I slept uneasily with a scratchy blanket on a hard floor. Was I cruel for tearing Katie away from her home and her father? The place of her birth? The pets, farm animals, and land that she knew? I had leapt out of an unbearable marriage into what? Into being a burden, an uninvited guest for people who had plenty of worries themselves. What right did I have to leave a man who provided for his wife and child? Many women suffered far worse, and they stayed married. The clench of guilt in my chest wasn't only about leaving. It was also that I couldn't bring myself to return.

Life at the hillside cabin was not so different from that at the ranch. Instead of pastures, they had forests and the echo of the river far below. Instead of cattle, they had fish. But there were horses to feed and chores to be done. I tried to help where I could, but Mary shooed me off. Whether she believed guests shouldn't work or that I was an incompetent assistant, I'm not sure. I kept peering up at the switchback, hoping for some new arrival en route to Vancouver to come along. No one arrived. But at least I saw that these people had no intention of throwing me out. If the tables were turned, would the white man show such peaceful restraint? I rather doubted it. In any case, when I fell asleep that second night, I slept deeply.

The following afternoon, I sat next to the elderly man while he tended a fire. His eyes were dark domes of night sky, sorrowful, twinkling, and expansive. His English broke into little bits and pieces, fractured and jagged in his mouth. They were shards of rock that hurt him to enunciate. Mostly, we sat in silence, watching the weaving flames. I hoped he didn't notice that I was studying him. With papery, soft hands, he poked a stick at the fire, under hanging strips of salmon. His face was trailed with years of laughter and grief.

I imagined what he would say: *that his life bloomed with exquisite griefs. All was bearable when his wife was with him. But she left—in spirit before leaving in body. He was a tracker, but he could not find the path back to her, back to the past, to the time when her warm hand rested over his heart, when her love was a force like a river, rushing through him. He sang into the night after she fled the earth, trying to call her back. But she refused her body, refused this world, would not meet him even in dreams. The magic of songs has weakened like so much else in this country of white folk.*

She took something from him. He was less solid now. When he looked at his hand, it seemed transparent—bones, veins nearly translucent. Every day, the cold river charged onward—a mockery of all that is finite. When he went down the hill to listen to it now, sometimes he forgot his name. If she could call it, he would remember. He would rise from this splintery bench to where she waited like morning mist at the edge of the forest. She would lead him into The After. He was waiting for that day.

He paused while poking the fire and pierced his eyes into me, sensing my intrusion. *That's enough snooping around,* his eyes said. A white woman and runaway wife, intruding on an old man's thoughts. Unacceptable. A wire of smoke coiled up. Whatever space had opened between us, closed.

15

MIDMORNING THE NEXT day, I was picking dainty leaves
out of huckleberry baskets when a couple of cowboys
kicked a carpet of dust up the trail. *My ticket to Vancouver!* One
was lean and gangly. *Harvey?* My heart leapt against my ribs—in
vain. It was not. Katie seized my hand. They dismounted and
began exchanging nickels for salmon jerky, sizing us up. Meanwhile, the elderly man asked if they could deliver me to some
other place—which sounded distinctly like *any* other place.

"Only half a dozen white wives around here," said the gangly
one, eyeing me with disconcerting enthusiasm. "And half of those
is up and run away! Reward out and everything!"

The other rolled a cigarette and looked sidelong at us as if we
were the sorriest packages he'd seen in some time. "No, no," he
said. "This is the same one we heard of, fool." The hair rose on
my neck.

"Nah, I don't think so. Look how they're dressed." He
pointed to my jeans and button shirt. "Cuckoos don't run away
looking all buttoned up and ironed."

"Yeah, you've seen your share of runaways now?"

"I know a *lot* of cuckoo lady folk and she don't look like one
of them!" His magnificent pride rocked him back on his heels.

"You know *hurley girlies*. That's not the same as ladyfolk."

Mary, standing on the stoop and wiping a cup, winced. The
elderly man stood watching the spectacle with folded arms and a
faint twinkle of amusement.

The long one was a born cowboy, I was sure. The skeptical one probably drifted into cowboying with the employment drought. The greatest sniggering came when they heard I lacked a horse. The long one erupted with gaiety, dancing in a circle, and slapping his knee. He kept looking over at me like I was in on the joke, rather than the butt of it. It's hard being rescued by fools.

"Mummy, you're hurting me," whispered Katie, and I loosened my grip on her hand.

Then, too, was this a rescue or a claim for reward money? I had to take the chance. If they were after cash, they might leave me here and send word to Hugh.

The skeptical one shook his head and spat a gob of tobacco at the dirt. "Running away without a horse, huh?" Katie bore her indignant eyes up at me. *They're making us look stupid!* Her small hand tightening around mine, too. She did not approve of this trampling over our pride.

Mary narrowed her eyes at them and threw a hand in my direction. "She's buying my horse," she stated, as if it were obvious.

"Mary—" I started, but she flashed me a reproachful glance and I shut up. How could I buy a horse and still manage the train fare to Vancouver? The cowboys leaned to hear what brilliance might exit my mouth.

Mary shooed them like bothersome flies. "We'll talk." She motioned me toward her. "You wait outside. She'll be ready soon." Katie and I strode stiffly past the cowboys' ogling eyes and into Mary's cabin.

Inside, Mary astutely noted, "If you don't go with them, they'll tell your husband and collect a reward." I furrowed my brow. My fingers stroked a strand of Katie's hair. Mary waited for the reality to settle. I resisted the inevitable. But a few minutes later, I relieved myself of my grandmother's silver earrings and half my money, and acquired some blankets, smoked salmon, bread, a saddle, and a white and quite elderly gelding—yet unseen—by the name of Ocktoo. The name meant "Winding

Trail," which seemed appropriate, given my very roundabout journey to Vancouver. It was a bargain, but I had little left. Not enough for a train ticket. As I stood to leave, I turned Hugh's gold wedding ring in my pocket. Superstition overcame me. Selling it might bring some curse.

Outside, a saddled and slope-backed horse loped forward—long-necked on account of his reins being pulled against his will. He resembled dirty snow. His ears were pinned above greying whiskers. When I took the reins, Ocktoo snorted gruffly, as if crossing the field exhausted him. I rubbed his nose and his long white lashes blinked with injured pride and feeble curiosity.

Understanding that we were leaving, Katie thumped down on Mary's step, locked her arms, and sneered. Mary's boy leaned in the doorframe, wide-eyed. Katie erupted into a furious cry, pinning Ocktoo's ears back and making our rescuers shake their heads. The boy looked bewildered by Katie's grief and tugged on his mother to lift him. In clear English, he asked me, "You come back soon?"

"We have to!" wailed Katie.

"Perhaps. Who knows?" I said, sweeping the hair from her face. "But today we have more adventure. And a brand-new horse to take us there." I lifted her gently onto my hip and turned to face the sagging horse.

When her wails slowed to a rhythmic gasp, she held her open hand to Ocktoo's mouth. He wiggled his soft grey lips, inspecting her for food. Her teary eyes twinkled.

I turned to thank Mary, but she was already gone. She had spotted the approaching goodbye—full of awkward gratitude and mute condolences—and had stepped inside to avoid it. I wouldn't fool myself into thinking she wanted me to stay. Yet my heart ached a little to leave her. I mounted Katie onto the saddle and hefted up behind her. The elderly man stood nearby, observing the fuss. We locked eyes. *Goodbye*, I told him with my eyes. *We knew each other deeply for a moment.* The cowboys slouched on their horses up ahead, waiting for us, the gangly one grinning hungrily, the other pulling seed puff from his sleeve.

16

T HE LONG ONE'S name was Tom. The disinterested one was Nick. We emerged from the top of the switchback to a dozen white-faced heifer Herefords lazing in the swaying meadow grass and wildflowers. Tom and Nick were tasked with driving them to a ranch just south of 108 Mile. This was doubly good news. First off, at last we were heading south! And second, the cattle provided rowdy entertainment for Katie and distraction from our sore legs and rear ends. Best of all, for Katie's sake, was Skippy, a keen, dark-eyed collie who was babysitting the herd from behind the camouflage of grass. When Tom, Nick, and I neared, she burst from her hiding spot and bolted at the cattle, who groaned and lifted their half-ton bodies off the grass and set off in wide rows toward the south, heads bobbing and heels thrashing through grass and dust.

For the next many hours, the mahogany-red backs wove before us, hoarsely booing their complaints or nodding their agreements. Nick gave a clipped whistle, pointed back, told Skippy to slow. Skippy dashed left, trotted to one side, ran ahead, nipped at ankles, and checked for approval, tongue lolling with the thrill. Katie barked her own orders to Skippy, which through sheer luck appeared to succeed on occasion. Ocktoo, meanwhile, impressed me with his steady patience and easy temperament. He'd win no bets at the racetrack, but he managed to keep up.

Nick rode in the rear and Tom in the front, while steady Ocktoo kept us off to one side of the heifers. Tom kept company with a flask of whiskey tucked inside his vest. He pulled it out whenever the scenery inspired—when brown shale hills appeared, when an eagle lit upon a gnarled snag, or when a cloud's shadow passed over the path. He slowed here and there to assess me, the way a man might assess a racing horse. Sizing up his bet. Ensuring I was worth an investment.

Mother instructed me to "always be charming and graceful," but stripping away charm and enchantment is an equally valuable skill. With a subtle rearrangement of expression and a rigidity of posture, I diminished my appeal by half. Unfortunately, even shoe leather looks tasty to the starving. Tom's smile grew wide and hopeful as airplane wings.

Katie, on the other hand, was merely weight in the saddle to him, wigglier and noisier than a bag of potatoes, but no more important. He looked around her at me. At least he likes women instead of boys, I considered. Nick didn't look over to us at all. When he wasn't signaling Skippy or spitting brown goo onto the dirt, he merely lulled along with the pace. If we kept up, we kept up. If we didn't, oh well.

In the Cariboo, May weather weaves winter with summer, with little hint of spring. The sun bestowed me with a crown of fire. I wished I had a cowboy hat of my own. A forgiving breeze rose from time to time to douse the flames. "How long do you expect it'll take us to reach 108 Mile House?" I asked Tom. A milky turquoise river roared to the left and a rocky hillside veered up to the right.

"We can make it take as long as you want." Tom chuckled at his joke, his head falling to one side like a puppet with loosened strings. He collected himself. "Now, don't get all dried up on me," he chided. He pulled his horse close to mine, pulled off his Stetson hat and passed it to me. "Put it on! Saves you from the heat!" he bossed. His dark blond tufts drifted in the breeze like duckling feathers. The hat pulled shade and breeze over my face. I was truly grateful, but I smoothed back Katie's curls and pressed my lips tight.

Katie's boredom, like old milk, was just beginning to turn sour.

"Poor Ocktoo," I distracted her, "carrying us so far on such a hot day."

"Poor, poor Ocktoo," she echoed, and bent over the horn to hug him around the neck.

Soon after, we rested the cattle and ourselves, hiding away in the shade of sharp-smelling pines at the creek edge. Nick snacked quick and quiet, then lay back and set his hat over his face for a snooze. Tom, thankfully, wandered down river to "water a tree." Skippy drank half the creek then flopped beside me with half-opened eyes, panting at a frantic pace. In a fine impression of a cow, Katie flopped on the grass, pretending to graze and regarding the scenery with disinterested content.

My thoughts kept fragmenting to moments from the trail, the reserve, the ranch. I leaned my elbows back on the fallen pine needles, unsure I should bother gathering my scattered pieces. I didn't want to see what it added up to. Hugh and the ranch felt like a hundred years ago, a country away. In reality, I'd barely been gone a week. That ranch life happened to another woman. Whatever happened next, she was gone. And I wasn't sorry. Let her cold story be buried in the dirt. Maybe I'd never speak of that event. No one would ever know.

When we resumed the trail, the Cariboo treated us to a whole gallery of weather. Golden sunshine painted grass, birds, and tree limbs. Wide ribbons of wind unfurled around us. A thin carpet of clouds seeped through the sky. Tumbling cumulonimbus billowed over the mountains ahead. The air filled with the scent of electric thunder. We were still hurrying to lift the saddles off the horses and hunker down under the tarpaulin, when the first cracks of lightning rumbled their guns into the earth. Katie screamed, but regained some composure after Tom cursed and claimed she startled him. Under the tarpaulin, Katie buried her face into me and whimpered, while Tom took the opportunity to "keep us safe" by wrapping a lanky arm over my shoulders.

The clouds let loose thick ribbons of rain. Then the rain—showing off its tricks—turned white, hard, and horizontal. Miniature ice comets launched into the dirt, breaking dry pine needles beside us. This feat of nature roused Katie, and she snatched a few and pressed the coarse, round snow between her fingers. The horses whinnied and stomped the dirt in disapproval, though they were sheltered by thick branches. Ocktoo's low head turned toward us to measure our sympathy.

I wasn't feeling too jolly myself. Tom's large hand squeezed my shoulder and released and squeezed and released, like he was kneading bread. The tawny scent of his clothes wrapped around me, too. Enduring his attention for a few more days and—worse yet—nights seemed irksome at best. He was the kind of fellow who mistook persistence for persuasiveness, certain he could succeed through relentless effort alone. Of course, I should have been grateful that he had any manners at all. Though most Cariboo menfolk were kind and honorable, some wouldn't give a lick for courtship at all. They'd simply take what they felt was theirs. I felt a little guilty for not appreciating Tom's merely irritating ways. I wagered a hopeful guess that he was not of the taking variety. The crow's feet about his eyes and earnest demeanor suggested a jovial heart shining with optimism. What optimist tries ruthlessness first? He believed he was compelling and dashing. He was just waiting for me to realize it.

I was stiff inside his embrace. When had he last touched a woman? Besides me, the nearest white woman might be fifty miles away. At the ranch, some cowboys—long in the company of men—would find any excuse to lay a hand on a woman. Any kind of contact at all. A touch on the elbow. A thumping hand on the shoulder like with the fellows. An awkward "thanks" and pat-pat on the hand after a meal. They would compliment Hugh on his "wife's fine cooking" and tap my arm with a finger for exclamation while I set down another bowl of gravy. One young man, a merchant coming all the way down from the Yukon, faced me to say goodbye and set a hand on each of my shoulders as if I might run off otherwise. The leathered clocks of their hearts creaked with longing.

For some, the remembering came like a taste of moonshine after a cold sober winter. They needed more. About three times during my years on the ranch, a cowboy stumbled in long after dinner, smelling of clandestine spirits, when all the other men had gone off to bed. He would lean against me or grab my waist as I soaped the dishes over the woodstove. Once, a cowboy who boarded with us every year set his hands on my waist and pressed a damp kiss on my neck. I brushed him off with a flush of embarrassment and some motherly "now, nows." Long after the cowboy was off sawing up his sleep in the cowboy quarters, long after darkness tucked into the lonely corners of my kitchen, I removed my apron and gingerly placed my hands on my own waist, to see what it was like. What was it like to hold me?

I never spoke a word about those incidents. But I pulled out the memories from time to time, studying them and elaborating the detail like a delicate piece of lacework. The thought made me relax a little inside the warm bay of Tom's arm. Some other night when I was safely away from this one, I could recover this moment too and mull it over. Polish it up to make it beautiful. A brief reprieve from solitude.

I've never been much for practicalities and planning ahead, but certain realities of my circumstances began to show on the horizon along with the ill-colored sky. Even when we did make it to 108 Mile House, I wouldn't have near enough money to catch the train to Vancouver. If luck and fate met, I could find a buyer for Ocktoo in a hurry, and maybe, just maybe, that would do it. If only that were the worst of my problems. Tom's comment about cuckoo runaway wives couldn't have been invented. Hugh already had the reward out for me. How many other folk might had heard about me, too? Hugh would expect us to take the train. If he was looking, he'd be clever about it. He'd send word or posters down the train route, all the way to Vancouver. Indeed, my cowboy detouring might have saved me from being returned to him.

I couldn't just walk into 108 Mile House and expect to find paying work. Even a wee broom and shovel job would be hard to find. Panning for gold in the used-up river might be more practical. Times were tough. People ate their own poverty and slept on scarcity. I knew a man whose wife had died, and shortly after he lost his job at the mill. He and his two boys survived on hunted raccoon alone. The schoolmarm said the younger boy practiced his reading by looking at the words on two empty soup cans. Other children ate butter without bread. Families of six shared two eggs for a meal.

Nothing was wasted. Bones were used for soups. Torn curtains became young girls' dresses. Worn girls' dresses were cut and stitched to patch holes in mattresses. Broken dishes were pressed into the mud in front of the house to reduce the muck. Newspapers, for the rare few who had them, were read and reread and shared with others before being used as wall insulation, or wrap to keep food, and then toilet paper.

It's selfish to ask for help from those who can't afford to give it. Despite the hardships, or perhaps because of them, people looked after one another in heroic ways. If a neighbor fell ill, someone bumpity bumped soup and well wishes a few miles down the road. No matter that the soup was just a few lonely potatoes, wild onion, and hunks of stringy moose meat.

I don't know if Hugh ever noticed, but a couple of times, more cowboy beds were slept in than paid for at our ranch. The mystery boarders made efforts to remake the beds, but clearly lacked the proper training of a British mother. If I heard Chester bark in the night near the cowboy quarters, I didn't wake Hugh to check. Probably just a deer, I figured, and if not, better not to know. Cowboys were honest folk. They would always pay if they could. Once, I found a nickel on the rumpled bed where supposedly no one had slept. It was much less than the cost of lodging. I ran a fingertip across it and swallowed a stone of regret. Probably it was his last.

Certainly 108 Mile House sprouted a humble boarding house or two. If they cost the same as ours, we could rest our saddle-weary bones for a week. The notion of a steaming hot meal set my mouth watering. Tom, sensing some change come over me, tightened his grip on my shoulder. A weeklong stay was surely too dangerous. I tried to think like Hugh. Clever and strategic. *What would he do next? How much did my presence at the ranch mean to him? How nervous would he be that I would reveal his ugly secret?* The questions left me in fog. I hoped against hope that some kind-hearted soul at 108 Mile House would loan me the money for train fare. Once I found a job in Vancouver, I'd return the kindness. A daft plan if ever there was one, but I could come up with no better.

That night, we slept in damp bedding. That is, the cowboys and Katie slept. Tom and Nick were out quick as light switches. I, on the other hand, wallowed in damp worry, listening to the night dripping down around me. The slow purr of Tom's snoring sent my thoughts to Harvey. In that soggy blackness, I felt no glow of hope for him. I'd needed him—to return, to love me, to help me, to rescue me. He hadn't. Anyone would have said it wasn't his fault, that he didn't know. How could he have known?

But . . . *how could he not?* I could see him, and the way he moved through his days, clear-headed and steady on his horse, waiting for life to come upon him as the earth passed slowly beneath. His thoughts about me were few and light, like the way he might glance at a wildflower—briefly noting the pretty blue hue. To him, my heart was like a place on a map he stuck a pin in, hoping to visit one day. But he was making no plan toward it at all. He couldn't feel my chest aching. The anguish in the center of my ribs. Though I could sense every step of his horse in the day and the weight of his dreaming head at night, he didn't know me at all. He was blind to my despair. Against all logic, I blamed him. My heart, like a shortwave radio, was tuned to his station. Why wasn't he tuned to mine? *Why can no one hear me?*

The jar where I stored life's disappointments brimmed over. I numbed. Thoughts came like memos onto a mayor's desk. *He doesn't love you. Not the way you love him. He doesn't see you. He won't come to rescue you.* I glanced at them with cool detachment before signing my name in acknowledgment.

At least Tom and Nick were gentlemen. They hadn't forced themselves on me. Or harmed Katie. At least we were safe from Hugh, for the moment. At least Edwin had gotten out. Run away. Probably buried in the cool hay of someone's barn or nestled between the wooly sheep. His chances in life were even slimmer than ours now. No parents. Ran away from his brother. No skills. Too young for real work. No schooling. Damaged by a man. Those were the memos he would be signing. Ugly work for sure.

17

B Y DAY TWO, Ocktoo's bony hips dug into the thin saddle, branding my backside with bruises. The cows loped and clopped ever onward, mooing, bellowing, and snorting with annoyance or boredom. Tom rode quietly, keeping to himself. Either he'd spent his whole pocketful of charm or was saving up for the next round. Skippy and Nick maintained their exclusive communication dance. What is the sound in a canyon an hour after a flood has rushed through, destroying and clearing out everything? That was the sound inside me.

That's when Katie got her instructions. Coded deep inside every child is the insistent need to test the durability of her mother.

"Mummy, where are we going? When can we stop?! I want to *be* there!" She flopped over Ocktoo's neck and lolled to one side, forcing me to catch her from falling off the horse.

"Not yet," I answered flatly. "It'll be a long time."

This perfectly unacceptable answer provoked a screeching cry and a gush of tears. Ocktoo rose up into a pinned-ear trot.

"I'm not magic, Katie. I can't make us arrive faster!" I snapped, snatching at the dregs of motherliness.

This struck Katie as a personal insult. She retaliated by bellowing louder. The fearful cows pounded their hooves to the earth and started scattering. This impressed or frightened Katie so much that she opened her lungs and wailed. I looked up at the sky, hoping for an exit door from the world.

Nick swiveled around in his saddle. His steely eyes punctured my weary guilt. I wanted to hit Katie. Knock her straight and sensible. End this wailing as quick as possible. But she broke through my numbness once again. *She's as broken as me though she doesn't understand it yet. And we two are in this together.* She was the innocent.

"Now, Katie, shhh." I stroked her arm and hair, mechanically.

"I want biscuits that are warm! I don't want hard bread!"

"Shh. Shh," I said for both of us.

"I want Chester!"

"I know," I offered, feebly.

As if she'd been trained as a circus girl, she up and stood on Ocktoo, turned around with tear-blurred eyes and, wrapped her arms around me, shoving her face into my chest. I covered her hot head with my hands. "Shh, shh," I said. She sobbed small, wet cries for us both. After a while, whimpers and hiccups were all that came out. "Shh, shh."

With her weight on me, my rear end went completely numb. Just like mother's milk, my love for her never completely ran dry. The cows had settled back into meandering compliance. Wafer-thin clouds diluted the sunshine while doubling its brightness. Skippy's eyes were half shut, squinting out the light. Tom spat onto the grass. We rode on and on, a rhythmic noise of travelers, warmth holding my shoulders upright.

At 108 Mile House, our horse-riding adventure would come to a halt. And then if every mountain slid down onto the train tracks and roads and some kindly cowboy offered to lope us along with a gang of beef, I'd launch him an icy look and say no. Katie would not tolerate another daylong horse ride anytime soon. I began to tell her a story about a swan and a castle in a faraway place. Both of us drifted off into the tale for a long stretch of trail ahead.

At last, Katie drooped heavily onto my chest. I wished I could nap and forget the world too. The cattle bobbed their pretty heads before us, a shuffle of hooves and hide, snorting and huffing. Tom rode slightly ahead with the flask still opened and resting on his thigh. The trail narrowed. Trees sloped down one side and sliding grey rock rose up the other. Nick rode in front, guiding the troops. Skippy, eyes half asleep, trotted and panted behind me. Ocktoo stepped cautiously around some fallen rock.

I tiptoed through the wreckage of my marriage, examining where the trip wires had lain. What had I missed? I remembered the dance where I met Hugh. Since few women were in those parts, I was a much sought-after commodity at the time. At the dance that night we met, the only unmarried womenfolk were little Louisa, who was too young for marriage, and me. I must have danced with twelve men.

But Hugh stood out. He came to me first, and he danced with me last. The dimness of the kerosene lamps hid my reddened cheeks. His dark blue eyes gazed without hesitation and he had a way of holding his shoulders like he always knew where he was headed. My breath caught as I looked up at him. He had a way about him unlike anyone I'd known. Like he'd sauntered back from the future to see how we were getting along in the present. Like he'd done all this before and was merely remembering his lines from last time. He held his hand out to me, and when mine dashed out, then hesitated above his, he grinned.

On the dance floor that night, other men chit-chatted with me as we swayed and swirled. *What's your name, miss? Mind if I just call you pretty? I hear you're the new schoolmarm. I sure like dancing with you. You got the prettiest face this side of the moon. Where you from? Thank you for the dance, miss. I'd sure be pleased if you'd see your way to foot tangle with me again tonight.* One small red-headed man with pudgy wet palms smiled twitchily and stepped on my feet every few steps.

But Hugh was different. He gazed at me intently, winning every staring match, while my gaze flitted across him like a blind butterfly's. His eyes slanted over his cheekbones like a wolf's. But a sprinkle of Irish freckles gave him a boyish charm. I believed his intent stare signaled desire and devotion. Just as in the early days of our marriage, I believed his clarity and knowledge would safeguard me, sturdy as house and sound as bedrock. But months or years later, I knew he behaved like that for his own purposes. Make people do what he wanted. Don't ask questions. Just do. And in that moment, he'd already decided I would marry him. He told me that later. He decided for me. When the last fiddler played himself out, Hugh squeezed my hand, then turned and walked away. My heart lurched sideways. Didn't he like me? Didn't he want to see me again? He did. But since he had already determined what would happen, he just didn't bother to ask.

Later that month, I asked around after him. He owned the Willow Creek Ranch, a sprawl of sloping meadows to the west of Eager Mountain. Well, the ranch, I later learned, contained not a trace of willows. No delicate streamers of leaves swaying out over the water. It had at one point, however, contained a lonely widow who renamed it before selling it for a dime. Hugh had come to the Cariboo direct from Ireland seven years earlier. He had never been married. He had proposed to Martha Ellen two years before, but she chose a jolly rancher instead. Don't think he ever recovered from that—not the heartbreak, but the insult. They said he kept to himself, didn't drink much, and worked hard. I ran into him a month later in town where we stood on the splintery sidewalk discussing weather, willing myself not to blush while he gazed at me over those high cheekbones.

The third time I saw him was the proposal. I was clacking the chalk brush clean after the children went home, when he arrived at the dusty threshold of the schoolhouse door. Wind drove autumn leaves in through the door as he entered. The last time a man showed up after school hours, it was Mackenzie Jones come to warn me of a wildfire blowing up from the south. The first time, it was Alister Rex coming to size up the new schoolmarm. He wanted to lend a hand with the board wiping, or wood chopping, or skirt lifting, or whatever else he could salivate his way into. A quick scolding and he went on his way like a beaten dog.

Quite understandably, I startled at the sight of Hugh and dropped the chalk brush to the floor in a mute firework of white dust. He wasn't out of breath, so he wasn't reporting an emergency. He stood holding a tawny hat loosely in one hand. Perhaps he wanted to steal the desserts of marriage without paying the price of a ring. I'd heard stories about other women, so I knew it could happen.

I glanced at his shirt pockets but saw no shape of a ring box. No awkward shuffling, either. That's the way men proposed, wasn't it? Earlier that week, I had learned that Donny, a cowhand from Whisky Creek Ranch, wanted to ask for my hand in marriage, but was still working up the gumption to do it. Donny was perpetually leaning his head to his shoulder and smiling about some joke of which only he was aware. He had wisps of hair pulled sideways over his bald spot like threads on a loom. His private cheeriness and general harmlessness sparked a thin flame in me that flickered and sputtered whenever he opened his mouth. After chatting with him, one wandered away wondering how sentences work, if one's hearing had become scrambled, and how the patterns of communication had become unhinged.

I lifted the chalk brush from the floor with a damp palm.

A true cowboy would say hello by tipping his hat, or touching his hat, or touching the place his hat would have been, or raising a finger to a forehead, or pinching an invisible brim. But Hugh was Irish, not cowboy. Rancher, not cowhand. He just stared from the doorway, a good ten paces off.

"Sorry about all the chalk dust," I said, motioning to the halo of powder at my feet.

"Chalk, snow, or dust. You can take your pick here in the Cariboo." He smiled, leaning on one leg and sizing up the room. "All three, going for quite a bargain round these parts." I smiled. He settled into a chair. I suppressed a giggle at seeing him sit in the naughty child chair. A missed omen, perhaps. "Well, after our splendid dance, I thought you would inquire all over town about me. Thought I'd save you the trouble and bring you the story myself."

Wide-eyed and curious, I masked my eagerness with a lot of fiddling about the edges of things—my desk, my shirt, my fingers. What came next was a sales pitch, though it sounded like earnest courtship at the time. The past is always changing. Months after our marriage I heard him negotiating with Vancouver butchers and grocers over the telephone. At sales pitches, he excelled. He spotted and exploited a client's emotional needs and weaknesses, knew what the client wanted better than the client himself. "I'm not selling beef," he told me once. "I'm selling self-confidence, stability, and opportunity." His product—whether beef, potatoes, or a marriage proposal—was presented as a solution to a person's inner needs.

His proposal to me described a worry-free life, a life of companionship and respect and "an end to the solitary life of a schoolmarm." He mentioned the pride a parent feels when their child has chosen the right partner. Indeed, my father would have been pleased and relieved to have me married. Hugh said he liked a woman who was "good and kind" and said I was both. Marriage, he waxed, was "an end to the lonesome austerity of the soul." A chill rose up my arms. Could he have known this secret of my soul? The childhood rooms packed with cold silence. Stiff sheets that whispered of spinsterhood in the night. My daydreams, lit like lamps on the cold streets where others walk arm in arm.

Two months later we had a small wedding with a handful of friends and family. With a nod toward his ranch, Mother remarked that he seemed "pleasant enough." We ate hard, white cake in a hall absent of flowers because the crocuses had not yet pushed through the icy soil.

Beneath me, my horse clopped with the rhythm of the cattle. Katie's weight strained my back. *Yes,* I considered, *Hugh is dangerous. And more clever than I.*

The cattle lowed and shuffled along with a rumbling of hooves and snorts, nodding heads and brown shaggy backs. Nick rode far up ahead, checking the front line. Tom was not far behind us, muttering finicky cuss words to his irritated mare.

I checked the horizons on all sides—soft, tawny hills; stands of pine; and thickets of fir behind. No sign of Hugh. He was not near. No sign of a lifeless body of a boy either. Where did he go off to? When people asked our names, I would lie. Katie would be Trina. I would take my mother's middle name, Ellen. I would tell the cowboys not to tell anyone who we really were. I would come up with a logical plan. *Stay alert.*

The town called 108 Mile House emerged on the horizon as a dark clump of minuscule buildings under a purple smudge of evening sky. The sight of it didn't cheer me. It's hard to go unnoticed in a town with five buildings.

I kicked Ocktoo into a trot and rode over to Tom. "Trina and Ellen," I instructed with a firm smile to seal the deal. Tom whistled in disapproval. He didn't like a crooked path. It went against his nature, which was straight as a proper arrow. The truth goes straight. That's the way to get somewhere. Nick, on the other hand, turned away from the conversation with indifference. He wouldn't give a hoot if we were called Buckle and Pushpin.

Katie delighted in the new names because she had recently begged me to start calling her Trina. When my mother visited us last summer, she had taken to calling her Trinie—short for Katrina. Katie loved that special association. The trickier part was explaining that if someone thought she was Katie, she should say she wasn't.

As the small town rose up like tombstones before us, Nick said, "We'll leave you here. We're off to the stopping house." He motioned to a corral to the east. "Best if we're not seen together." I thanked him for taking us so far.

"Yup," he replied, spitting tobacco onto a piff of dirt.

"Sure you don't wanna keep cattle driving with us? We'll be in Vancouver in ten days or so. And we won't charge you hardly a thing," Tom offered.

Nick turned his horse away. "Hey, we ain't no lady transport service."

Tom took offense. "See here—that's the problem with you. You don't know a good thing when it's sitting pretty on the saddle in front of you!"

"No, that's okay." I straightened. "We should be able to train it from here." I glanced with trepidation at the town before us.

"Thank you, Tom." Something caught in my throat. Tom was the last. The last of anyone who knew me, who knew us, who cared a little about what happened next. My eyes pained with suddenly inexplicable tears. I looked off in the distance until they passed. *After all,* I reminded myself, *I'm not entirely sad to see him go.*

"At your service, missus," he offered with melancholic bravado. After so much levity, gravity had gotten the best of him. His eyebrows, mouth, and shoulders sagged as he touched finger to hat brim and turned his horse toward Nick.

I pulled hard on Ocktoo's reins to prevent him from following. He yanked at the bit in disagreement, turning his body to one side as if the rear could go where the head was prevented. He huffed and grumbled, alleging that my efforts were misguided. And that was the last straw for Katie.

"I'm going down!" She threw her arms straight up and slid out of my grasp down Ocktoo's side to the ground. With Katie and Ocktoo conspiring against me, I rapidly dismounted. I grasped Katie with one hand and Ocktoo's reins with the other. Calmly, we three strolled into the unknown town. The dust trail left from Tom and Nick was still settling. Besides a couple of dopey-eyed mares hitched in front of the saloon, no one was around.

The boarding house was a two-story log building, plain as a hay bale. I tied Ocktoo to the post and knocked timidly on the door. The woman who answered the door had dark blue bags under her eyes and brittle blond hair that looked like a wig, but was not. Indeed, she resembled a man with a wig and stuffed brassiere. Her decades—three, four—had knocked her around, leaving her shoulders high and ready for battle and pudgy, short fingers curled in a loose fist, ready to sock someone.

Her aggressive curiosity dissolved into bored annoyance as she sized me up. Whatever she hoped for in boarders, Katie and I were not it. I explained our need for a room, and she waved us in. Then she leaned out the door and hollered until a lanky teenaged boy dragged Ocktoo to the stable. We stepped into a dining room containing an elegantly carved table battered by knicks, scratches, and grime. On the wall hung four small and very faded paintings of women in flirtatious poses. Years of sunlight had turned the models' rosy cheeks to cold porcelain and dresses to pale blue, and made an elegant hat look like a bird hitting a woman's head. There was enough dry muck and dust on the floor to welcome in the cattle. A large man at the table rose quickly with a crust of bread still dangling from his mouth. He too was uncharacteristically round where everyone else in these regions was lean from hard work and food shortages. He sized me up with impolite curiosity, then turned to the woman for explanation.

"She wants a *room*," she pronounced, as if boarders typically requested something else—a yellow barn, a traveling circus, a line of cancan girls in ruffled skirts. Her answer satisfied him. He nodded once, dropped back down to his chair and resumed ripping apart the carcass of bread, Katie was watching the bread with pity on her face. She rearranged the tightness of her grip in mine. What an odd manner for a boarding house, I pondered.

After paying the woman, who never did tell us her name, we followed her up a creaking staircase to the room at the far end of the hall. Inside was a single bed with a woven and tattered bedspread. The mattress sloped in the middle like an elderly horse. Next to it, a cock-eyed, half-burned candle perched on a wooden apple box. The window curtain was the color of an old orange. A chipped enamel pouring jug sat beside a chipped enamel basin on an upturned bucket. The scene might have been disappointing under other circumstances. At that moment, however, it suited me perfectly. We were far, far from Hugh. No damp bedding. No animal footsteps padding through the trees in the night. Katie squeezed my hand and looked up at me for approval. I nodded to her. She let go of my hand and petted the bedspread delicately, like beds were rare creatures she had never before seen.

"Well, that's it," the woman said. I nodded and she closed the door behind us. We stood listening to her tromp back down the wincing stairs. Exhausted, we stripped to our underclothes and crammed into the tiny, sagging bed, grinning at our luxuries. Katie asked, "Can we stay here forever?"

"We can stay a couple of nights." I lay on my back with my hands behind my head and peered gleefully at the melting pink horizon out the window.

Katie whispered, "I don't want to ride Ocktoo again. Don't tell him. I don't want to make him sad."

I giggled, "All right, I won't."

We whispered and giggled for a while before the warm flood of sleep swept us under.

18

THE TAILS OF dreams slipped into the shadows as the waking world sharpened. Morning glowed through the orange curtain. Today I would inquire about the train to Vancouver.

Fear pressed a bony finger to my chest. A week had gone by since I'd left the ranch. I pictured one of the new farmhands coaxing porridge into bowls while Hugh muscled up his jaw and schemed beside him. What would Hugh do next? I lay on my back, staring up at—but not seeing—the angled wooden ceiling. Hugh's tense face, closed fist, and penetrating eyes flashed before me, like a shuffle of photographs. The first night I was gone, his anger had spilled like a blood-red sunset. Now, it had tensed and contracted into stone. *She's my wife, for Christ's sake. She'll do the obeying. Our vows said the same.*

He was plotting how to bring me back. I could feel it. But what would he try? He would not send a farmhand to look for me. That would be too easy. And he needed to prove to everyone—especially himself—the wretchedness of my departure. He would revel in the pain of it, put it on display. He would inquire after me all over town, watching folk watch him, shaking their heads on account of his poor suffering. He would shore up sympathy to be put to use at some later date—when borrowing a steer or hiring a cowhand. It was a chess game, and he was three steps ahead of the rest of us. A thread broke in my fingers. Without realizing it, I'd been pulling at the loose ends of the blanket. I pressed my fingers to my aching temples.

Hugh would ponder over the truck parked outside Edison's Market. Why hadn't I put it somewhere else? Mr. Edison promised to keep my secret, but Hugh would stare at him like he was on trial at the Inquisition. In his bewildered and guilty confusion, would Ed relent? My heart flip-flopped. Yes, I felt it. Ed had blurted it. *Oh dear, yes, she headed north with a cowboy.* Goosebumps raked up my arms. *Yes. Yes. She was here. Wouldn't say why. Didn't want her to go. Said so. Now don't come down too hard on her when you find her . . .* He would leave out the part of how he himself arranged the escape.

I felt queasy. One trail would lead to the next. Once he knew my initial direction, it was all toppling dominos from there. So Hugh would head north. That would buy me a few days, since I was far south of there now. I saw Ed wringing his hands after Hugh left. *Something amiss. Something not right in that Annabelle's husband,* he'd be thinking. Then with bustling urgency, he would rearrange the cans on the shelves to distract himself from the unsettling notion.

All of this I knew. I knew and no one could have talked me out of it. For the next while, as I lay in bed, fear dressed up as practicality. Fear said go home to him and apologize. Tell him and all the townsfolk you had a case of hysteria. You'll have food and shelter. You can live with danger once you understand it better. You can live in the shadows. You can listen at night for his footsteps into Katie's room. Listen in the day for the barn doors sliding shut. Fear said it was a stupid experiment to run away. Fear said Mother would want you to go back. Fear crawled under the covers, filled my lungs, and hurried my breathing.

But when I imagined returning, my body felt grey as ash. Better the danger of freedom. *Let hope be my guide, not fear.* I tried to picture Harvey. The ceiling planks before me were blank.

Careful not to disturb Katie, I put my legs over the side of the bed and sat up. I crossed the splintery floorboards and slipped on trousers and a plaid shirt. Mother didn't believe in women wearing trousers. Even Hugh smirked when I suggested trying them. When I lived in Vancouver, skirts weren't bothersome at all. But in the Chilcotin when I squatted by the laundry basin, gathered armloads of wood, and raked garden weeds, a skirt felt like a net for mud and twigs. In the city, women wore trousers as a sign that they supported women's equality. But in the Cariboo, I wore trousers because it's depressing to wash laundry while one's hem drags in the dirt. I support women's right to do less laundry. Nonetheless, I wore them infrequently and felt rather bold when I did.

When Katie awoke, I would head downstairs for breakfast. I didn't want to frighten her by leaving her alone. That's always mothers' excuse: pretending to protect our children, while needing the security of them by our sides. A small hand in one's hand. A small tug at one's skirt. The shiny loops of Katie's hair lay across the pillow. Her delicate red lips were parted slightly, faintly revealing the rhythm of her breath. The humble room was beautiful because she was in it.

Later that morning, after warm porridge and hot tea—oh, the luxuries of being off the cow trail!—I worked up the nerve to ask. The sole other boarder, a quiet gentleman on some kind of government work, had left the table. The woman came in to remove the dishes, sighing heavily over the table.

"I beg your pardon, ma'am." I squeezed the napkin on my lap. "I wondered if I might be able to have a word with you about something."

She stopped in her tracks, frozen, as if in the next moment I might pull out a rifle. I shifted in my seat, hoping she'd sit down so we'd both be more at ease.

"You see, I'm on my way to Vancouver, but my trip there has been delayed for unexpected reasons. And this means I've spent more liberally than expected."

She nodded, but didn't blink.

"I wonder if you might have a bit of work I could do in exchange for being here. I've got a couple of days' wait for the train. Perhaps the dishes or a bit of weeding in the garden, or something of the like."

She looked at me. She glanced at Katie and back to me.

"Felix!" she bellowed into the kitchen. Felix marched heavy-footed and grimacing into the room.

"The missus wants some work." She pronounced each word carefully, as though Felix might misunderstand. His eyes went from her to me to Katie and back again. Something peculiar was going on. It occurred to me that I didn't like these two very much. They made me ill at ease. They were odd and unusually lacking in warmth and welcome. My heart was beating fast despite attempted self-control.

Felix thumped down into the chair beside me, leaning a bristly chin and pale lips uncomfortably close. "Listen here," he whispered, so Katie wouldn't overhear. Katie sat erect and alert in her chair, sharp ears tuned to every word. "Where did you say you came from?" His eyes searched mine to fish out the answer. *Where was I supposed to be from again?*

"Up north," I muttered weakly.

"And you want work?"

"Well, yes." *Wasn't that already clear?* "If it isn't too great an inconvenience." I tilted back to create some space between our faces.

"Hmm," he grumbled, puzzling it out. He turned back to the woman and knocked his fist on the table, exclaiming, "Send her to garden with Glenda." He nodded firmly at me. His job done, he stood, turned and left.

"Thank you," I rushed to say as he left. To the woman, I said, "That's very kind."

"Okay," she said skeptically, slightly shaking her head.

19

SOMETIME LATER, WHEN the rain stopped and Glenda had been located, the woman gave Katie a shabby, one-eyed doll and a glass of milk in the kitchen, and I donned my still-damp coat and met Glenda in the garden. She stood leaning on the end of a shovel. Was she a youthful forty-five-year-old or a weary twenty-five-year-old? Pale blond curls wrapped a babyish face. Thin lines that sloped under her eyes and around a voluptuous mouth revealed a history of disappointment. She wore tight grey trousers and an oversized coat, clearly not her own. She propped up a tired smile.

"I'm Glenda," she intoned, like an actress who has lost conviction for her role.

"I'm . . . Ellen," I returned, setting my hands on my hips and scanning the garden to deflect her gaze. "Well. I suppose we ought to start with the weeds around the potato bed."

"Sure," she agreed indifferently. She stretched the shovel handle out in front of her like a dance partner, passing it hand to hand.

I yanked fistfuls of soggy weeds. Spring potato stalks wriggled up through last year's dead mess of old vines. Glenda stepped closer and kicked her toe at a clump of dirt.

"City life takes a toll," she remarked. Apparently, country life didn't enthrall her, either. "Wears down the bones with worry," she continued. "Got a lot to fret about there. No money. No jobs. Hard if you got a kid, too." Was she talking about herself?

"Do you have a child?" I asked.

"Me?" Her eyebrows raised, incredulously. "Wouldn't be able to keep one if I did!" I blinked at the weeds. A tangle of questions caught in my throat. Sensing this, she added, "No. No child. No child now."

"What's your girl like?" she asked, propping hands and chin on the shovel handle.

"Well, she's—she's fine," I stammered, uncertainly. "She's smart and stubborn and all the things three-year-olds are."

"Good, good." She considered. "That's good. You want them to be healthy." Glenda stuck the shovel into a patch of grass. Repeating the action, she seemed more intent on insulting the grass than removing it. I wiped loose hairs from my eyes with the back of my hand. The sky was knotting up with clouds. The boarding house mistress peered at us through a window. Glenda glanced at her, then lazily sank into a squat to pluck at dandelion leaves.

"Lots of work here," she offered.

"That's good. I need some work right now," I said, surveying an overgrowth of weeds choking out the stray vegetables. She threw her head back and laughed.

"Not *that* kind of work," she smiled. "I mean keeping the menfolk company." Of course the boarders would enjoy chatting with her. She was pretty enough and chatty—and most importantly—female.

"You don't understand." Her face was deadpan, so for a moment I couldn't see where the joke was going. My smile faltered.

"I mean keeping them company, so as they're not lonely," she explained. In case I was still plodding my way toward the obvious, she added, "Company *in bed*." She stood and resumed her dance with the shovel handle. "Pays room and board. And the men are okay. Mostly."

"Oh," I said as kindly as possible. I glanced at the house, worrying about Katie. The woman was watching. Not a boarding house mistress. A brothel madam. She's assessing me—wondering if I would make a good whore. I turned back to the weeds. *Now where do we go?*

"It's not as bad as you think," she sniffled, kicking a clump of dirt. "I never thought I would do it either. Not why I came to the Cariboo."

I sat back and looked at her. A spent beauty with oddball charm. I queried, "Why *did* you come to the Cariboo."

"Well, it's a funny tale." She smiled sadly at the dirt, so that I knew it was not funny at all. "I broke with my family when I started dating a fella they didn't like. I moved in with him, but then one day I found out he's cheating on me, so I up and left. I was working at that time at the fish cannery on Dundas. I asked my boss if I could sleep in the spare room there just until I saved enough to be on my own." She glanced at the house. "My own family wouldn't talk to me anymore, see? So he let me. But after a week, he decided he should sleep there too—with me. We had a bit of a tussle, and he said he was going to call the police and tell them I broke in and was stealing. So I left. Walked all the way to Hope. Took me three days. Didn't know where I was going, but had to leave Vancouver. The boss had given me a nice shiner, too, so I wasn't too pretty.

"By dawn on the third day, I was having coffee at a diner, when in walks this tall handsome man, a hardware deliverer. Offers me a ride to Kelowna, and I says yes because I was thinking I could find work anywhere, and the boss might throttle me for good if he saw me again. Anyway, I stayed with the deliveryman and we were married a month later." She gave up on leaning against the shovel and plunked right down onto the damp dirt. She kept looking over at the house, as if part of her story were stuck inside there. She plucked at the tips of some grass, trimming them rapidly, blade by blade. "Well, he was at the bottle a lot. And, uh, that made him vicious mean. So I left. In the middle of the night, I left." She paused the story there, checking me for understanding.

"Oh." I tried to console her. "You've just had the most miserable string of luck!"

"Yup." She smiled and rolled up her sleeve. On the back of her right arm was a welt the size and shape of a quarter. "He did this with the poker." She peered at it with melancholy. "So I found myself here. Felix and Alice had a boarder who wanted something extra, so they offered that I could help him out for cash. What else was I gonna do? After that, one thing led to another." She pressed her lips and held my gaze. I pressed mine and tried to smile.

"It's not so bad. Most men are just a little lonely. Felix and Alice look after me. When my husband came up here looking for me, they fired a rifle over his Stetson." At this, she chuckled, looking out to the road where her husband must have gripped his hat in fear.

"But, Glenda, is this where you want to stay? I mean, I'm leaving—I'm going back to Vancouver, and perhaps you could come, too."

"No. I won't never go back. But I won't do this forever. I make the men real happy here. Soon I'll meet a nice gentleman who wants me all to himself. He'll take me away, and I'll lead a new life. Kick this life off me like mud on a shoe." Just as well that she wouldn't look at me. The doubt in my eyes didn't match the hope in hers. We were silent for a while, letting the shadows of clouds pass over. The breeze bounced the curls about her face and shivered the grass beside her. We each contemplated the complexity of womanhood, the struggle for independence, for safety, for peace.

Reaching a conclusion, she tilted her head toward the house. "Guess I'll tell them you ain't the right kind to do this work."

"It's—it's not like that," I started. But we both knew it was precisely like that. I didn't judge Glenda. In fact, I admired her. She pushed on past one affront to another, making her own choices. But she was right. I was not more righteous or moral than she was—just more stubborn. Gentle and yielding on the surface, but unbendable inside. I'd more likely die in a ditch of starvation than lie beneath the bodies of man after man.

She looked down at her boots, making no effort to hide her disappointment. For a brief moment, she had imagined she could have a friend in all this. A sister at the brothel.

"I'm sorry," I offered. But it was time to go in and fetch Katie.

She picked at some invisible mark on the shovel handle. "Not your fault." She leveled her gaze at me. "But Felix and Alice won't like you lingering about if you're not working. They worry about authorities finding out. And they own the whole town—grocery store, bar, this place."

I peered down at the bowl of my laced fingers. Green juices from weeds stained my hands. It was Wednesday morning, but the train was not due until Friday afternoon. I nodded, grateful for the warning, and walked quickly toward the backdoor.

Up in our room, I scrubbed in the washbasin while Katie looped around my leg, swaying back and forth like a sail in a storm. 108 Mile House was not a town I could stay in or try to earn money in. My money purse was light, but I needed to leave the brothel at once. The smells, the scuffs on walls, the assessing looks from Felix and Alice carried new meaning now. I grimaced at the washbasin, imagining its purposes.

Panic quickened in my throat. How could I reach Vancouver and Harvey? Which one of these barred roads would carry me toward the future? I couldn't take a train or bus to Vancouver because I was short the fare. Tom and Nick were long gone down the road, impossible to catch. Alone with Ocktoo and Katie, we'd be trampling in tangled, disoriented circles by nightfall. If I wasn't going to be a working girl, Felix and Alice would see us as a nuisance, rats who might squeal to police. Glenda had done her best to escape a man and ended up here. Mother said if the road looks blocked, you're looking at the wrong road. What road had I not seen?

I dried my hands. What would it be like to entertain just one man? Just one. That would be enough for a ticket. The fare for a new life. Maybe he wouldn't be so awful. Not leering. Not stinking of sweat, lust, and beer. Not claiming my body like his private property. One bitter compromise on the road to freedom. *What makes me so different from Glenda?* I interrogated myself. *Foolish stubborn pride. The gumption to think I deserved better—that I deserved love not sacrifice.* I pressed the hand towel to my tears. Nausea tingled my skin.

I couldn't give up yet. Perhaps no one in the world understood the self-sacrifice Glenda had made just to stay alive, to have food and shelter. An unlucky man can become a vagrant, a drunk. But an unlucky woman is a whore or else dead. I peered far over the edge of temptation, but pulled back just in time. Katie and I weren't going to starve to death tonight. Still time to try another way.

Katie was humming as she rocked side to side on my leg. Now she looked up at me and with disconcerting timing sang, *"Mummy's a dummy."*

20

AN HOUR LATER, I had a plan. I put my change purse into my bag and put it over my shoulder. "Come on, Katie." I held out my hand. "We're going to the bar."

"The *bar*?" she asked. "But I don't like the bar! Someone might throw their glass at me!" I wondered what cowboy stories she'd overheard.

"Don't be silly. You've never been in a bar. No one's going to throw their glass at a little girl."

"But they might throw one at *you*. They might be mad at you. *You* ran away. They might hit you with glasses to make you stop running."

I swallowed fear. "No, Katie, no one is going to throw a glass at anyone. That's not what bars are for."

"Fine," she huffed haughtily, perching her hands on her hips. "*You'll* see."

I shook my head and bundled her into her wool coat. "We're only going there to see if some cowboys will take us to Vancouver."

She contemplated this while wrestling with the coat sleeves. "How are they going to take us?"

"By horse, of course." Rhymes soften the truth.

"And Ocktoo?"

"Yes, with Ocktoo."

"No, Mummy, noooo! Ocktoo hurts me." She pointed to her rear.

"Calm down. We're not going on Ocktoo right *now*. We're just seeing if we can go down to Vancouver really soon."

"I don't like riding on Ocktoo anymore!"

"Well, then, you can walk!" I snatched her hand and we went out the door, with Katie whimpering the whole way. My teeth tightened. Felix was standing on the front step, chatting with Glenda, who stared at the floor when she saw us.

"Hello," I managed as we passed between them. They said nothing. Glenda toed at a rock with her boot. Felix stared at Glenda aggressively, blaming her. Her recruiting efforts had failed. His profit was walking away.

I pulled my slow-footed daughter over the dirt road. A wood sign next to an eight-pane window said simply: BAR. It wasn't much to look at. A couple of skinny, white-washed posts held up the sagging clapboard awning. Two mares tethered to the hitching post dozed with swishing tails next to a dusty Ford. The afternoon sun lit the wooden sidewalk before the screen door. A golden mutt beside the door raised his head, contemplating whether to bark. He puffed his cheeks, but apparently we weren't worth the effort. Katie leapt forward and stuck out her hand, and he swept his tail over the sidewalk.

I lifted Katie up onto my hip for confidence and careened into the door, which flapped open with a loud whack. I had been prepared for a few curious expressions but, indeed, I was the headline show. Silence shot through the room. Glasses half raised to mouths stopped in motion. A half dozen heads turned toward me with bewildered, amused, or ogling expressions. *And now gentlemen, please welcome Annabelle! The disheveled, stern, and pretty Annabelle and her miserable daughter!* Katie's hot face banged against my neck. I moved toward the bar counter. *Where has she come from? Why is she here? Gentlemen, let your imaginations run wild!*

I sat down at the bar with Katie clinging to my midriff like an octopus. I smiled tersely at the bartender, scanning the bottles behind the counter. I patted Katie's back, waiting for folk to go back to their liquor, thoughts, and talk. They did not.

At last, the bartender broke the silence. "Can I help you, ma'am?" he inquired, doubtful that he could.

I spoke softly, but all manner of rough, drunk, and sober men listened on. "I'm trying to make it home to Vancouver with my daughter. I'm wondering if you might know a kind fellow who's cowboying down that way in the next few days. I could use a guide on the trail, and I already have a horse."

The bartender started to shake his head, but a fellow with a shiny, round face sitting across from him interrupted: "No, Leonard, I can take care of this." He splashed the last of his whiskey down his throat and stood. He wasn't as lean and weathered as most of the men in those parts, and he was wearing a bulky flannel jacket. Probably a ranch owner. He sauntered over to the door. When he held it open, I realized he meant for us to follow him. And I hopped off the barstool with Katie still bundled around me and followed him. When I glanced back at the bartender, he was smirking at another fellow, like they knew something funny. As we stepped back outside, someone swore and we heard a glass shattering. Katie flew a look at me.

The ranch owner led us right back to the boarding house steps. Glenda turned and went inside the moment she saw us coming. But Felix stayed put, curious and amused. My arms were hurting, so I set Katie down. She clung to my leg.

"This here young lady says she wants a ride to Vancouver," he explained.

Felix paused, and then his eyes flickered with recognition. He bloomed with excessive jolliness, opening his arms to welcome the notion. "Why didn't you say so? I'm driving to Vancouver myself to visit a friend. Leaving tonight. You can come along for the ride!"

"You are?" I blurted out in disbelief. What timing!

"Why, yes, I am!" he cheered.

"Well!" I smiled with relief. "What extraordinary luck!" I grinned at Katie, who looked scornfully at the men.

"Yes," he agreed, eagerly. I glanced in the direction in which

Glenda had disappeared. I felt stung that she didn't tell me. Surely in such a small household, she would have known. Her need for a friend had outweighed her compassion.

"But what about our horse? I have to sell him before we leave."

"He's really not much of a gelding, is he?" Felix offered sympathetically.

"Well, he's—."

"His back is bowed like a tarpaulin tent. Looks to be about a hundred years old. Won't be worth much." He glanced at the shiny-faced man, as if daring him to challenge him on his assessment.

"Suppose I could take him off you for free, as a service," the shiny man said. "I don't need another horse. Especially an old one. But I'll make sure he don't starve to death."

"But," I swallowed hard. *What would Hugh do?* "I paid for him. I won't let him go for nothing. He's worth *some*thing."

"Well, ma'am, I'm not too sure about that." He brushed finger backs against his chin scruff and gazed off in the distance. He was lying. Hugh would say so to his face, dare him to disagree. I clutched my arm, too embarrassed to call him out. I gazed down the road where he was looking, as if the answers lay there.

"He's worth something," I offered. Somehow saying so made it feel less true.

His small blue eyes curled up with amusement while his thick mouth curled down with pity. "All righty then. I'll give you fifty cents." He glanced at Felix for input. Felix mirrored his frown and nodded once in solemn approval. Without waiting for me to respond, the shiny man reached into his coat, opened a coin pocket, and plucked out two quarters. He held them out, waiting to drop them into my hand. And, I saw my hand reach out of its own accord to catch them, though I was quite sure Ocktoo was worth many times that amount.

Upstairs, we ate a dinner of Mary's salmon jerky, and then I stuffed our belongings back into the sack while Katie sang *so-long-Ocktoo* at the windowpane. An ashen-blue dusk settled over the valley, and Felix was helping us up into the truck. A decrepit Chevy, it seemed to have more rust than siding to it. The door squealed in protest when he slammed it closed behind us. Katie was on my lap, but she quickly noticed the back bench, covered in pink blanket and crawled back there to claim her spot. Felix hopped in grinning like Christmas. He blinked at me and started humming "Puttin' On the Ritz" as he rumbled the engine to life.

I felt as if I were in a dream. So many horrible things had happened, I couldn't believe one good one was about to occur—a ride all the way to Vancouver that very night. We would arrive late, very late. Likely too late to knock on a friend's door. But I wouldn't think about that now. I felt dazed with uncertain glee, relief, and fatigue, and my nerves jangled around inside me like loose coins in a purse.

The buildings of 108 Mile House were swallowed up in the distance behind us. That puny stake of mankind gave way to the endless expanse of wilderness. Katie, who was already lying down on the blanket, was quickly lulled to sleep by the bouncing truck. Then, the moment turned inside out.

"Felix, oh! We're going the wrong way. I'm sure Vancouver is the other direction. This is where we came from." I checked to see if my blurted observation had accidentally wounded his pride, but he only chuckled.

"Oh, I've got to make a stop in Lac La Hache tonight. I'm going to see someone about a property there. Then we'll be on our way to Vancouver by morning." He glanced back at Katie.

"But," I asserted, "you said we were going to Vancouver tonight."

"Sure thing." He smiled without a care in the world. "But we'll make a little stop first." He studied me. "You're not in a rush, are you? Why are you in a rush?" He paused for me to answer. I wished he'd stop looking at me, since worry shaped my face. "Are you running away from something, *Annabelle*," he asked, teasingly. He knew who I was. The rumor had spread.

Behind us, Katie was drifting in a more welcoming place. I faced the road. "Are you really going to Vancouver? Are you even going to Lac La Hache?"

The frankness of the question momentarily stumped him. Weaseling, roundabouts, and tricks were his forte. He pulled in a breath and resumed an authoritarian posture.

"We'll just have a little talk there. Don't worry. I'll take care of you." His tone was paternal, but he squeezed my knee when he said it. The headlights bore an eerie white hole into the forest ahead. "You need some help," he clarified. "And, luckily, I want to help you." The habit of politeness arranged my face.

For a few minutes, the truck did all the talking, bumping and creaking with warning as it pushed grimly through night's canopy. We were definitely moving too fast to jump out. And with Katie sleeping behind me, I couldn't grab her quick enough to try.

"I think you are worried that I'm going to give away your little secret. Yeah?" he teased.

I tensed. I didn't know what he would do. The alarms in my head were too loud to think.

"I wouldn't do that. And bring you back to your husband? No. He must be a very bad man. And you're a good woman. You deserve better. Like Glenda. She is a good woman too. That's why we helped her leave that terrible man. Some husband he was. You see, we are good people, too. We try to help everyone. But this is difficult when someone won't accept our help. When we know we can help them and they try to do something dangerous or foolish instead. You see, I don't want you to have to go back to your husband. I don't want that. And yet, we could use a hand at the boarding house." *Or a whole body*, I thought.

"It's *not* a boarding house," I snipped. "I'm well aware of what it is."

"Oh, but it is! It's the best kind of boarding house! A place where men who are lonely can get some tender care. That's all. You don't like tenderness?"

"Certainly not in *that* manner with strangers!"

"In what manner? I think you have the idea wrong, my dear. Nice, good men visit us, and Glenda sits and chats with them. Perhaps she makes them a drink. Perhaps they just need to sit alone with a woman and talk, share company. That's all. If Glenda wants to give more than that, that's her own business. I don't pry in her business. I never ask what happened. But she's a very kind and good woman. And we keep her safe."

My stomach tightened. Had Glenda known Felix might pull this kind of trick? I imagined the way she had turned on her heel and disappeared when we approached the boarding house. Yes, she suspected. "I have no interest in working at your boarding house. None at all."

"Well, see, I don't think it wise to drive you to Vancouver when you have entirely the wrong idea about our business." He paused to let the implications sink in. "We don't want the Mounties up here poking their noses around. How can I say to them that we're doing nothing wrong? I can't even prove it to some runaway ranch wife?"

Some runaway ranch wife. So he knew everything about me. I touched my hand to my coat pocket. He didn't know I put our money in there.

"Oh, I believe you. I do," I offered, changing course. "It's just that I can't stay there. I'm sure you can ask some other woman."

At that he released a hearty belly laugh. "How many women do you think there are in the Cariboo, my dear?! I count five, including you!"

"Yes, but in Vancouver . . ."

"Vancouver is worlds away."

Out my window, the trunks of trees passed like bars on a cage.

"I guess I can't go to Vancouver after all," he announced

extravagantly, like he'd just resigned himself to the decision right then. He tilted his head at me and smirked like we were in on an intimate joke. "It would be bad for business. Also"—he set a large, meaty hand on my thigh—"that husband of yours has offered a sweet little reward for anyone who turns you in." I pushed his hand off and set my sights on the road ahead, plotting, panicking. He scolded, "Hey—don't wake the little one. I don't want her to be scared. Do you?" His thick, warm hand fell between my legs. I gasped, shoved him, and pressed into the corner of the truck. He drove with one arm on the steering wheel. He tried to pull my thigh nearer to him. With effort, I pried his heavy hand off me again. He took hold of the steering wheel with both hands, glancing rapidly from me to the road, strategizing.

I glanced at Katie jostling along on the back seat. She was rolling over. I hissed at him, "Stop it! Stop this nonsense!"

Katie woke with a mewling cry, as if from a bad dream. I pulled her up from the back seat and plunked her onto my lap, while Felix gibed, "It's OOOkay. It's OOOkay."

Katie whispered something to me. An idea came. "We need to pull over. My girl needs to go to the bathroom."

With great pomp and self-confidence, Felix shifted down to slow the truck. "You go past the road's edge into these forests and you're cougar food," he bellowed. Katie gasped and whipped her head to measure his seriousness—exactly as he planned. If the daughter is terrified of the woods, she will scream if the mother tries to run. For added measure, he continued, "Thirty miles from 108 Mile House now. And that's the closest town by far."

The truck grumbled over to the side of the road. Felix turned to stare at me. His wide, wet smile turned down at the edges. He found pleasure in my discomfort. It puffed his sense of control. I hoisted Katie onto my hip, glanced at our belongings tucked behind the seat, and turned empty-handed away from the truck.

We walked slowly to the edge of the woods. The floor of twigs softly cracked beneath my feet as the truck rumbled in wait.

I whispered in Katie's ear, "*Trust me.*" Her breath quickened. Her hand on my back caught hold of my braid. When we were a good thirty feet away, I peered over my shoulder to see if he was coming. One arm rested on the steering wheel and his other on the seat back. Too self-assured, I thought. One more step and the light of the truck gave way to the mottled shadows of dusk and forest. I set Katie down and whispered urgently, "*Run!*"

She flashed me steady eyes, and we charged into the dark. Together we were breath and snapping, thumping steps, flying through trees, rising over fallen logs, scraping past brush, running on and on, while behind us the voice of that man bellowed into emptiness. Threats, verbal injuries faded into the dark with the truck lights. We were swift and panicked. Behind us the forest floor cracked heavily beneath his weight. Katie's hand was in my hand, tight and damp.

In the distance, the truck door closed, opened again. A moment later—two rocks smacking hard. A rifle. Our rhythm jolted. *No, Katie. He won't get us. These woods will protect us.* We ran until the only sound was the padding of our running feet. Dirt, moss, twig beneath. Held, hurried, panting. My legs burned. Sharp pine air cut my lungs. Katie's hand grew heavier in mine. I swooped her up and ran for us both. I could run forever.

21

I STOPPED WHEN we came to the edge of a creek, where smooth rocky sides glistened over with grey moonlight. I recognized it, I was pretty sure. Tom and Nick had stopped with us for a bite of salmon jerky and bread before continuing on to 108 Mile House. Under the swath of nightfall, I couldn't be sure. It didn't matter.

I lowered Katie and scooped up a palmful of sweet creek water, just like the cowboys taught me. Katie did the same, slurping and gasping and smacking her small hand to her mouth. We walked toward a twisting oak tree. I pulled Katie into my arms and sat with my back against it. He wasn't following. He would drive up and down the road for a couple of hours, waiting for us to reappear, haggard and frightened, resigned to his aid. Alone in the woods, we were as good as gone, he would think.

He didn't know us at all. I stroked Katie's hair. I kissed her head. She threw her arms around me as though the forces of night might wash us apart the moment we let go. She trembled from fear. A chill breeze picked up from the north, hinting of the night to come, but I did not feel frightened or cold. I unbuttoned my jacket and wrapped Katie inside.

"Go to sleep." I patted my chest.

"The forest will protect us?"

"Yes," I answered. "The forest is our friend." Katie leaned against me, tossing one way and then the other for a long time. She didn't complain. She didn't ask for her bed or an explanation.

Finally, she dozed with her ear over my heart. I lay awake, listening to the clean breeze hum in branches, the language of wind speaking of far-off places. I listened the way rocks listen, nestled in my own utter quietness, without time, listening to the motion of the world. After a long while, deep and sudden sleep settled upon me.

The wind carried images of Harvey into my dreams. My hand rested on his, as he spoke to me with a glance. Instructions. A coding. Direction. In another dream, he said, *I am a compass, not a watch.* Teeth so white. So white. In another, his arm brushed my arm, but I lost him in the darkness.

I awoke with daybreak. The wind shook darkness loose from the trees. My legs were painted with a cold dew. My back ached with the print of the tree trunk. I readjusted Katie. She was a hot, heavy lump of slumber. I buried my nose in her hair to regain the scent of love.

The dreams of Harvey did not dissipate at the edge of waking as dreams are apt to do, drifting into the soon-forgotten fog. Harvey's presence stayed with me; his hand under my hand felt like memory. I was calm, as if I knew exactly which direction to take. In fact, I didn't know anything. But some stubborn pull inside me leaned me out into the day, and we walked. If it were July, the woods would be filled with huckle-, goose-, and thimbleberry. We could feast like the bears off the wild fruit. But since it was still early May, we had to make do with a few pale, hard huckleberries.

Somehow—certainly not owing to my doubtful sense of direction—we found a cowboy trail. Was it the only one in these parts? A sort of north–south cattle-blazing road? I didn't know, and whatever landscapes and landmarks I'd seen with Tom and Nick had drifted off into Neverland, so I couldn't recall if we'd been on this same trail or not. We headed in a southerly direction. Thankfully, the sun elbowed away the overcast, and I could at least discern the directions from shadows. If I was right and this was the same trail, we could make a wide detour when we came to 108 Mile House, then walk far enough south to, I hoped, stumble on a ranch before nightfall. I would leave Katie at the edge of the woods and spy on the occupants. If I determined that they seemed like good people, I'd fetch Katie and call upon them. If, on the other hand, they were liquor-swilling slobs—the type that provided Felix and Alice with regular business—I'd wait till nightfall to steal just enough from their garden to keep us from starving. It was going to be a hungry day.

Because of the novelty of searching for huckleberries for breakfast, Katie didn't complain during the first couple of hours of walking. But finally, all the tears, fear, and hunger from the night before shook loose, until it seemed that only her wailing carried her onward. Each cry throbbed the metal of my eardrum, but I stayed patient. *Let her cry now. She was magnificently silent and obedient when I needed her to be.* When the shattered cymbals of my ears strained my patience, we struck a deal. I promised to carry her on my back for a whole hour, so long as she stopped crying immediately. Instantly, she folded up her cries into a hiccup.

It was Katie who heard them first. "Is he coming?" she whispered, with her ear leaned out over the path.

"Who?"

"The fat man from the truck."

"No. No—I don't think so." I stopped walking and listened for the faintest noises. What sounded like the rushing of wind through flapping leaves a moment ago, now sounded like the steady plod of a small herd of cattle heading toward us from the direction of 108 Mile House.

"No, Katie, this is someone else." Felix wasn't driving cattle. But if Felix knew about the award being offered for us, how many others knew?

"Who is it?"

I set her down and took her hand, preparing. She was fast on her little legs, but I was slow with her on my back. "I don't know." If the cowboys coming had a mind to turn us in, perhaps I could convince them otherwise. In any case, we had little chance of surviving alone. When I left our sack in the car, I left the last of our salmon jerky and biscuits, and extra clothing. We weren't even wearing enough to survive a May cold snap.

On a particular day about two years before . . . Katie was asleep in her crib, the men were out in the fields, and I was scrubbing desperation into the floor. Why? I had a working marriage back then. I had a roof over my head and a kitchen with food in it. I was not running for my life. No one had shot a rifle at me and my child. Yet at few moments of my life had I felt so utterly alone and defeated. My mother had visited us prior to returning to England. My heart ached with her absence. That day, the diluted sunshine and shallow clouds set a coolness into the bones, into the heart that craves warmth when no warmth is coming.

If I could just keep scrubbing the floor, my world would not fall apart. If I just stopped letting thoughts play circus with my head—thoughts that I could go with Mother to England—thoughts that I could be kicked in the head by a horse and someone else would be left to scrub the floor. If only we had never left England, I wouldn't be so alone on the ranch now, without a father, without Mother. A morose chuckle had escaped me. *I'm surrounded by horses and ponies, Daddy. But now I don't want them.*

The tumble of cattle hooves grew in the distance. This day held no certainty of food, shelter, or safety, but I was free. If the warmth of love didn't wrap me, at least the fine breeze of freedom did. Morning sunshine brightened countries of cloud. The heart-shaped leaves of poplars jittered in the breeze. My dream of Harvey was lightening my step. Sometimes we go digging for hope, prying at the rocks and scratching through the dirt. But this morning, hope trickled easy as creak water.

The cattle dog found us first and rushed back to tell the cowboys. Next, dozens of unamused cattle tromped past as we pressed our backs to the tree trunks. Then two cowboys strolled in on slow horses. And when I saw that one of them truly was Harvey,

I was relieved—but somehow not wholly surprised. My heart didn't leap, it unfolded with a kind of knowing, like the feeling one has settling the last puzzle piece into place. The two cowboys touched the brims of their hats. Harvey and I held each other's gaze, letting sweet silence do the talking.

22

KATIE PULLED LOOSE from my hand to rest on the ground. The cattle dog bathed her fingers with its tongue. I clasped my hands tightly in front of me, smiling at Harvey. His eyes crinkled. Mutual delight. Or at least it looked like delight, if I didn't look too close. Something else lingered in my heart. *This is what you wanted*, I admonished myself. I turned away from Harvey and nodded to the second cowboy. He looked at me, winced skeptically, stole a glance at Harvey, and, raising his eyebrows, looked away. He'd leave us to sort it out. Harvey was first to break the silence.

"Out for a stroll, are yah?" He smirked.

"Well . . . ," I faltered, pressing my teeth. What could I say? I couldn't tell anyone what had happened on the ranch—not even Harvey. Yet somehow I blamed him for not already knowing, for not rushing down from his horse to hold me, for not sweeping me up into his arms and carrying me to safety. He couldn't see the sear of pain inside me, the bruises Hugh left, the uncoiling grief of loneliness. I needed to weep in his arms, in grief, in fear, in gratitude. It was exactly this kind of irrationality and excessive emotion that repulsed Hugh. "We, uh, needed to get on the road," I uttered. It was not an answer I expected anyone to believe.

"This here's my cousin, Fred," Harvey offered.

Fred nodded. I smiled but didn't tell him my name. He looked off to the hills. Inspecting us more closely, Harvey asked,

"Got any food with yah?"

"Well . . . we've eaten some berries." I looked at my hands, embarrassed by our poverty.

"Well, that won't do," Harvey reflected, and I relaxed a little. Fred rested an elbow on the horn of his saddle, as if preparing for a long and rather unlikely tale.

"You going someplace particular?" Harvey inquired.

Katie leaned against me. I stroked her hair. My fingers snagged in a knot the size of a mouse nest at her nape. "I'm afraid we're a little aimless at the moment. Can't go to 108 Mile. Can't go back to the ranch." I stared at him, hoping he would catch my meaning.

He didn't hesitate. "Then you better come along with us." I stepped toward him, realizing this was what I'd been resisting all along. He nodded his head at Katie, then his riding partner. I caught the meaning.

"Katie, you're going to ride on this horse." I lifted her into Fred's hefty arms.

She kicked and writhed and whined. "No! I want to ride with you!" Fred bunched up his mouth and set her down in front of him. Thankfully, she knew enough not to squirm on a horse. But her whine and whimper created an unpleasant backdrop, and I was determined to make this moment solely lovely. Harvey took my hand and guided me up onto the saddle in front of him. Warmth radiated from under his clothes against my back. Shallow, inaudible breaths escaped me. I tried not to think about the hot skin beneath his rough clothes. It was a would-be-perfect moment, except for Katie's mewling kitten noises. Fred looked over his shoulder, catching our eyes, hoping we appreciated his sacrifice. A hot-cheeked apology rose on my face.

Eventually, Katie settled. I was left to contemplate—or resist contemplating—the feel of the saddle pressing my hips together with Harvey's in a constant sway of squeaking leather. He wore a grey-blue, snap-up shirt with an ivory kerchief tied at his neck, both faded with sun and years. He smelled of cedar and smoke.

The low purr of his voice came over my shoulder. "We're heading up to the ranch where I work. Me and my cousin picked up new cattle just south of 108 Mile House for the ranch owner." Almost to himself, he added, "Lucky thing."

He wants to take care of me, keep me safe and close. My smile warmed me. "I guess you were pretty surprised to see me out wandering the trail on my own." I told myself I wanted to gauge how far the rumors had spread. *Did common farmhands know?*

"Yeah, well, word got out from here to Mexico that you cracked up. Up and ran out on that 'hard-work husband' of yours and stole your daughter along, too." I tensed, turned to catch his expression. His dusty-rose lips were flat, but his eyes twinkled.

"But, Harvey," I rushed, "you're not going to try to bring me back to him, are you?" I hoped the question didn't sound as desperate in his ears as it did in mine. As soon as I asked, I knew the answer.

He scoffed, "Any man who's got to pay for his wife's return ain't too qualified a husband." I sank into the saddle with relief. The mare snorted beneath us. "Besides, a woman's got a right to be free, just like a man. You can live your life as you see fit." I smiled but my chest cramped with the question: *does he intend to be part of that fit?*

I probed, "And what's your rancher going to say about me showing up?"

"Old Bert? He ain't going to know. You're gonna be a secret," he whispered, salaciously. His smile over my shoulder heated me all the way through.

The trail petered out into a mucky field. Low-roofed cowboy shacks sat to the right while the rancher's grand log house settled by a small lake. Harvey and his cousin herded us into the cowboy quarters, then left to corral the cattle. Katie flopped like a leaden kite onto Harvey's bed.

"Katie, don't do that."

"Why can't I?"

I couldn't think of the reason. Except the bed would smell of

Harvey—his hair, his warm skin. The pillow would hold ghosts of thoughts—of memories, of desires. If I lay in the bed—if I sat on the edge of it—I would be carried away by the current of his longings. I imagined his hand at the back of my neck, pulling me into the warm breath of his mouth.

"Do as I say, Katie. Now." She lifted herself with exaggerated effort. I peered through the tattered, gauzy curtain. *Don't think.*

A robin's egg sky decorated the day with blue. Muted sunshine entered the room. A towel sat neatly folded beside a metal basin. A grey wool jacket hung from a nail by the door. The candle in a brass stand was burned down to a nub. A tin of chewing tobacco, a white comb, and a jar of ointment perched on a wood dresser. What caught my eye most, though, was a dressy cowboy shirt, freshly laid out on the back of a chair. *Where would he go in such a shirt?* The question quickened my breath. I dismissed it.

Overtired and weary from travel, Katie flopped against the bed like a heavy rag doll. To keep her quiet, I perched on the bed and made up a story. Perhaps a lot of words would lull her.

"Once upon a time, in a faraway country called Australia, there lived a dingo."

"What's a dingo?"

"I'm going to explain. I told you before—don't interrupt stories."

"But sometimes you don't explain, and then I can't understand anything."

"Yes, well—" *Were we still talking about stories?*

"Just try to tell it *right*," she scolded me. "You're hard to understand."

"Katie, that's not polite." I was stung. She looked up at me, as if to say: *Let's not pretend. You know what I'm saying.* I pressed my lips. I would not respond to rudeness with more rudeness—or to truth with a lie.

"A dingo," I began again slowly. After a while, Katie slumped against me under the weight of sleep. Despite my unease, soon I was overcome with sleep myself.

We must have slept much longer than expected because when we awoke, Harvey was lit up with a lantern, standing in the doorframe with a bedroll. The daze of sleep gripped me. Dusk had pulled long shadows over the room. Harvey flopped the bedroll onto the floor with a thump of dust. The sight of him should have caused elation, but I was still disoriented from sleep. My heart felt flat. He looked over at me with those crinkled, smiling eyes. For once, I couldn't make sense of their meaning.

He leaned outside the door and grabbed a pot with two forks sticking out. He set it on the bed beside us. "It's none too fancy," he explained. Wide-eyed, Katie lifted the lid. Roast beef and mashed potatoes with a couple of boiled carrots bending off to one side. My mouth watered instantly. "Dig in," Harvey encouraged, pleased to please us.

The beef was tough as shoe leather and the gravy a mass of lumps. We gobbled it down far too fast, murmuring sounds of pleasure. Katie and I didn't take our eyes off the pot. I was trying—despite hunger—to leave the best bits of meat for her. In my periphery, Harvey shook sheets over the bedroll.

When my mouth was still full with the last bite, I gushed, "Thank you!" I hesitated to speak his name. "You've been so kind." He smiled. Teeth, so white. A funny thought came into my mind: Surely I wasn't the only woman drawn to such a charming, attractive man. The notion slipped under the skin like a sliver.

I wanted to talk to him, to be with him alone, but Katie was wide awake. She inspected dried bugs on the floor. She bounced on the bed and sang to herself. She threw her socks at me, fetched them, and threw them again. If I'd had more pride to begin with, I might have hoped to appear elegant and refined. Fortunately, humility couldn't carry me much lower. Harvey tried to interest Katie in drawing on the floor with a crumbly piece of sandstone, but she promptly stomped on it, and that was the end of that.

It was hours before that petite, rebellious clown spent enough energy to be cajoled into sleep. Harvey had given us his bed and was now lying on the bedroll against the opposite wall. He propped his hands behind his head, enjoying the entertainment. He grinned as I told Katie a long, slow story about not much of anything. At long last, I bored her into slumber, one of my limited motherly talents.

"So, Miss Annabelle," he said, omitting my married name. "Where does the road take you from here?" His voice was warm sand poured on gravel. His eyes spoke mischief. Comfortingly, he couldn't see the heat in my cheeks in the dim lantern light. *Was it a veiled invitation?*

"Well, Vancouver," I said to the bedspread, avoiding his eyes. "But I'm clear out of money. So I'll have to find some fellow to take us for free or else—I don't know. Find a small job." I fidgeted with my fingers, turned to stare at the wall as if discerning answers from the roughly hewn wood.

He didn't take his eyes off me. "Probably lots of folk would be willing to offer a free ride, excepting that one hundred-dollar reward might turn them in the wrong direction."

"Yes, I've—." My breath caught. "I've already experienced that." I pushed Felix out of my thoughts, over a cliff. If Harvey couldn't sense the thorns inside me, I didn't want to show him. I hoped, however, he might chivalrously volunteer to escort me to Vancouver. *Day after day, pressed against each other in the saddle.*

"Hmm." He studied the lamplight. "That husband really put you in a bad spot, didn't he?"

"Yes," I exhaled. Harvey understood. He wanted to help me. I could sense it. And his help was what I wanted the most. No knight in shining armor for me—just a cowboy in a plain shirt, a bit of unshaved scruff, guiding me away from danger.

"Well—." He picked at a bit of wool coming loose from his bedroll. "We got a cattle drive heading out of here in a couple weeks. Long ride for a lady and little girl. Lots of bumping around on a horse, staring at the backsides of cows. Food's not too gourmet neither. Take about fourteen days to get to the city's edge. Don't know what you'll do from there."

"You're going?" My heart jumped. "You'll take me?"

"Sure. Improve the situation if you had a horse." He paused. *Faster*, I thought, *but not better*. "How'd you get this far without one?"

"I had one. I gave it to a man from 108 Mile House in exchange for a ride to Vancouver."

"Oh. Seeing as how you're not yet in Vancouver, but you've been relieved of your horse, I guess someone took advantage."

I wasn't going to tell him the whole story about Felix, but he asked so many questions. So much concern. Finally, the whole story was out, lying between us like a dead animal giving off stink. I turned away from it, folded my arms. My arms twitched with leftover fear. I hoped he couldn't tell.

"Oof," he said. The weight of all that trickery, danger, and lewdness sank him down onto his bedroll. He contemplated the ceiling. "Got a might lot of trouble, lady."

I waited for him to say more. My breath was shallow. I felt like a scolded child. I had let my life escape the corrals and run wild. I sat there peering at my interwoven fingers, waiting for some worthy explanation to enter my mouth. But I couldn't tell him about Hugh. Or Edwin. I wouldn't tell a soul for the rest of my life.

At last he spoke. "Well," he said in that voice cool as sand. "Got a cabin 'bout an hour's ride from here. Ain't nothing but a shack, really. Place for us road-rough cowboys to lay down when we take the herd to the south pasture in winter. Some folk got grander outhouses. But if you're willing to give it a go, I could take you up there at dawn, before old man wakes up and starts sniffing around. That boss's got a nose for trouble. He'll sniff around like a pig rooting truffles. Anyway, I could drop in on you every couple days with a bit of food till it's time to get south with the herd."

The deck of cards fell open to a perfect hand. All aces and kings. "Yes!" I blurted. "That's a perfect plan. And I'd be grateful eternally." Harvey seemed too tired for more talk. He wound the lantern flame back into blackness and whispered good night. I lay awake enjoying the swell of hope, love, and relief beneath my ribs. I arranged the furniture of my daydreams: Katie and I relaxing in a meadow; Harvey arriving with the day's meal; Harvey and I sitting out on a ramshackle porch watching the orange haze of dusk light the gold in our eyes.

A certain kind of daydreaming can make itself real. Maybe it already is real, and just makes it known. I've done this before. By accident to start. My daydream looked like this: *Katie asleep inside the ramshackle cabin, Harvey and I talking long into the sunset, he touches my hair. Not just touches. Touches it oddly. Softly, longingly, grabbing a fistful near my shoulder.* If you grab the daydream, if you grab it by the throat and pin it to you, you will surely lose it. It will become the impossible—the one thing that will never occur. Rather, you have to wait for the daydream, like a wild bird, to alight on your open hand. Some want to land. Others will not. I looked and gazed longingly, patiently, at that daydream—and it landed.

23

FATE IS A finicky thing. Sometimes it pins you so strictly to events that it might as well be a sewing machine, piercing you down to every point of the day. The great mundanity of the inevitable. That was life on the ranch. Do this. Now you shall do this and this and this. Each day, the same. But when Harvey put his arm below mine and guided me up onto the grey mare early the next morning, and Katie settled cheerily onto the saddle blanket before me, life broke wide open. Above me, gossamer clouds spread wings over a pinkening sky. These rolling meadows and forested mountains were becoming part of me. I was beginning to truly see this land: a place of endless possibilities.

The mare, Katie, and I moved in rhythm. Harvey's horse waited obediently a few yards up the trail. He mounted with an energetic leap. He turned back to stare all the way through me. I let him. This time, I hid nothing. The breeze lifted stray wisps from my braid. It felt good to be on the move again. Harvey smiled to himself, which made me smile to myself. Off we went.

The cabin, a rather generous moniker, sat in the elbow of slow-rise hill, the place where the hill hesitated before deciding to continue. Wind had convinced the shack to lean west. Rain had painted it with moss and lichen. Gravity sagged the shingled roof. It appeared so humble—whisper to it to fall down, and it just might. A breeze picked up and it creaked and groaned like a codger with aching bones. It held our weight up the single stair. It let us cross the puny porch. It sighed and moaned when it released the rust-hinged door. Wan light came from one grimy, warped windowpane. The dust from past visits and long ago events lay thick on the floor.

Nonetheless, a half-decent bed with a wool blanket sat in the far corner. A small wood table supported a tin washbasin, a handful of candles, a single bent fork, and a chunk of mirror. How endearing that cowboys out minding the cattle checked their appearance in a mirror. In another corner sat a pot so blackened and sooty, it might have been pure charcoal.

Harvey didn't step inside with us. He needed to head back to the ranch before the boss woke up. He loosened the straps of the saddlebag. If asked, he was going to say he was seeing to a hole in the fencing. He pulled out soda biscuit crackers, a jar of last summer's peaches, and a bag of oats from the saddlebag. My heart swelled as he set them on the deck for me.

"You can take these. I'll be back tomorrow with more. There's a trail to the creek over there, down the back side of the hill." He lingered with something less pleasant to add, scuffing at the dirt with his boot. "Might be a pretty lean couple of weeks." He eyed me to watch how the news took. But that morning, I was fed and rested, calm and content. At that moment, I was with the people I loved the most with the scent of spring leaves around me. All the world was right.

"You've been so kind." The words revealed my surprise. Besides Ed, no one had been quite so kind and generous to me in a long time.

He turned away then, eyes crinkling. He snugged the belt on the saddle and nodded goodbye. The pull between two people can be like a magnet. The only choice is to pull far away or surrender into each other. I sat on the deck cuddling Katie on my lap, listening to the day—the fading horse clops, the chick-a-dee-dee-dee from bushes, hearts beating, and the near inaudible hush of lifting mist.

The warmth and contentment of that day slowly gave way to fatigue and hunger. Katie and I curled up on the bed. By late afternoon, I lulled both of us into a nap with another nonsense story. When we awoke, shadows filled the room and the sun had already slipped below the horizon, which was unfortunate, since I'd forgotten to look around for the matches. Katie sat grumpily on the bed unhelpfully asserting, "You should light the candle," and "Then you should *find* the matches," and "You should have found them when it was light out!"

I ran my fingers over rough table edges and smutty cobwebs, under the table, over nailheads and floor dirt. After a long while, I gave up.

"Tonight we're going to have special light," I suggested.

"Like a lamp?" she questioned.

"No. It's like having hundreds of candles, but they're all really far away. Hold my hand and I'll take you outside to see."

"Woooaaahh," she whispered, as if her whole childhood hadn't been freckled with twinkling night skies. "Are those really candles?"

"They're tiny fires, each one. Some sitting on tables. Some in fancy candlesticks. Maybe some the angels are holding as they drift through the sky."

"Wow." Her big eyes twinkled with starlight.

We sat on the stoop of an old porch on a tiny cabin under millions of tiny candles. I fetched the jar of peaches—since I couldn't cook the oats without matches—and we ate with juice dribbling down our chins, sharing the one warped fork. An orchestra of late spring mosquitoes hummed in our ears, and we slapped them off legs and cheeks. We talked about whether bushes slept at night, and if mosquitoes feel bad for biting people, and what happens when stars burn out. For a spell, poverty, fear, and uncertainty faded away. We were consumed with the great beauty and wonder of the world, with the rotation of the cosmos, grey starlight on leaves, the warmth of our shoulders touching. Katie's head grew heavy against my shoulder, and I carried her inside to sleep.

The following day, I went down to the thin creek—more

stone than water—and filled the basin. Katie undressed and splashed in it with squeals and gasps, while I absentmindedly wafted her drying dress in sunshine. The cowboy was upon us before we heard him coming. I looked up. Fred. *Not Harvey*. Katie leapt away from the basin and scurried over to hide behind me.

"Harvey asked me to give you this," he said, pulling a brown wrapped package from inside his jacket. As he set it in my hand, warmth emitted through the paper. My mouth watered.

"Thanks—thank you," I stuttered. "Thank you for coming all this way."

He leaned an elbow heavily on the saddle. The air was laden with blame and guilt, and I had difficulty taking a full breath. "It's a lot of trouble. I see that."

"Yeah, well." He paused to find an explanation. "That's what cousins are for." He didn't want to help me, any more than I wanted to trouble him. He was here out of obligation to his cousin. Perhaps a debt owed. A returned favor. He glanced at me from under his brim. But there was something else, too. Some curiosity to his being here. He liked it. The flicker of judgment. Peering down from the saddle. Looking down on a fallen woman.

"I'm afraid we don't have any matches to light a fire with," I asserted pragmatically.

He snickered. Alone in an abandoned cabin with no matches. That iced his cake. He made no move or motion, extending the moment as long as he could. Finally, he stuffed a chubby hand into his jacket pocket and pulled out a tiny box of matches.

I looked at the match box. They were nothing so special. "Thank you. Thank you very kindly."

"Yup," he confirmed. He steered the horse back up the path, touching his fingers to the brim of his hat. Off he went. Tight air released from my chest.

Katie wound around my legs and grabbed at the package in my hands. "Hold on, hold on. Get dressed first."

"But my dress is wet!"

"Fine," I sighed. No one was there to watch us. She plunked down on the deck in the mild May sunshine. The package contained two roast beef sandwiches and several boiled spring potatoes. I contemplated this. Who took the time to make sandwiches for us? This was normally woman's work, but there were no women on this ranch like most ranches north of Kelowna. Harvey did this? Heat filled my chest.

Katie grabbed a potato. "Potato!" she delighted. Such a simple vegetable, bland, pale, and plainer than dirt, but it looked like the stuff of miracles. I took one in my hand. It had the warmth and weight of love. I took a bite.

After we finished the potatoes, we moved on to the sandwiches. We were so hungry, it didn't take much to fill us. We kept eating, but had to slow our chewing. *Why hadn't Harvey delivered the food? Probably ranch duties occupied him.*

24

I DIDN'T HAVE to wait long to see Harvey. By late the third day, the tiny daisies near the cabin had all been ripped off their stems. The oats had been tossed into the boiling pot once, twice, and three times for meals. And the night sky was unfurling a crisp, white bouquet of stars over the darkening sky. The horse hooves I'd waited for finally thumped down the path. A warm shiver rose on my arms. I left Katie complaining in the bed, while I tiptoed onto the porch to check.

The candlelight willowed and flickered behind me. I registered the faint shape of his shoulders, his height in the saddle.

His silhouette came closer. "Glad to see that the runaway didn't run away yet," he joked.

I giggled. "Will you wait just a minute while I put Katie down?" But he was already sliding off the saddle. The mare grazed on the moonlit grass.

Like all children, Katie could sense a mother's need for privacy. So, she stood on the mattress and looped arms around my neck. "Take me outside to see the cowboy!" she gushed.

"No, no," I soothed. "It's bedtime."

"But I want to see what the cowboy brought."

"If he brought any food, we'll have it in the morning. Not now."

"But what else did he bring?"

"Well, nothing else."

"Then why did he come?"

"He came, well, to see us. To say hello."

"Well, he can't say hello if I'm in bed!"

"I'll tell him you said hello."

"You're not listening! I want to know what he came here to say!"

"Well," I pondered, "he didn't come here to say anything."

Her blue eyes brimmed over with tears spilling down her cheeks, past her pout. She crossed her pudgy arms and turned away from me. Bedtime had come and no amount of argument would shift it. I pressed a kiss onto her head and settled her under the blankets.

"If the cowboy tells any interesting stories," I soothed, "I'll share them in the morning."

"No, you won't," she muttered, back turned toward me.

"Of course, I will," I replied.

"You don't pay attention! You don't even *know* the story." A sob escaped her but she pressed her lips tight and muffled it with pride.

Startled by her rebuke, I patted her shoulder once and stood. The candlelight unsettled the shadows on the walls. I stepped back outside to Harvey.

Outside, crickets strummed small wings beneath the tall grass, calling out for love. The porch creaked as I sat down next to Harvey.

Wordlessly, he passed me a package, identical to the one Fred brought the day before. I smiled and set it gingerly beside me. I didn't want to appear ravenous. In truth, I'd eaten only oatmeal all day, and not much of that, since most went for Katie. My stomach panged just imagining what might be inside.

I turned back to him. "I hope it's not too far for you to come all the way out here."

"Nope. Kinda nice slipping off in the night to meet a beautiful woman," he said, brazenly. When he looked at me, I remembered things I normally forgot. The wave in my hair, which I'd carefully brushed with the old comb earlier that day.

The slopes of my shirt over my breasts. The curve of my knees. There was some comfort in remembering my thoughts weren't as evident as news headlines.

"Well, I hope I don't get you into any trouble," I said, brushing invisible dirt from my pant legs. Night was settling fast. Already the sugar-scented dew invisibly dampened our clothes. I told him about our day. He recounted a struggle with an ornery mule the day before. We talked about the night sky and the strangeness of our meeting on the trail. Fear and hope crowded for space inside me.

He probed, "Tell me something about a woman who wanders out on her husband and ends up on a muddy cattle trail."

"Oh," I gasped, "I can't imagine what you'd want to know."

"I want to know everything. What's it like to be Annabelle?"

I scanned the darkness for answers. "I'm just a ranch wife, Harvey. Just like that."

"No, you're not." He shook his head. "You're different. I've seen ranch wives." His gaze was penetrating. Moonlight touched his brow. I looked at my lap. "You got something different. That's why I noticed you."

I froze. I could hear the blood jump inside my ears. *Did he know? Did he know about my daydreams? Could he see into me the way I could into him? The thought sprung a dreadful yearning.* A thin voice escaped me. "Everyone is different in some way, I suppose."

"That's not what I mean," he scolded, playfully.

I stared across the meadow. I didn't want him to see the surprise in my eyes—the wide-eyed fright of having been discovered. I held my elbows close for warmth. I did know what he was talking about.

Finally, I stuttered breathlessly, "Yes. I suppose, a little different." I looked down at my hands. "Hadn't realized that it was obvious."

"Only to me," he cooed, grinning. "You think a lot. Your thoughts keep you preoccupied."

"Yes. Thoughts, or daydreams," I admitted.

"Well, I'd sure like to know what you think about."

So, he couldn't read my mind. I sighed. And maybe he wouldn't understand my words either. "I guess I don't belong here," I said, cryptically.

"Then where do you belong?"

"Maybe the next muddy cattle trail will lead me there." Against my will, my mouth opened and out fell the stories about a childhood in London and the move to Vancouver. I told him about my mother going back to be with her sister. I told him about being lucky to get the teaching job during the roughest years of the economy. I told him about meeting Hugh. I even told him about my father's death and the almost pony.

He listened quietly to everything. And when I was done, he said simply, "Yeah. Yeah, I know," and looked down at his lap. He was quiet for a long time. I heard him swallow, saw him watching the thick weaving of his fingers coming together. Finally, he said, "Perhaps that's all this place is. A bunch of folk who got chased and bumped out of other places."

"Right. A big patchwork of personalities and odd journeys."

"Exactly. I was raised in Oregon. Left there when I was ten. Folks died. My uncle came down from British Columbia to get me. Brought me to a ranch, then another, and another. Finally, he went north and I ended up here with Bert.

"Funny thing, hadn't never even been on a horse before I came north. Didn't need to. Lived right in the center of the city. Folks worked for a packing company till they got laid off."

"Must have been difficult to come here."

"Yeah. Traded a school for a barn. Streetlights for moonlight on cow patties," he chuckled.

As we talked, the night rolled a dark, translucent shell over us. The moon rose higher, and the sorrel, wild grasses, and pines turned luminous grey.

Stories are the first gifts of romance. The tragic, the comic, the dubious, the formative, all of them given, received, and—one urgently hopes—accepted. Harvey told me of the hardships of the orphanage where he awaited the arrival of his uncle. He told me of an early winter chill out on the trail, threatening to freeze and splinter his bones in the long creaking night. I told him of the great fog I lived in at the ranch, days and days of soapsuds, clouds in the head, the warmth of Katie's hand against mine, shafts of sunlight.

We talked until we found the moment our stories led to each other. Silence pulsed between us. One day, scientists will learn that love doesn't stay in the body. On certain nights, the moon wears a halo, a shimmering ring of light. Our bodies shimmered, too.

With a voice soft as wheat fields, he turned to me and re-vealed, "Yeah. It's good to be here. I *like* you." Even in the moonlight, I could see the dusty rose color of his lips. He reached up and touched my hair, oddly. He grabbed a fistful near my shoulder—*just as in my daydream*—the look in his eyes, all longing. Just when I thought he would lean over and kiss me, he pressed his lips to my forehead and rose to leave. Swift and quiet as a fox, he wiped the dew from his horse, patted her on the neck, mounted, and turned back up the trail.

He left with a moonlight twinkle in his eye. But he didn't completely leave. His scent, his warmth lingered behind with me, so I could imagine him beside me as I sat on the bed, carefully unwinding the thick braid in my hair. As I unbuttoned my shirt, my hands were also his hands. As I slipped off my jeans and pressed my face into the pillow, he was everywhere. How could I miss him? *He must feel halved*, I thought. *Surely, he'll want to return to be whole again.* I reconsidered the theory. No, love didn't halve us, it expanded us. Harvey was in his cowboy quarters back at the ranch, *and* he was next to me, whole in two places.

I had a neighbor back in Vancouver who, upon hearing of a cousin's divorce, said, "They'll pay in Hell for that one." My own mother, if she saw what was building between Harvey and me, would have pursed her lips tightly, her admonishment too nasty to utter. The red-faced priest at my childhood church in

London would have shaken the marriage contract in my face. *God has witnessed this contract! And the signature was sealed by the Holy Spirit. It's a commitment of love till* death *do you part!*

But there are many ways to die. Death of the body is only one of them. My marriage to Hugh lasted until the death of hope, of faith in integrity and safety. What goes on living in a marriage like that is a husk of a human. A shell. I'd heard of wives who kept the heart—which brimmed over with emotion—but lost the mind. Perhaps they couldn't reconcile the knowledge of love—its gifts, potentials, and omnipotence—with the reality of love—their husband's cold shoulder turned toward them night after night.

I rejected it. The whole notion that ending a marriage is a sin—I rejected it. Does God care more for contracts than for life itself? What if the only way to live—to truly be alive—was to become unmarried? The feeling I had for Harvey was a thing of beauty. I could not believe God would punish me for feeling it. Supposedly, God made man in his image, but the way some priests and pastors spoke, one would think the reverse. Man fashions God to suit *his* image.

Surely there must be greater rules to living than those confined to small, black curls of ink on a marriage contract. In my mind, I saw the words of the Bible lift their clipped wings from the pages and fly higher and higher, past the place where blue atmosphere gives way to infinite black. That's where Harvey and I were tangled together. Some bigger place. We can't imagine the plan from here. Our small specks of bodies stuck on the earth, trying to look up. We get it wrong. Other contracts are designed in the black ink of space while, down below, we clutch thin slices of pressed pulp and ink pens.

At dawn, I awoke to birdsong. I lay in bed, feeling him more faintly than before. For a couple of days, I was content in our small universe. We had just enough food and time to ponder the passage of clouds or pulsing fingers of branches.

Katie felt it, too. "We'll live here forever!" she announced, as she sat in the meadow, snapping the heads off tiny daisies. I laughed, but I was daydreaming about it, too. I wanted Harvey to ask me to stay. He could tell the ranch owner who would smile and delight in what he called "Harvey's luck." Everyone would decide my husband should let me go. No one would want to return me. Harvey would pay the rancher to purchase this ramshackle cabin and we'd build a real house and start our own ranch, right here. Humble, but full of love. Katie would call Harvey "Daddy," and he would love her, protect her, be a trusted friend for life. Our marriage would be signed high above in the luminous dark of night.

By day three, something had shifted. I didn't notice until it was too late. Harvey's presence—that I'd been wearing like a precious, invisible robe—was altogether gone. I was alone again. Just me. Just a woman running away from a husband, alone with her daughter in cowboy country. *Don't be silly*, I told myself. *Too many daydreams play tricks on the mind.* But all day, I was unsettled. Katie wanted to go to the creek to pick thimbleberries, but I grumbled that I was exhausted and if she stopped making messes everywhere with ripped-up grass and mud on boots, perhaps I'd have more time. She crumpled into a lump of tears. Guilt and annoyance knotted inside me.

He did not come that night though surely he knew our food wouldn't last. *Why hadn't I asked him when he'd come back?* What if he intended the food to last us for a week, and I'd let us gobble it up in two days? We'd have long days ahead with four measly and stale soda crackers and a handful of thimbleberries. It was my fault. He and his cousin came all the way out to bring us food, the least I could do is ask how long I should make it last. Assumptions. Was I making assumptions about everything? I felt in my heart for the warm blanket of his presence. But I was too distracted by hunger to feel him. *Be logical*, I told myself. It's something my mother would have said in these circumstances. *Lost in the clouds again. Touch a foot to earth once in a while, for all our sakes.*

If I'd had a father—I mean if I'd had one past the age of

five—would he have given me good counsel? That's what fathers are supposed to do. I'd seen it before. My best friend in high school had a father like that. "Don't let any man love you who treats his own mother like a maid" and "When all the doors are all shut, it means you're knocking at the wrong man's house." He put an arm around her shoulder, and she tilted into his embrace, in perfect safety. He kissed the top of her hair.

If I had a father now, here in Canada, or right here at this cabin . . . But I couldn't imagine it. I couldn't make it seem real. The father I imagined for myself—the one who went off to war, seemed made out of wood, immobile, mute, and unbelievable. A caricature. I couldn't begin to imagine what he'd say. I leaned on the porch rail where Katie and I (well, mostly Katie) ate our soda crackers. I waited for this father of mine to eschew his wisdom. To guide me. *How do I find my way home, Father?*

Quiet. Katie turned the cracker over and over in her hand. She couldn't hear the voice of *her* father, either.

25

ALL DAY, I waited. I waited for Harvey or Fred to deliver food, comfort, a contact with the outside world. I waited for my imaginary father to guide me. I waited for love to come thaw the frost of loneliness. By afternoon, Katie was hungry again. She leaned against my leg, whining. Guilt tamed my irritation. Reluctantly, I broke the last soda cracker in half and gave it to her. I eyed the trail to the ranch. A dragonfly halted over the wildflowers, had second thoughts, and darted back the way it came. Katie threw the cracker on the deck in disgust.

"I don't want a stupid cracker! I want *food*!"

After providing her with a brief overview of the lives of famished children, I agreed to take her down to the creek to look for more thimbleberries. Who knew? They might be our only sustenance for the day. Katie ran ahead, stopping occasionally to trip on a tree root. I lingered with the thought, unreasonable though it was, that one of the cowboys might arrive while we were away.

The silvery creek gurgled under the dappled canopy of balsam leaves. Water poured like glass over rocks. The water talked endlessly to stone, air, and the audience of trees and bush. We wandered along the bank, getting scratched by bushes and nearly slipping on rocks. Katie, more agile than I, scurried under bushes where animals had bent branches into tunnels. The creek's mineral scent mixed with the sweet spring foliage and dark, damp earth. A month later, the pink huckleberries would ripen. I might even stand a chance of snagging a spring Chinook. The thought of barbecued salmon made my hungry belly cramp. I pushed the unripened thimbleberry bushes away with my arms, shooing mosquitoes, and paused.

"Katie, we're going to have to go down creek until we get to a sunny spot. These thimbles aren't ripe enough."

"Okay. Come, come, come, Thimble-Thimble!" Katie called.

Farther downstream, the trees parted to make way for waist-high grasses, spotted with purple lupine and fireweed. This forest of flowers came up to Katie's shoulders. Excitedly, she launched herself into a dense thicket of grass to stare up at the sky. I sighed. Despite hunger and worry, life was good. The world offered a bouquet of beauty. Purple, azure, and spring green. Katie's exuberant smile was contagious. I lay down beside her and contemplated the walls of grass and flowers and ceiling of sturdy blue. A breeze came and shivered the stalks and stems. The whole world, swaying and shifting beneath the permanence of sky.

Something on the air smelled different here. We were a good forty steps from the water. I couldn't detect the mineral scent of splashing. Here, the fruity scent of lupine mixed with something more pungent, ripe, musky even. A second later, instinct snapped a twig inside me and I bolted upright. *Bear!*

She was on all fours, not twenty paces away, staring at me with small, sharp eyes. The hairs of her fur were matt black and waxen stiff. Her damp nose, as large as the palm of my hand, lifted into the air and the nostrils flared to pull in more scent.

Katie started to get up. I slammed a hand on the ruffles of her shirt and hissed, "Shhh." I could feel her looking at me per-plexed—surely just on the edge of blurting something out. The breeze moved in and trembled the grass and strands of my hair. Something black bounced out from a nearby stand of trees towards the bear. *A cub.* It moved up next to the mother. She grunted softly, studied me briefly, blinked, and turned away. She lumbered back into the trees with the bouncing cub before her, off to fill their own bellies with thimbleberries.

"What is it?" Katie said in stage whisper. I pulled her up under the armpits and pointed, keeping one arm wrapped around her, just in case. She lifted her own small, human paw and waved them goodbye.

I made Katie stand still in the field with me until we could no longer hear or smell the bears.

"Why didn't the bears eat us?"

"We're not really their favorite food. They're a little frightened of us too."

"Do they think *we* will eat *them*?"

"I don't think they think about it. They just know to be afraid."

"Do they know Goldilocks?"

"Oh, well—"

"Could we find their cabin and eat their oatmeal? I don't mind if it's hot."

"Oh, Katie." I pulled her head into my chest and pressed my lips to her warm head.

We walked with a new caution, as I illuminated for Katie the discrepancies between fairy tales and reality—a position for which I was hardly qualified. Katie was as altered by the conversation as she was by a puff of cloud passing unnoticed overhead. As I suspected, the thimbleberry bushes were picked nearly clean of ripe berries. Katie did manage, with some assistance, to eat a whole handful, enough to temporarily allay hunger.

As we searched, I contemplated. Animals were largely predictable. Even I—knowing little about bears—knew that the she-bear and her cub were wandering downstream now, putting a safe distance between us. She treated us like fellow bears. Mother and cub of the tall and furless variety. She would hesitate to return to this area for a couple of days. But since this was her territory, she would most certainly be back, and we would be wise to be absent then. If she had encountered humans before, she knew what I knew about them: they're defined by unpredictability.

I squatted by the side of the creek, inspecting the one thimbleberry I saved for myself. Who knew what any of us would do next? Harvey. Hugh. Me. The only reliable one of the bunch was Katie. If she didn't get dinner, she would whine with woeful eyes, plucking the heart strings of motherhood. I tried to maintain faith that Harvey would come that evening. Faith and denial share a seesaw. Perhaps hope was merely light-headedness. The May sun tilted toward the horizon. I'd eaten half a cracker and a thimbleberry all day. It occurred to me that this land must be full of food. Perhaps Mary and her people would know where to look, but I was at a loss.

When we returned to the cabin, I soothed Katie into a nap with a rendition of "Bye Bye Blackbird": . . . *Where somebody waits for me, sugar's sweet, so is he, bye, bye blackbird . . .* When she awoke, we went outside to the meadow to see if I could determine anything edible. I've never been much good at naming things out in nature. A tree is a tree. Deciduous or evergreen. I could identify only a handful. I knew the difference between the long sharp needles and pitch-pungent scent of pine and the soft, short needles of fir. I knew maple and could tell some fruit trees apart. I knew lupine, fireweed, and dogwood wildflowers. But the rest was all a muddle. What's a birch? Is everything that dangles strings of leaves a willow? What's the name of the tiny white-pink flowers hanging in bunches upside down? I felt the blind burn of hunger in my head. My stomach cinched tighter in pangs. I pushed through the field grass, going nowhere in particular. Hunger and inexperience led the way.

Then I remembered fern fronds! The spiral heads of spring ferns were entirely edible. My mother made me eat them the first winter we were in Canada. Boiled with butter, they were fragrant and pungent with a hint of vanilla and asparagus. I hated them. We only ate them twice. Perhaps mother's own pantry was bare. I cut sideways through the grass to head back to the trail to the creek. I'd walked right past ferns earlier in the day. Now they would be dinner. At the creek, I found the patch and quickly snapped off a cool green coil.

Alone with my thoughts, I pushed through grasses, snapping at fronds. Memories of the last few days flashed before me. Katie falling into armloads of wildflowers. Evening sunshine breaking golden dust over a meadow. The sound of Harvey's voice, the heat from his shoulder. In those moments, the world teemed over with abundance. And in all the moments between, I walked through a world of scarcity. Impoverished. The sound of my footfalls. The coolness of my hands. The silence between mother and daughter wandering into the unknown. My arms and legs were weighted with fatigue. Weary of the stoicism that masks exhaustion, despair. I squatted down with the gravity of eight measly fern fronds in my hands and a sob in my chest.

"Mummy, what?"

I couldn't answer her. Had there been a time when life was full? Perhaps, holding newborn Katie in a marriage bed blanketed with crisp denial. Was that happiness then? Playing in tide pools with childhood friends down by the bay in West Vancouver. Mouthfuls of blackberries. Mouthfuls of mother's apple pie and strawberry jam. The distant quietness of her kitchen was a kind of peace. Wasn't it? The tug of buried grief ached beneath my eyes. Salty tears splashed onto my hands. Hard times hit everyone, that I knew. But it was the paucity of love, of the loneliness that depleted me most. Hadn't I spent my whole life alone, waiting for the other to return? Home alone, waiting for Mother to return from work. Alone at the ranch with the men all gone into the field. Alone in the tall house in London, waiting and waiting for Father to return from war. Alone in a marriage bed with a man who wouldn't touch me.

Deliberately, I slowed my breath and set my shoulders right. I would do what I had always done. No one was coming to rescue me. I would take care of myself. Myself and my little girl. Scoop up all the loneliness and bottle it under a different label. Call it "a penchant to daydream." Or "a touch of the aloof." And I would carry on with all these stacked-up and shelved bottles inside me.

And one day, if I ran out of room for them, what would that look like? What would become of me then? I thought of the old drunks who wandered around Chinatown in Vancouver, torn lumberjack sleeves, scruff of unshaven faces. I envied them their abandon. I wanted most to be free, but now, even with freedom stretching mile upon mile in every direction, I was locked inside the prison of grief. A great hunger no one could see.

I smudged hands over my cheeks. I settled the fern fronds into my coat pocket and stepped back up the trail. I took Katie's hand in mine, avoiding her wide eyes. Deliberately. *One foot in front of the other*, like Mother says. As if they might veer off the trail without such concentration. As if they might run away with me, like the Devil's red shoes, running, running on and on.

26

THE BOILED FERN fronds mushed in our mouths as we sat next to the smoky fire pit. Night cracked open its can of amber sky and haze. I drank in the darkening blue. Beauty is a kind of sustenance. My hands performed motherhood, wiping away tears, spooning food onto tin plates, holding the hot and heavy hand of a tired daughter. Hunger breeds fatigue. Katie tucked in before the sun swept up the mess of orange scattered over the horizon.

"This is going to be our home forever, Mummy," she yawned. "And we're going to go back and get Chester and some apple sauce and roast beef, and we'll live here and eat berries and be friends with the bears."

"All right," I agreed, comforted by her daydream.

"And then I'll sing you songs, and you'll make me food all day, and nobody will cry anymore."

"All right," I managed, nodding.

"Let's go back and get Chester soon, Mummy."

"Let's talk about that in the morning." I touched a kiss to her forehead.

As soon as I stepped outside, I heard a horse trotting in the distance. Someone was riding up. I was too weary to cheer. Harvey's horse swayed up with a swoosh of tail and a soft snort. As for Harvey, his quick dismount and speedy unlacing of the side sack suggested that he hadn't exactly forgotten me. He knew I was hungry and his shoulders bent with regret. The realization softened my own stiff posture. I set the lantern on the deck beside me.

"Hope you haven't been too starved out." He looked at me with worried eyes.

Yes, we had. Starved by emptiness and abandonment, too. "We made do, if lightly," I lied. I kept my gaze on the dirt. Irrationally, the daydream flashed before me—him holding a lock of my hair, putting his mouth over mine. Worried he could read my thoughts, I looked away.

"Old Bert was stuck to us like flies on cow patty last night. I couldn't get away. Couldn't even sneak some food till today." He handed me a package. I tried to unwrap it gracefully, but my fingers trembled.

We sat down on the deck stairs. I offered the open package to him, but he waved it off. "That's for you and the girl," he said. *Katie*, I thought. *Doesn't he remember her name?*

I devoured a slice of cold roast beef, before deciding that I really would need to fetch the fork from inside before plunging into the mashed potatoes and boiled greens. When I returned, Harvey was leaning on his knees and staring into the weave of his fingers.

"I know you were hungry out here." His long gaze made me blush, though only the darkness knew it. I nodded and chewed. I would save Katie the biggest portion.

"How long should I make this meal last?"

"Gosh. I dunno. I want to come back here tomorrow, but with Bert snooping and poking around . . ."

"Does he know someone's here? At the cabin?"

"No, he doesn't know nothing. He's just nosy like that. Comes and checks in on us. Doesn't have a wife, see, so he's got extra time to pill around."

The logic was lost on me. Wouldn't having a wife *save* him time? "I should think he'd be worked to frenzy without a wife to cook, clean, and garden."

"Nope. Got enough ranch hands for that. One of the biggest

ranchers north of Kelowna. Just bought a dozen more Herefords. That's what we were doing when we saw you. Man's got a mind like a razor." He cocked his head. "Maybe a heart to match."

I was uneasy at the idea of a razor-headed, nosy rancher only an hour down the trail. But Harvey assured me that while his business sense excelled, his social competence lagged. Even if he figured Harvey and Fred were acting oddly, he wouldn't piece together why.

And so, Harvey had neither abandoned nor forgotten us. He had fretted. By not coming sooner, he had tried to protect us. For that and for all his trouble, I should be grateful. He told me about his days on the ranch and the restlessness he felt. What a relief it was when the cattle drive was underway so he could be out on the trail. With a full belly and the comfort of good conversation, I began to relax.

"That's a long sigh, Miss Annabelle."

Pleasure spread across my face to hear him say my name.

"You going to tell me what's going on behind that pretty smile?"

I carefully rewrapped the meat, mash, and greens for Katie. "Just glad for your company." I shook my head. Then boldly, I met his gaze. Iris to iris. White specks of stars reflected in his eyes. Crickets on high-pitched accordions pulsed the night. In a flicker of daydream, I saw his arm wrap round my shoulders.

"Then there's two of us glad." And his warm arm gently circled around my shoulders, just as I imagined. My heart was a galloping horse. With his other hand, he fiddled with a strand of hair loosened from my braid. His lips were soft and dry and curious against mine, searching—searching for the meaning of this thing between us. Curiosity grew more fervent. His hand slid over my shirt where it covered the collarbones. A small gasp escaped me. My arms tingling. In the kiss was the answer, the question, the direction. A trail leading outside the world where only two people can follow. I held the soft square of his bristly jaw. He led me and I followed, and when I hesitated, he found me and reignited my courage. And when finally, we found the last aching kiss, we pulled slowly apart and the world reformed itself around us. Touches of light, surges of shooting meadow grass, headfuls of stars.

That deep, long kiss happened just as I'd imagined. Except I hadn't imagined the new gravity pulling me to him, the nearly unmanageable urge to discover and rediscover this secret embedded in both of us. A kiss, of course, was only the beginning. We pulled away, breathing in unison. I was lost in the heralding of our breath, the concentric rippling of heartbeat, the wonder. Slowly, he pulled me to him and set a kiss on top of my head.

He was up. The tall, shifting, magnetic wiriness of him moved to his dozing horse. I couldn't make thoughts, so lost was I in that daydream come to life. I watched him pat and mount his mare, and still no word nor idea came into my head.

"'Night, Annabelle." He mesmerized me even while I ached to see him go. He and his mare and the crowds of forest behind and scattered constellations above.

I wanted to ask him why he must leave, but I saw my hand wave goodbye.

27

I SLEPT EASILY, dreaming of wild horses crossing a ridge. I wished I was riding them, but I was held back by an invisible force. The beauty and grace of those beasts sparked a yearning in me that couldn't be satisfied.

Katie was awake before me. She played itsy-bitsy spider against the wall, while I hoarded the last remnants of sleep from the edges of my dream. When dawn had cleaned the last bit of slumber out of night's bowl, I rose and made her a dish of cold potato mash and roast beef.

"Mummy. Mummy!"

"Hmm?" I was rebraiding my hair, pausing to touch the strand that he'd touched.

"Can't you make this hot?"

"Aren't you starving? It would take an hour to get the fire going and warm it." I pulled my fingers through the slippery weave of my hair.

"Mummy. Mummy! Did you eat yours cold last night?"

"Yes, I ate mine last night. I want to be careful that we don't eat too much, since we're never sure when the cowboys can come back with more." I shook out my mane. It was a lot of hair. I should have trimmed it before I left the ranch. It hung down past my breasts.

"They're not very nice to let us go hungry out here."

"Oh, no, no! They're very nice. They have to ride all the way up on their horses and it takes an hour! They're being very kind and helpful to us." With reluctance, I started pulling the tired old cowboy comb through my thick hair. Too bad we'd lost our pack in Felix's truck.

"Tell them I want applesauce next time."

"Katie. We'll take what they give us." I looked at Katie's hair. Had I remembered to comb it the day before? Her curls kinked and bent with the evidence of bed and play. Later I would comb them back into order.

While the morning unfolded, a faint stirring began in my stomach. It began with an out-of-the-blue thought. Would Hugh know where I was—because of the kiss? Would it light me up like a beacon and lead him to me? A silly notion. Yet the thought wouldn't let me go. By midday, I was bumping up against it whichever way I turned.

Is this what guilt does? I asked myself. *Allow me to feel great joy and then poison it with distress?* Except, I didn't feel guilty. Sure, the thought of Mother or Mr. Edison flashed feelings of contrition, brief as lightning. But when I thought of Hugh, I knew our marriage was over—if not on paper, then in my soul. Nonetheless, the sharpness of his presence disturbed my thoughts.

After a tiny portion of mash and dandelion greens for lunch, Katie and I left our little cabin—our blankets and sweaters, our remaining bit of food—and sauntered down to the creek to look for more fern fronds. Katie chatted to herself and turned over rocks in the creek, looking for "gold." *What a lark if she found some!* Peering downstream, I wondered how far we could go before trespassing into bear territory. The creek gurgled its ancient song. A picture sprang to mind. So clear. As if someone had surprised me by flashing a photo inside my mind. Hugh was scratching his bad elbow in the gruff way that he does when he's mad. He was walking.

Then I knew—I knew and I didn't know how—but I was certain. Hundreds of miles of Cariboo, but Hugh was *here*.

I turned and looked upstream, roughly the direction of the ranch. "Katie, we have to go!"

"Not yet. I'm playing rock family."

I grabbed her by the arm and pulled her up, taking huge strides over the damp earth. "Now!" I half carried, half pulled her.

Katie jogged beside me as I pulled her. "Why? Why do we have to go?" She looked behind us, checking for a bear.

There wasn't time to explain. There wasn't a way to explain. Mother's voice rang in my head. *You're being absurd! You cannot know such a thing.* I slowed my pace, listening. Was I going mad? My heart thumped inside me. No. It was Hugh. I could neither see nor hear him. There was no trace of him. But I'd married that man. I'd breathed the breath of his sleep for years. I knew the imprints of his every movement. They were part of me. And I knew. He'd found me. He was close.

"Are we running from the bear? I want to stay and see it," Katie objected.

"No." With every step, I was also listening. "Stay quiet."

In an angry hush, she complained, "You're hurting my arm!"

"Sorry!" I whispered back. But I didn't release her arm, only lightened my hold. "We have to keep going *quickly*."

"Stop pulling me!"

"Then I need you to run. But run right beside me, don't go ahead or behind me, unless the trail narrows." I released her. Luckily, with a full belly from lunch, she had energy enough to keep up. And she was quiet. She launched ahead over fallen logs and over stones but kept a watchful eye that I was right beside her. With every step, I listened and my mind raced ahead.

When we got near the place of the bear sighting, I began snapping my fingers.

"That's not quiet!" Katie admonished.

"I want the bears to know we're coming, so we won't startle them. But I don't want to talk or call very loud with my voice."

"Why not?"

"We need to be quiet."

"Are we playing a game? What game is this?"

Yes, I thought. *We're playing the game of mother goes crazy and drags her daughter with her.* We crossed all the way through the lupine and fireweed of bear meadow and into the thicket of deciduous trees and brush on the other side. And there, I yanked Katie to me and huddled at the base of a tree. Katie's cheeks were rosy, but she had hardly fatigued. My heart banged and lungs gasped.

"Mummy, I don't like this game," Katie whispered.

"I don't like it, either," I confessed. "But we have to play a little while longer. Let's sit here quietly for a bit. And when I say it's alright, we can go and look for thimbleberries."

"But the bears ate them all."

"I know, I know. Shhh."

The creek water trickled in skittish song. The leaves above us flapped and waved as if trying to escape the trees. I concentrated on slowing my rapid breathing. Katie curled up tight against me, either enjoying the game of danger or sensing her mother's fear. She was silent and still as stone.

"Are you all right?" I asked quietly.

"I'm just listening," she said with adult-like concentration.

"What are you listening to?"

"The man's voice."

My heart caught. "What man?" Then, with hope, "Harvey?"

"No. The big man."

"Fred."

"No. I don't know him," she clarified with an irritated tone.

"Then how do you know he's big?"

"Because," she was straining her patience with me, "he *sounds* big."

I remembered a trick my childhood friend had taught me. I imagined my hearing lifting above the grove of trees into the sky like an eagle. My ears became eyes and I peered at everything. His voice broke above the trees. Sturdy. Big, just as Katie said. I didn't know him. Talking with authority. Loud like only his words mattered. Not Hugh. Hugh spoke quietly, made people

lean in to hear him. Not Harvey, nor Fred. Perhaps Old Bernie—
that puzzle piece that fit.

"Now there's two," said Katie.

"Who's the other?"

"It's Daddy."

I pressed my fingers to my closed eyelids. I was rigid with
fear. When I spoke again, it was in a strained whisper. I couldn't
look at Katie, though her inquiring eyes scanned me thoroughly.
"We have to go. We have to keep moving." I forced myself to
unfold from hiding and pulled Katie up. She stared at me with
heavy cheeks and worried eyes.

"Mummy," she whispered, "is he going to hurt you again?"

I swallowed. My chest twinged. I could sort out her observation later. I clasped her small hand between mine. "No. Because
he won't find us."

28

THE SOUND OF our steps and flapping leaves conflicted with the urge—the necessity—of listening. I compromised. We charged ahead for a few hundred yards, then stopped and widened our ears. Sometimes we heard nothing and began to believe we were safe. Sometimes voices, the big man. Another, too faint for me to hear. Probably Hugh. A horse whinnied and then the sound of a horse in a trot. As we moved, all things dark and round in the periphery caught my eye—a rounded stone wet from the creek. A broken log, poking up from the grasses. An unusually large burl on the side of a tree. These were the not-bears. The almost-bears. But bears or not, we had to keep moving.

We pushed through the soft snapping necks of Scotch broom and fern, crunched over cracking twigs and last autumn's leaves. The sun bore down on our faces, like a pitcher of milky bleach, diluting the scenery. Only a moment later, it turned sullen as clouds overtook it. After some distance, bush gave way to a pine forest. Our feet crushed red-brown needles, dashed over the sponge of eons of decay. We were neither fast, nor quiet. Deer moved through these forests soundlessly. We stomped and cracked and banged along, weaving through an endless gallery of tall bark pillars. A maze with no meaning. When several stops in succession revealed no voices, I spotted a burned out stump with a cave-like opening.

"Let's go hide in there." Katie ran in front of me. She ducked in first and squealed. I grabbed her and yanked her out. Looking past her, I saw why. Foxes. Two of them, curled together and looking at us with dazed fear.

"Not here, Katie. Let's keep going." We'd find another spot. Farther down, the stream opened up to a sweeping meadow. White-faced Herefords grazed in the distance. We'd made it all the way to someone else's ranch lands. But that was not good. We couldn't hide in open meadow. I pulled Katie back into the forest to a huddle of tree trunks and a fallen log.

I sat on the log, pulling Katie onto my lap. Her thin arms nearly strangled me, but I hugged her close. We panted and waited. We didn't speak. I stroked her hair. *My courageous girl, full of fortitude.*

When her breathing settled, tears leapt over hot cheeks. Bravely, she tried to muffle the sound in my jacket. Trembling, I bore her small chokes and whimpers and pretended I could soothe her.

"If we see someone, don't make a sound. Let me do all the talking. It's better if nobody finds us."

"But who's trying to get us?"

I pushed her hair behind her ear. "There are just some people who don't know what's best for us. They think we should go back to the ranch, but that's a no-good place."

"Okay," she ceded, whimpering.

A flash of speckled fur dashed around the trees not two steps away. A squealing cry burst from Katie as I muffled her mouth. *The cattle dog!* Harvey and Fred's dog. Smiling a big, dopey dog smile. Proud that she found us. She hurried back to spread the news.

I set Katie down and peered over the log we were resting against. A dark jacket and hat sat on a brown horse in the distance. It was Fred. He saw me. I was a miserable school child who had just failed a game of hide and seek and now would be taken in by bullies. I trembled all over. Horse steps grew more pronounced. *What's in it for Fred to return us? Could Hugh murder us in front of others?*

Fred and the dog came around the tree. The cattle dog stood panting, no longer interested in us. Her work was done. Fred kept a distance between his horse and us. That's his way, I thought. Kid gloves. He seemed uncertain what to say. He couldn't look at us. Something gnawing away at him, I figured. Perhaps the guilt of returning a woman and child to the man who would harm them—or worse.

He squinted in the direction of the others. He went to wipe some chewing tobacco from his lip—and for a terrifying moment I thought he was going to whistle to them.

His voice was a low hush. "Don't go any further west." He tipped his hat toward the cattle pasture, but kept his eyes fixed in the direction of the others. "Stay here a while. Then, follow the tree line east. Maybe an hour—hour and a half. Past the cattle trail to a wall of rock on the hillside. We'll try to come out there tonight or tomorrow, if we can. Can't promise." He turned and looked at me like I was real trouble—or, perhaps, like he had private news about me—ideas, opinions, that he wished he didn't have. The burden of knowing was evident in his gaze.

I wanted to thank him, but words shattered in my mouth.

"Here." He shoved a hand into his inside jacket pocket and pulled out a wrapped sandwich. And because I sat there, stupidly, gaping—trying to find words, he said, "Take it." He nudged it toward me. I set Katie down gingerly. The horse flipped his ears back and swished his tail assertively. If he weren't so tired, he might nip. He smelled fear. Fred put the sandwich in my hands. For a moment, he studied me. I don't know what he was looking for or what he saw. But in his eyes, I saw longing, concern, and regret. He had judged me before, but apparently, he judged Hugh worse now. He averted his gaze to the leather stitching of the saddle and said nothing else.

"I don't know what to say—" I started.

He shook his head. There weren't words for either of us. He tipped his hat at Katie, whose eyes fixed on him like a wildcat's.

He turned the horse west, keeping close watch for the others. His horse swished its tail side to side over its rump. Panting with half-mast eyes, the cattle dog picked up the rear. She had not won the prize after all.

When he was out of sight, I unwrapped the sandwich and broke off a large piece for Katie. My own belly was too full of worry. I couldn't add food to the mixture. Fred was on our side when it mattered most. I'd misread him. Perhaps his coldness had been closer to envy than judgement, since Harvey held my interest, not him.

Katie ate quickly. Then, timid as deer, we tiptoed through the woods, riding the tree line. We would find the rock and let the rest unfold from there. The future was busy forming itself behind closed doors. A magician garbing up for act two of an unbelievable, beguiling, death-defying show. My hot feet ached inside my boots. From the height of the sun, I guessed we had three more hours of daylight.

The lives of the young are not yet patterned. It takes a while to emerge. As we get older, though, patterns do emerge. Even the rough, grey-brown legs of trees around us began to develop a pattern. Evenly spaced and tightly spaced and snug together like the cold legs of a girls' gym class. As the trees moved past us on both sides, I considered all the times in my life when I felt buffered by some invisible force of separation from the world, the way the forest now separated me from those who would find me—for ill or for good.

I'd been a lonely child. But I was lonely the way fish are wet. An invisible constant. I was born into lonely, a room with greying walls, down a hall that led to the bedrooms of the brothers or sisters I would never have. Mother told me this once when I was a teenager. Home from a long day cleaning the Mansons' house, she sat with a rare glass of brandy, a gift from her employer. The house where I was born, in the center of Camberwell, was a hand-me-down house that belonged first to her cousin. But when her cousin died of influenza in the first months of her marriage, her husband walked out and was never seen again. They say he walked all the way to the Thames and right off the bridge. Either way, he never returned and the house stood empty until the family feared it would rot with abandon. So, they offered it for a song to my mother and father, also newlyweds.

"And when we saw the upstairs, we were delighted because the three little bedrooms in a row were perfect for children."

"But you only have one child," I clarified.

"God did not bless us with more," she said in her clipped way, which always meant there was more to the story.

"What does that mean?"

Looking indifferently down at her glass, Mother assessed the color of the brandy. She swished it, and a wave of amber curled round and round the glass. "We were too poor after we had you. And then the war came."

I stared at the table, and she squinted at the window. We always paused after mention of Papa's death, but in that moment it annoyed me. I wanted Mother to keep talking.

"Did you want to have more children?" I pushed on.

"In the beginning, yes. Later . . ." She shrugged her shoulders. "There wouldn't have been enough money for another. It was hardly enough with you."

Their poverty filled hallways, rooms, and hearts with dust. I was given the end room, the brightest. I was going to be the oldest, so I could be farthest away. My room had a view of the street, so I could watch the comings and goings of other folk. The early morning bicycle ride of the newspaper boy. The whacks upside naughty children's heads. The singing sisters swinging hands. The hugs hello. The goodbye forevers.

The floorboards creaked their familiar song several times a day, as I passed the closed doors of my ghost siblings. I could open them if I wanted. I often did. I didn't know then those rooms were waiting for my brothers or my sisters. Yet I felt a strange yearning when I entered them, like looking at a coloring book and having no crayons. I wanted them to be filled with something. Sometimes, I snuck the door open only a sliver to see if something had manifested in secret. Dust. The wan light of London weather. Floorboards with less familiar songs.

My childhood in that house carried a particular kind of lonely. Blank spaces separated me from my own parents. It's a lonely that doesn't know its name. It doesn't breathe. Air stale as dead matches. The scent of grief for what never began. I carried that scent inside of me. I thought every child lived this way, surrounded by an unbreakable quiet, down a long hall, sucking tips of her hair in secret so that something was touched, something was made real. All children have irrational fears, and mine was that I might slowly break apart, the way dust drifts apart in the sunlight. I wouldn't even notice until I was half gone, and then— poof!—a small gust from the crack in the window. Mother would come looking for me, but I would be everywhere and nothing. I would become the emptiness.

Years later and a continent away, I felt that fear again, standing in the kitchen at the ranch, stirring a pot. All the men were out in the fields, of course, and I was pregnant with Katie. A wave of light-headedness came over me, so I sat down on the bench to gather myself. But I wasn't easily gathered. My mind was floating far atop the castles of clouds, my hands danced with the apron fabric far away. And in some other country, a baby thumped with downy feet, inaudibly. Water brimmed over my line of sight and sailed down my cheeks because I'd accepted a life where I was alone in the midst of empty rooms again.

The backs of my hands wiped and wiped at the slosh of tears coming down, but I couldn't make them stop. Finally, I banged the lid onto the soup pot and sent myself upstairs. When Hugh came in that evening for dinner, a morose mass under the blankets on the bed rasped that he should serve the meal himself.

After that unpleasant episode, I resolved to be more upright, to draw upon the familial tradition of stoicism. But I couldn't quite get the feel for it. When the ache of emotion or memory or longing burned inside me, I tried to extinguish it with reason. But the bonfires of yearning would not be easily doused. So I tried to distract myself with doing things. But the mundanity of peeling potatoes or scrubbing sheets made my eyes glaze. Instead, I distracted myself with daydreams. I filled the vacant rooms of my mind. I went on sailboats that caught storms. I found my childhood home and painted it. I met a stray dog in the woods who would let me—and only me—pet him. I passed so many hours living in a world in my mind, that reality faded.

One day on the ranch, I was thinking about my mother and whether she worried about me living up in the Cariboo with a man she hardly knew. I imagined what it would be like if she were visiting me and if she revealed her innermost thoughts.

"Not worried," she said from her imaginary seat on the bench. "I'm disappointed."

I turned to her, shocked. "Disappointed? You're disappointed in me?"

"You're not quite the child I wanted." She turned to look at the wall, not facing me. "A boy would have been better. Would have been able to provide for me."

"Mother, how can you say that? Is this *really* how you feel?"

"Yes," she emphasized. "But I would never tell you. Life is just bitter that way. I shouldn't have expected more."

Too stunned for grief, I turned back to the bread dough before me. The wooden spoon turned the stubborn mass in the bowl. *Could this be true?* I felt kicked in the gut. *Could imagination alone make me this miserable?* But once the notion of Mother's disappointment came to me, I couldn't shake it loose. That night, the next morning, I was still reeling from the news.

I began tracking the evidence like a detective to see what clues I'd missed. She sent letters every other month and signed them affectionately, but she only visited for the wedding. She claimed she couldn't help me after Katie was born because her employer urgently needed her. However, she departed quickly from Vancouver—and seemingly for good—when her sister fell ill back in London. Was Aunt Rose really ill? Surely she was.

What was it mother had said to me in congratulations after the marriage ceremony? "Well, you won't have to worry about having enough beef around!" It was the only comment she offered that day.

Over the course of weeks, the notion of Mother's disappointment fixed a deep, unshakable root through my soul. As true as sky is blue. I just hadn't seen it before. She had carefully masked the evidence. That's the danger of daydreams. They can take you by the hand, like Yeats' faeries, and lead you to cold river bottoms.

Yet there was one door I hadn't opened, in daydream or reality until it was too late: the barn door. And that one had been the most important. I did not daydream often of Hugh. Why dream of potatoes as you peel them? When I did contemplate him, I dreamed of sudden accidents. A slip of the ladder, me running to help. Or Will, out of breath: "Hugh's been kicked by a horse." Or rolling over in the night to silence. No snoring. No breath. I bang his chest. "Hugh!" Died in his sleep. I didn't *want* him to be hurt or to die. But I suppose I felt that he was perpetually slipping away from me.

Remembering that now, as I lugged Katie in my arms through the trees, regret cinched my chest. Probably I'd been a horrible wife. What were the things good wives did? I brought tea. My cooking wouldn't win awards but nor was it slipped under the table to Chester. I thought I had done what Hugh wanted the most: I gave him space. I respected his peace. I didn't impose upon the carefully guarded privacy he kept for himself. How different we were. I tried to escape from haunting rooms while he built the very same around himself and locked them from the inside.

The daydream, like a good dowsing rod, can guide one to satiation and maneuver around at least some land mines. That's what I'd done with Hugh. His coldness in the bedroom every night. His disinterest in relating to his own daughter. His "luck" in locating younger men—boys, really—to work on the ranch with him. All of this, I'd stepped around as long as I could.

29

FEAR AND EXHAUSTION quavered in my arms. I set Katie on the ground. I'd neglected to fill us up on water when we left the creek, and now Katie warned that she "would die of thirst." We curved around a hillside, around pine and over fallen logs, hoping to find a trickle somewhere. A grey wall of rock made regular reappearances between the shrubbery and weeds. At last, I spotted a lush patch of moss stuck to the stone, and with a flash of inspiration, ripped it away and revealed a silent trickle of wet slipping over the stone. Awkwardly, I lifted Katie so she could suck the water. Then, it was my turn. The cold, sweet liquid filled my mouth as it tinkled like the smallest faery bells. I closed my eyes. Cool, minerally sweetness slipped over my tongue. Two nights ago, I was kissing Harvey, and now—a stone.

A twig snapped, and I whirled around. But it was only Katie, squatting down to examine an elbow-shaped opening in the hillside. A den of sorts.

"Katie, step away from there."

"It's empty!" She pronounced gleefully.

"Even still." I pulled her by the hand, but she began the slanted dance of rebellion.

"No! I want to go in the cave! Let me go!"

"Fine!" I released her, and she lunged toward the den. I added, "But don't get dirty!" As if dirt, a bit of soil on the clothing of a soon-to-be-starving and destitute child was important. I turned away from the den and folded my arms.

"Come in here, Mummy!" Katie's head reappeared through the dangling moss.

The words filling my mouth were sharp edged and unkind. I pressed my lips to hold them in.

"Mummy! Mummy! Look!"

"Katie, come out of there *now*," I snapped. "We have to go back to our *spot*."

"No! I like it here!" She sat cross-legged inside the den, folding her arms like the ruler of her own private, dingy castle.

"We can't stay here. We have to go where Fred told us to meet him and Harvey."

"No! They let us be starving! I'm staying here." She pressed her back farther into the den, so all I could see were her kneecaps, shoes, and shadows.

"Katrina Jean, come out of there this instant! We have to go!" The day's anxiety turned my nerves into a fine glass web. I could feel the shattering.

Katie continued, "NO! You chose all the other stopping places. I choose here!"

I tried reason. "But, Katie, we can't stay here. They won't know where we are. They won't be able to bring us food."

"We can listen for them. I have good ears. You *told* me I did."

"Yes, but—" I looked around to try to assess how far we'd come from the meeting spot. It was a good hundred feet around a slight bend. Could we really hear them from here? "But, Katie . . ." I'd run out of fight. I searched myself, looking for the part of me who could haul Katie out. I was empty.

"For a little while," I mumbled, and half squatted, half collapsed at the den's mouth.

"Welcome inside," Katie intoned sweetly. "I'll show you where your bed is."

Once inside, the den cleared my head by only a foot and if Katie bumped me an inch, I wouldn't be entirely "in" the cave anymore. All the running, all the momentum had drained out of me. My belly knotted up where food should have been. While Katie chattered about, making us an imaginary home with pillows of moss, blankets of fern, and a fence of pebbles, I listened to the din of emotion inside me.

For hours, Katie chattered of make-believe house making. I fed her bites of Fred's sandwich. Her day ended when she crawled onto my lap and laid her head on my chest—as if sleeping on top her mother in a den were the most natural thing. She asked for a song. Quietly, so I could listen to the silent spaces between notes, I sang "Somewhere a Voice Is Calling": . . . *Dusk and the shadows falling, o'er land and sea. Somewhere a voice is calling, calling for me . . .*

The day tucked below the heavy lid of dark. Stars and moonlight dappled the forest floor between the shadows of fir boughs. A chill touched my arms and legs, and pinched my cheeks, but Katie's hot weight kept me from shivering. Her curls warmed my chin. I wriggled this way and that, trying to find comfort where there was none. The ache in my back evidenced this fact.

No one came. No Harvey. No Fred. Harvey would know I wanted to be rescued. He would know and so would Fred that I was cold, hungry, and scared. Perhaps they were threatened with losing their jobs or being dragged to the Mounties if they helped us. On the scale, our comfort and safety measured less than their freedom and employment. They looked after themselves. I wanted heroes. These were just men. Hungry cowboys living in lean times. They didn't owe anything to a woman and child curled in the dark and damp of the cave. Perhaps too they were shot dead somewhere. But I hadn't heard gunshots, and Hugh's anger aimed at me, not random ranch hands.

I felt I would run through a field of flying bullets for Harvey. For him, I would abandon my plans for Vancouver and live in a cabin the size of a walnut shell. I would put my whole life on a plate and served it to him warmed with honey. But he did not come for me. Even with a great imagination, I could only bend the laws of reality so far. He was just a cowboy flirting with a ranch wife, enjoying female company in this land of men. I had made him a hero, my future, but he was not. That wry look in his eyes did not mean he saw me. He was only reading me, seeing how far he could take the flirtation. He wanted me to fall for him because that would polish up his self-worth. He wanted me to believe he was serious about me, so he could decide if he was. With that kiss, I'd invested everything. I'd made him my partner, but he was merely sampling.

I couldn't sleep. Everything had fallen apart. All my plans of escape. I was no farther away from Hugh than the first night I left him. We were caged inside this land, this vast Cariboo, caged inside the endless loop of a wedding band. I'd left behind a ranch, a boarding house, a cabin, a horse, my suitcase, my bag, my money. I had nothing now but my daughter, and no way to care for her. I wanted to live a life free from brittle-thin winters and sun-smacking summers clouded with bugs. I wanted escape from the bruising, the hand that brought the bruising, the threat beyond mere bruising. Hugh had never really cared for me. I was a commodity. I wanted protection and a father for my daughter. I had wanted Harvey. I had wanted the warm embrace of love to come and find me, to sweep me away from this life. I wanted to believe I wasn't alone to fix my life, that someone wanted to do it with me.

Above all, I had wanted to be free to love and truly live. But the more I ran toward that freedom, the more caged I became. I was a cornered animal now. I couldn't go back to the life I had lived. I would rather die. Yet, running away was not working.

Then I must not run anymore. The idea flashed. *I must not run.* There is a child's toy made of two metal loops that need to be pulled apart. Try to pull it apart the obvious way and it remains stuck forever. But try something completely unexpected, counterintuitive, and *voila!*—the pieces come apart.

If I couldn't run away, then I would go toward. I would go to Hugh and meet him face to face. I would tell him—something. I wasn't sure what. I could ask for a divorce. I'd tell him I was leaving, taking Katie, and never coming back. He would be so stunned, maybe he wouldn't know what to do. I was squeezing Katie too firmly. I made my arms ease off. I nodded to myself, pressing my teeth tightly.

Dawn spilled grey rain over the forest. Were it not for Katie's insistence on sleeping in the cave, we'd be drenched. Fir boughs and pine needles shed droplets in patternless rhythm. The bent metal sky brightened. The rain stopped and only the tree droplets pattered on. Chickadees scattered their calls in the distance. Puffs of clouds crossed overhead, like white ponies in mid-gallop. Auspicious. My back ached with a night-full of worry, cold, and cramped spaces, while the full spell of sleep lay over Katie.

Were I a practical person in a practical state of mind, I would have plotted what to say when I faced Hugh. Were I strong, and not sore and worn down, the pinpricks of fear up my arms would make me reconsider. Shivering bewilderment and resoluteness defined me in that moment. The sleeplessness of the night had fortified me with grey resolve. My mind was a white sky with a single bird in the middle, and in my arms, a rifle. *Go to Hugh. Face him. Make him look you in the eye. And tell him there, that you are never going back. Bang!*

Katie awoke like a drunk—with a squint, a rub of her head, and a lopsided look of disorientation.

"Let's get up," I said. "I have someone to see."

30

A S WE NAVIGATED toward the ranch, my heart stomped in protest. I couldn't decide if I was more afraid of humiliation or death. Both loomed menacingly. It was a long way for Katie to walk, and by now we were completely out of food. I wasn't hungry myself, but for Katie's sake, I constantly scanned our surroundings for food. I gave her a few pinches of huckleberry buds. Not tasty, but edible. When we came back to the creek's edge, we scooped up handfuls of sweet water. I found four unripe thimbleberries. Katie's face twisted from their chalkiness. I broke off the fresh tips of new dandelion leaves. But those proved too bitter for Katie, so I ate them myself, for strength and for courage.

I ran through scenarios in my mind. *Would Hugh be so angry, he'd carry a rifle?* I searched the landscape of my mind for a trigger. *Could I tell? Could I identify his mood?* But my own thumping anxiety prevented me from discerning. *Would he get me alone—pull me into the truck with Katie and somewhere on the road back to the ranch—turn and strangle me? And how to protect Katie? Would Harvey's boss encourage Hugh? Side with him?* I would hide Katie in the trees and approach Hugh alone. If he intended to drag us back to the ranch, he would have to find Katie first, and that would buy me some time.

Still, I hoped for the best. An argument. Yelling. He'd threaten me with the back of his hand, but perhaps with cowboys and a ranch owner watching, he wouldn't hit. Most men would think he had a right, but it would reflect badly. Even if he did hit me, I could withstand the blows if I knew they were the last. And I would tell him: *I am not yours anymore. This marriage has dissolved in lies. I go my own way now. I belong to no man.* And I would turn and walk away, into the woods. Pride would prevent him from pleading. Pride would also implore him to humiliate me. He was unlikely to attempt murder in front of other men, but he would salvage his pride as a husband. I slowed my pace trying to imagine how.

All too soon, the forest gave way to the lumpy muck and shorn grass of cow pasture. "Katie, you need to wait here by this tree, okay?"

"No! I'm going with you. I want to go to that house and eat porridge!" I glanced at the rancher's home.

"That place is not for us. If I can, I'll get some food." I bent and pressed a kiss into her curls. "It's not safe for you to come with me. I need you to be here so you can keep safe." *Poor girl*, I thought. *Leaving her in bear territory, so she'll be safe from her own father.*

She huffed in protest, but plunked down on the ground. She folded arms over her chest and pouted at the dirt.

"Be a good girl. Don't come unless it's me who calls you, okay? Only me. Just stay here until I come." I lifted her chin to see her eyes. Her steely eyes looked at me with the stubbornness only a three-year-old can have.

I stepped out into the clearing. Katie's whimper trailed after me like a shadow. The clods of dirt mismatched my steps as I fumbled up and down over them. The sky opened up to a great upside-down stage. A pale blue platform above a new drama. *Go. Go,* I told myself, hoping I wouldn't lose courage.

It was not as I expected. I'd pictured Hugh switching this way and that through the ranch paths with an angry glare. Instead, he was leaning calm as Cain against the rancher's truck, sipping steaming tea and chatting about cattle. I walked toward him, fingernails pressing into my palms, chest taut with undefined emotion. The rancher flinched at the sight of me, and Hugh turned in my direction.

His eyes widened but he quickly hid his surprise. An unexpected chess move. How would he respond? I registered the alarm and anger in his eyes. I stopped a few steps away from him. The rancher motioned at me and raised eyebrows to Hugh, and mumbled cheerfully, "Well, speak of the Devil and up she turns!"

A jolt ran through me—it was Katie—pressing against the back of my legs. I resisted the urge to turn and scold her for not staying put. Hugh shifted backward when she looked at him. He swirled the tea in his cup, glancing with agitation between me and the rancher.

"I'm not going back with you." The words flew out from me, lancing the silence. The rancher looked bemused. The most entertainment he'd seen in a while.

"Now, Annabelle," Hugh reprimanded, passing his mug to the rancher. "Just settle your fret and be calm. Don't do something you'll regret." *Don't blurt about Edwin to the rancher or you'll regret it.*

"Be calm?" *After the incident and the choking and days of sleeping outdoors on the run and near starving—he wanted me to be calm?* I shook with a rage I didn't know I owned. He chuckled paternally, catching the rancher up in the joviality. I saw the pattern. He'd made a story. He'd told the rancher, and who knows who else, that I was nutty. Unstable and unsound. Like a mentally defective child. The smirking rancher saw now the character Hugh had created: disheveled, unreasonable, toting a hungry daughter through the wilds. Meanwhile, Hugh had established his own role as the ever-patient and calming husband—more caregiver or father than lover. He was bringing his hysterical wife back to civilization. With arms folded over my chest to mask the shivers, I stared at him, wondering how to untangle his story.

Smiling for show, Hugh straightened up and, with a nod, announced flatly, "Time to go on home now. That girl of yours needs some care." The intensity of his eyes belied the calmness of his voice. He *hoped* for obedience. I had to outmaneuver him.

"No." I hoped he couldn't see my knees shaking. My eyes fell from his face to shirt to dirt, but I made myself look him in the eye. More calmly, with more control, I asserted, "No. I'm not returning to the ranch. Not now. Not ever. You've treated us callously and put us all at risk." I had it now—the way to unlock the puzzle pieces. Pure defiance. Complete obstinance. He never expected that! He would not *drag* me forcibly into the truck. Beyond the grueling embarrassment of it, he simply would not want to touch me as much as that feat required.

He shifted uneasily. His carefully constructed story was teetering. "Annabelle," he spoke as if to an unruly child, but fear pulled at the words. "I'm telling you. You need to. For the good of the child." He motioned to Katie who instinctively squeezed my hand.

"No."

"Well." He shifted to the other foot, felt inside his jacket pocket for a toothpick. "Well. Then I'm leaving you right here," he threatened. An ultimatum.

"Whoa." the rancher backed up a few steps. "She ain't a cowhand. I can't use her here."

"See, Annabelle," Hugh tried. "You've got no place to go. Probably spent most of your money already." *We own the clothes we wear and nothing more.*

"Oh, give her a few bucks so she can train out of here. Nothing for a single mother in this town, except Felix's house." His eyes fell down the length of my legs. "Not her style, I suspect." Excited to be a player in the action, he motioned for Hugh to toss some money.

Hugh grimaced, tension raising his shoulders. He was stuck. He couldn't drag me. He couldn't reason with me. He wouldn't openly threaten me. He took a long moment to work the toothpick through his teeth. Then he sank a hand down into his pocket. With a face of granite, he pulled out a five-dollar bill. "You don't deserve it. Give it to the girl," he said, holding it out with whitened fingers. My hand reached out and plucked it from him. He spat the toothpick to the ground, and gave a nod to the rancher. He looked angrily at Katie, whose puzzled eyebrows couldn't make sense of him. Then, slowly, he turned on his heel and sauntered off, casual as day. As if this is what he planned all along.

The truck door slammed. The familiar engine chugged to life. A thin dust carpet unrolled behind him to the orchestra of car springs, creaks, and grumbles. We listened to the sound grow fainter and fainter.

My breaths were long and loud, but I no longer trembled. I could hardly believe it. *Free.* Katie and I. *Free on the earth!* The rancher turned to us. He said, "Come inside. You can make the lunch for the boys." The drama was over for him. Back to the dullness of the day. He turned and walked toward the house.

I picked up Katie. I pressed her to my chest, savoring her sweet pine scent. She sighed from the strain of this unfathomable world. As I rocked her gently and carried her into the house, a light warmed me from the inside.

31

I N THE DARK interior, the kitchen resembled a wartime mess
hall. The rancher motioned to bread, the icebox, plates, and
things. His words were crow-talk because I was full up with the
shock of relief. His arms lifted and fell like heavy, bald wings as he
pointed out this and that. When he left, we were wonderfully
alone. Basking in a novel and astonishing solitude. I turned myself
to the task of assembling sandwiches the way people do in
ordinary moments. A mundane thing turned extraordinary.

Katie sat on a stool by the wall, staring out with eyes too old
for her age. With still-trembling hands, I sliced and buttered a
sliver of bread for her, setting a wrinkled blanket of cold roast
beef on it. She looked at it like it was a strange creature she felt
sorry for. She cradled it between two tiny hands on her lap,
waiting for it to move by itself. A sigh shuddered through her.

"When is Daddy going to come back?" she asked softly.

"I don't know, Katie." I pressed my tongue into my teeth.
"We're all done with the ranch." The words tumbled out
heavily. "We don't live with him anymore."

"Where do we live?"

I pulled the knife through the dry roast beef. "I don't know
yet. But eat up. You're hungry."

She lifted it to her mouth and bit gingerly. She was not the
kind of hungry that has one drooling at the sight of food. She was
distrustful of the sandwich. A reluctant participant in the business
of living. Eating ties us to things. To people, to our bodies. Most

of all, to life. But just then, she was wary of life. She negotiated the sandwich with dignity and hesitation, chewing and sighing.

My feet firmly on the floor, I cupped her shoulder in my hand. "We'll be all right. The future is calling to us. We only need to follow it." She smiled with relief and tears spilled down her cheeks. I understood her pain. Her father seemed not to want her. And now he was gone. But the deeper pain was her soul's recognition of what came before this moment. She never did have a father in the real sense, not like I did. Hugh hadn't held her in his arms, told her stories, delighted at her questions, cared for her like a beloved princess. All those things my father had done. At best, Hugh tolerated her. Often, he hadn't.

I lifted my gaze to the heavens and prayed: *please let the future bring a man who will be a real father to her.*

One way or another, I would find our future—for her sake. The map in my mind was blank. Vancouver still called to me, but what then? Ten days ago, Vancouver seemed simple, obvious. But there's a difference between running away—which I had now accomplished—and running toward—which I didn't know how to do. I had a few school friends in Vancouver, Betsy and others. Surely, they would be willing to accommodate us for a short time, days or weeks. *But after that? How would I pay for lodging on my own? How would I feed us? Where would I work? How could I work when Katie was too little to leave on her own?* It was different when Mother left England, asking those same questions. Vancouver was advertising for all kinds of workers, jobs were abundant, and I was old enough to be left alone. The questions inside me, previously hovering like distant clouds, consolidated on the horizon like a storm front.

Any minute, the men would be inside and ready for their lunch. The rancher, eyeing me up and down, Fred, and Harvey. The familiar wheels of daydream turned: Perhaps Harvey could promise to take care of me. He could do extra work to compensate for my room and board. The rancher said he had no use for me, but Harvey could persuade him. He would see my needs. He would make the decisions. He would save me, and my new life would begin. I would go back to looking after Katie, and basking in the intense affection of his eyes, his touch. My only skill is to open the door that's right in front of me. If Harvey led me to it, I would open it.

I focused on these slippery daydreams, not the chasm of uncertainty beneath. I couldn't make out the greater pattern. I was transfixed on one piece of color inside the kaleidoscope, even while I sensed the impending fall and shattering.

Harvey, Fred, and the rancher bustled in with the day's heat and dirt. A flock of birds broke loose from my chest when I saw him. But he smiled apologetically, and sat down with hunched shoulders. Mother's voice rang through my head: "Made a muddle of it this time, haven't you?" The men ate. Katie lay sideways on her bench, dancing her fingers in the air. The rancher chewed loudly, inspecting his sandwich for errors. Fred offered a flattened grimace—his attempt at a smile.

As I wiped the counter, I snuck glances at Harvey. He didn't meet my eyes. His elbow lifted when he reached for the water pitcher. He brushed imaginary crumbs off his legs with big, long swoops. He launched a bite into the sandwich with slightly showy enthusiasm. But my feet were on the ground now. I could see him. Had he always been this evident?

Harvey liked what he could get for free. He didn't want to pay for anything with commitment. He feared becoming someone's property—shackled by heart or groin. His own needs tempted him to give in. But he was a coward and refused to surrender to love. Like many other men, he mistook vulnerability for weakness. He was going to pat himself on the back when I turned away from him. *Let her go, just as I should. Didn't need more than a kiss anyway. And got that.* I stood mere paces away from him. A free woman. That availability didn't appeal to him. It threatened. So, he was cold and sheltered.

I also knew when I stepped away from this ranch, he would lie in the cedar-scented blankets, stoking the fires of yearning for *the one who got away.* And when I was long gone, he would stare up at moonlit walls indulging in the sweet pain. For him, love was a coin with only two sides: possibility and loss. Love was the ache of love lost. In going away, I would give him what he desired most. An unattainable love.

Harvey finished first. With a cheery grin and an odd hop in his step, he nodded a brisk thank you to my apron and left for his work. I turned to my waiting sandwich as storms broke loose inside me.

The rancher decided I would leave right away. One of the men would drive me to the train station and from there, I'd be on my own. But time moved more slowly in those days. So "leaving right away" meant first spending three more nights at the ranch. Then they could take me to town when they had a reason to go, to pick up more supplies and not waste money and time with an empty trip. The rancher made sure I had plenty of work to do, earning my keep. I stuffed canvas bags full of greasy sheep wool. I scrubbed all the men's rough work clothes with a washing powder so weak, I couldn't muster a single sud. I ladled the oatmeal, and then ladled the lunch soup, and then set out the dinner roast.

At night, I slept on a lumpy, yellow sofa in a living room piled with boxes and smelling of truck grease. Katie slept on a bedroll on the floor beside me. I daydreamed about sled dogs, the whip snapping over their heads, threateningly. Running and running, paws on snow, mouths open. That's what they live for—to be on the move. Sled dogs like the whip. It keeps them from thinking. The rancher's blustery commands throughout the day had the same effect on me. They prevented me from sinking too far into the cold unknown. The grief of loss. The beautiful thing between Harvey and I had turned inside out. Its shiny fur hidden away. The gore of veins and organs fully visible. I was afraid to touch it. Afraid to go near. I turned the other way. Avoided his gaze. Spoke to no one but Katie. Expected nothing. Lived in the limbo.

Supposedly, I was free. Hugh had let me leave. But I was leashed and pulled by the urge to flee—to move and keep moving. Sleep outdoors under crowds of stars. Sleep in old shacks where moonlight fell in thin shafts. Gallop on horseback. Feel the rhythmic sway of a train. The beat of my footfalls running before me.

My own rhythm. My own path.

I wanted to drift beneath the roaming clouds, and listen to the swaying pines whisper of far-off places. Beneath the flights of geese, swallows, and dragonflies. All of us in motion. I missed Ocktoo. A horse, a bedroll, and a bit of dried food. That was the cowboy way. The springs in the sofa squeaked as I rolled over. Perhaps I couldn't decide quite where to go because I didn't want to arrive anywhere. I used to wander only in my thoughts, but now my whole body needed to move.

I could take the five dollars and buy a train ticket to Vancouver. I could stay with my school friend for a short time while I tried to save money. Then I'd buy tickets to England for Katie and me. We'd visit Mother and Auntie. Find more work. Start a new life. Keep moving. France. Some odd jobs. Down to Italy. I could school Katie myself. No one would hold us down. No shackling bonds of marriage. I laughed at myself. Perhaps Harvey and I were not so different after all. Tears crested my eyes. No, I thought. We are not quite the same. Freedom was my consolation prize. What I had wanted most was love.

The morning of our departure arrived. Fred volunteered to drive. He and Harvey thumped sacks of sheep wool over the sideboards of the truck. Fred went to grab more things from the barn, and Harvey leaned against the truck, folded his arms, and drank me in with a gaze. The toe of my boot pecked at the dirt. Katie was peering through the sheep pen at the shorn and sleepy creatures. I shivered with the coolness of morning. Harvey was preparing to miss me. I disliked being right. I couldn't look at him with anything but hurt, distance, and disappointment, so I tried not to meet his gaze.

But he caught me by the hand and sang my name. "Annabelle." A smile spread through him. "I'm sorry that . . . Well, you know, if I had my own ranch . . . I mean, maybe we coulda . . ." He cocked his head toward the ranch house. "This ain't a good place for someone like you. You need better." I didn't look up. I imagined his lips on my forehead. Then he leaned over, and fatherlike, kissed my forehead. I sighed, trying to forgive. What right had I to disappointment? He had only ever been himself. His promises of long-lasting love, protection, and soul bonding—those were all mistranslations. The miscalculations between courtship and hope.

"Goodbye, Harvey," I breathed with a cracking voice. I wouldn't see him again. Of that, I was certain.

"Gooodbye, Haarvey!" Katie hugged the stiff jeans of his leg.

Fred was exiting the house and hurrying toward the truck, leaning forward in his slow, perpetual hurry. I opened the passenger door and set Katie down. "Take me to the future, Mummy," Katie cooed. I squeezed her hand.

Like a gentleman, Harvey's hand lifted my elbow as I stepped inside. "Yup," he said, to no one in particular. Fred nodded at him and kicked the engine into a sputtered, rhythmic promise. The satisfaction of escape overcame grief. We kicked off over the dirt, mud, potholes, and rocks of the driveway.

"Oh—I didn't thank the rancher!"

Fred turned over his shoulder to look furtively back at the ranch. "Nope." He shook his head. "He was about to ask you for boarding money!" His head fell back in laughter.

32

THE DRIVE WAS long, bumpy, and quiet. I jangled about on the seat with my worries. Nonsensical as it was, I half expected Hugh to show up at any moment and demand that we return to the ranch—grab us and drag us there—or have me arrested and put into an asylum, torn away from Katie. But we made it to the train station without incident.

Katie was floppy as a rag doll from her nap. I lifted her out of the truck and pulled her along as I said a hurried farewell to Fred. Despite my indebtedness to him, I was anxious to be on our way, as if excess gratitude might stick my feet to the ground and trap me. I covered curt actions and worried thoughts with a tense smile. I thought I was in charge. I thought I, alone, was carving the path to our future, hacking away the path with pure stubbornness and will. But I didn't understand the pattern of things. We never know when the future might arrive. It might be already waiting outside the door, hand raised, ready to enter.

Fred chugged off in the truck, and we hurried inside to purchase tickets. The bow-tied old-timer who sold them parsed out words like they were in short supply and he regretted losing even one. The train was leaving in just over an hour. Five dollars wouldn't take us to Vancouver, but we could make it to Whistler. Fair enough, I thought. I'll figure out the rest later. Perhaps I'll find a ride with a friendly delivery driver. Whistler was only seventy-five miles from Vancouver, not unmanageable. *If we have to, we'll walk!*

The imminent boarding of the train should have calmed me. But instead I was agitated like one fighting unseen ghosts. It was a peculiar kind of irritation, like my ancestors were lifting strands of my hair, the corner of my blouse, pointing at obscurity.

From the hard bench inside the station, I watched men preparing for their trips. Perhaps unnerved by my tension, Katie set off to explore spiders in window frames and the stacks of baggage and packages near the door. I wished to be alone with my thoughts, to settle down and examine the source of my urgency, but Katie required constant intervention, which rattled my nerves all the more.

"Katie! Don't touch those bags. Those aren't ours."

"No! Stay inside the station. Don't go outside."

"Step out of the man's way—Katie!"

When people go on trips, their spirits arrive before their bodies. That way, when the body arrives, part of the spirit is already there to greet it. And that's why one's last days in a place have an empty feel. We're already part gone. We send ourselves ahead of us, and we must travel out into the world to meet ourselves and be whole again. But if you don't know where you're going, how can you be there to meet yourself? And if we're utterly determined not to stay in a place, then we are simply half-selves. The rest is scattered, woven through thick grey bands of clouds, brushing over the grasses in a field, touching down in the forests of mountains, then off again. While I've never experienced real homesickness, I imagine this must be the root of the problem. A homesick person doesn't send themselves out ahead to scout. Instead they leave themselves behind. So when they arrive, rather than feeling whole again, they feel halved.

In the last few minutes before the train arrived, I pulled Katie onto my lap and explained with great regalia of detail what a train ride was like. Finally, a small ticking sound in the distance grew into shushing and grinding. With an elated hoot and happy snorting of steam, the great metal stallion rode into the station. Katie was rigid, wide-eyed, and mute with gleeful excitement.

A boyish attendant stepped off the third of five cars and hollered, "All aboard!! Pemberton! Whistler! Squamish! Vancouver!"

There were not many of us boarding. Perhaps only eight passengers. They all looked the same to me. Landowners, potential landowners, and former landowners. No women, needless to say. The gentlemen very kindly made way for us to go first, which only increased the audience for my next feat. I passed the attendant my ticket and began to ascend the stair when a second train attendant emerged a few cars away. I gasped in shock, recognizing his face. *It's the boy! It's Edwin!* In a flash the barn—Hugh's bare legs—Edwin rushing past me—flashed before me. I misjudged the train floor and—in a whirlwind of limbs and a pop of my ankle—fell backward onto the ground.

"Mummy! Mummy! What are you doing?!" Katie yelled from the train threshold. I tried to catch another glimpse of Edwin, but he was gone. *Was it really him?* I was enveloped in a sea of men and questions and reassurances.

"Ma'am? You all right there?"

"Crashed right down, you did."

"Up you go. Now watch your step." Unfortunately, once they set me upright, I was lopsided and toppling over. My foot throbbed with numbness. I looked for a place to sit. Since there was no place, a couple of kindly men continued to hold me by the elbows.

The young attendant blushed, believing himself responsible for my accident. "I'm so sorry, ma'am. I can fetch you a doctor." I didn't want to be the center of attention a moment longer. I wanted to say it was all right—that I could continue on my journey. But those words would not come. And I found no others. I was suddenly mute.

Sensing the rudeness of my silence, Katie thrust hands on hips and scolded me. "Mummy!"

The sturdy man at my elbow confirmed, "Yeah, she's gonna need a doc. Go see if you got a doc or a vet on board. No doc in this town since Wilbur left. An' vet's way out at Moonie's

Ranch. Two days' ride."

Another man offered, "Grady's on board. Laid eyes on him myself when I got on in Kamloops. He can inspect her." He and the attendant hurried off to fetch him.

The men hobbled me over to a nearby bench. Katie trailed after, squeezing her hands with worry and darting between the men's long legs. The men settled me onto the bench. I pressed finger and thumb to the corners of my eyes and reached for Katie's hand.

The men discussed me in the third person, hashing out the specifics of the injury. Meanwhile, I focused on the throbbing pain, embarrassment, and tightness of Katie's hand in mine.

"Ma'am? Do you want us to notify anyone for you? Husband or someone? Send out a wire?"

"No. No, thank you," I croaked hoarsely.

By then, the conductor had stepped off the train to survey the commotion. With dark boots and navy slacks, he walked into the midst of us. He stood silently, trusting his status and authority would provoke the needed answers.

After a moment of collective silence, one man offered, "Fell off the train. Just stepping up and fell right off." It sounded profoundly idiotic.

He shifted weight. "You'll be all right, ma'am," he announced, as if he believed just saying it made it true. *Oh, to feel so powerful!*

The thumping of hurried feet announced the attendant's return. I looked up to see his youthful face washed with shock. I wished to reassure him, but if I opened my mouth for words, tears would come too. I refused to let tears drench my dwindling pride. The attendant looked sheepishly at the conductor, who—in the split second before the older man slapped the attendant reproachfully—I realized was his father. Katie flinched. "It's not his fault," I began to say, but the words were stuck and small, hard to hear.

A larger man pushed past the attendant and knelt down by

my foot. He carried the floppy triangular bag of a doctor, and yet he wore jeans, two layers of button shirts, and a faded red bandanna around his neck. He lacked the cowboy hat, but everything else about him spelled C-O-W-B-O-Y. At best, he was a farm vet. At worst, a loose-headed mountain man with only snake oil and bluster. Regardless of his doubtful expertise, I was somewhat grateful. Left to my own cleverness, I probably would have sat mute on the bench a long while, with little clue what to do.

Without a word, he lifted my heel into his hand and pressed fingers and thumb on the ankle in several places, gently turning it this way and that. He had wavy, unkempt hair in need of a trim and very broad, rounded shoulders. His fingers were thick and long. Indeed, he seemed more fit for helping birthing mares than for inspecting female ankles. I wondered dimly if I should be suspicious. The other men stood around respectfully quiet. *Or suspiciously quiet?* He attempted to move the heel back and forth, and I yelped. He looked up at me in assessment. He glanced at Katie, who was squatting on the bench, still anxiously squeezing my hand.

"Don't worry," he assured her with a smile and a nod. "We'll take care of her." He stood up, towering like a bear next to the other men, the tallest of whom only reached his eyes. "If you're up for it, we'll get you on the train, and I can better attend to you there." This sprinkle of gentleness over my damaged pride mildly irritated me. But I nodded. Although he could have easily carried me over his shoulder like a sack of potatoes, I lifted my arms over the shoulders of men on either side. The bear-man mountain vet stepped out of the way, while Katie pushed ahead to clear the way.

They settled me down into the plush red seat at the front of a train car. The locomotive whistled long and loud, and with a clamor and chug of the engine, we began to move. I winced in pain. *The train toward Vancouver at last. How many times had I imagined this moment? Yet none of my daydreams looked like this.*

As we picked up pace, metal wheels squealed along the rails. Katie gawked at the passing station, shrubbery, and peak-roof houses. The train chugged forward, building slowly into a great rhythm of speed. It rounded a bend and billows of grey steam obscured the view. I leaned against the train wall, with my leg up on the soft bench seat, craning my neck to take in the view. Katie turned to me with an exuberant grin. I loosened her grip on my hand and touched her arm softly. We celebrated in silence, catching each other's eyes and smiling. My chest cramped from the soreness radiating up my leg. But perhaps—*perhaps*—somehow everything would work out all right.

33

S OON, THE BEAR-MAN returned and positioned himself on a short stool in the foot space between our seat and the wall. I saw that he was armed with a cloth filled with ice chips, a towel, and a pillow. Beneath my short brown boot, my ankle throbbed. With only a cursory glance in my direction, he began unlacing my boot.

"Oh. I can—" I tried to assert.

"It's quite all right," he said. He seemed mildly amused by something, or at least contented. It bothered me. After all, I was crossing a vast chasm of fear, pain, and hopelessness. I'd been through so much. What did he understand of a woman's life? Of *my* life? Here he was, grinning at my bootlace like this was the best thing that happened since the invention of pie. I knew a twisted ankle might take days to recover. It was all too much to endure someone else's cheeriness at that moment. Why must some spend every cent of their soul to earn freedom, peace, and contentment, and others pluck it up—free—from the ground without ever tossing a penny? I was utterly spent.

With a self-assured grin, he raised my leg, and set the pillow, towel, and ice beneath it.

I recovered my voice. "Might take a few days to heal, I guess." It wouldn't hurt to draw his attention to the obvious inconvenience.

He stood. He was tall indeed, with shoulders wide as a griz-zly's. Hands on hips, admiring the awkward architecture of ice, ankle, and pillow. "Oh." He paused. "You'll be resting in bed for a good three weeks before you can walk again. And then another two or three with a crutch. Got yourself a second-degree sprain there. Tore it halfway through."

"What? No, no." I had to make him understand. "It *can't* be that bad. I'm sure if I see a doctor, he'll agree."

The man grinned even wider. His face had a boyish quality, though a few white hairs showed in his stubble. Politeness tightened my face.

"I *am* a doctor." He mused. "Name's Grady."

"No—" I blurted illogically. "No, that can't be right. I can't stay in bed for three weeks. It's not possible. I can't." And then I bit down on my lip to stop the rest of the story from tumbling out of me.

He paused to assess my anxiety. He was waiting for the dust to settle before speaking again. Katie hummed and talked to herself. Apparently, her concern for me had dissipated like the engine steam behind us. Her face was so close to the window, that every time the train turned, she bumped chin and nose against it. The doctor lowered himself onto the stool again, staring at me as I glared out the window, willing away the tears. The train's engine churned and churned, grinding away.

When he spoke again, his voice was soft, kindly. "Are you heading home?"

A simple question—never mind the impossibility of answering. "I—maybe. I don't know," I whispered, unable to fashion a lie.

"Hmm," he said. Then, more seriously, "Hmm." He studied the carpet pattern. *Now he'll question my mental condition.*

I attempted an explanation. "We're getting off at Whistler—but only temporarily. Until we can make it to Vancouver." I spoke to my hands, to the window. His dark eyes made me uncomfortable. He seemed to want more than words could offer.

"Do you have someone to stay with in Whistler?"

"Not as of yet." My mind raced. "But . . ."

"Know anyone there?"

"Not yet, but . . ." I swallowed the rest of the words.

"And no money for a hotel. Is that right?"

"You don't understand," I whispered, even though he obviously understood perfectly. "We're transitioning. Starting anew. New life."

"Right." He nodded solemnly. He sat silently with clasped hands over his knees. I was wholly discomforted by his accurate assessments. He had figured me out. I had no one and nothing, only my pride, which I was lugging around like a heavy stone. I folded my arms, focused on the view out the window.

He studied my ankle. "Well," he announced pragmatically, "I think you better come home with me to Pemberton."

"What?! No, no. That's all right." I added suspiciously, "Very kind though." I straightened up in my seat, still avoiding his gaze. "We've had an ordeal, that's all. And now we are en route to Vancouver. Whistler is just a stopover, anyhow. I mean, maybe just one night. But no. I can't."

"What's waiting for you in Vancouver?" He folded his arms across his chest and pressed a knuckle to his lip. A lot was waiting for us in Vancouver, but the birds in my head scattered. I couldn't get ahold of the answer.

"Um," I stalled. The pause was tense. Even Katie turned to observe it.

"You will be safe at my house. You will have a room to yourself. My assistant, Eloise, is there too," he announced. "You'll be fed, and you can recover until you're well enough to continue on your mysterious way." He spoke with complete self-assurance.

I fumed, "But surely there must be some way to speed the healing. You're a doctor," I challenged. "Surely you know."

"I *do* know. Rest is your medicine."

I felt like I was falling. I didn't want to go to Pemberton. Pemberton was barely out of the Cariboo. Not near as close to Vancouver as Whistler. Besides, Pemberton was a puny, stopover town created for gold miners and rosy-cheeked farmers. I shook my head involuntarily. I glanced at his hands. *A wedding ring. He's married.*

"It's such an imposition."

"No imposition at all. But ma'am—forgive me, I didn't catch your name—"

"It's Annabelle—" I caught myself from pronouncing my last name—Hugh's name.

"Annabelle." He said it slowly, considering its meaning and shape. "You can't walk on that ankle. Can't walk at all. If you don't believe me, try it. I've treated these before. And arms and elbows the same." I shifted uncomfortably under his unwavering gaze, as he gauged my reaction. "Your daughter can sleep on the cot beside you." He spoke to my ankle. "I can't let you go away on your own like this. You won't even be able to make it out of the train car."

I bit down on my tongue and settled my shoulders. Pressing my lips, I surrendered. "All right."

"All right," he echoed, smiling sadly for my sake. I felt like a reluctant loser handing over a trophy. "I'll leave you to your rest, then. Train arrives in Pemberton in about three and a half hours, but I'll be back before then to see if you need anything." *I won't need anything,* I wanted to snap. Rising, he looked back at me, hesitated, then slid the noisy door and disappeared into the next car.

Katie was fixated on the slow bending of the metal snake, hissing along the tracks. Children are acutely aware of their mothers' moods in some moments and oblivious in others. Outside, wide valleys gave way to mountains so steep, they crowded out the sky. I slumped on the seat, arms folded, my corrupted ankle perched on the stool. One by one, tears spilled down the hills of my cheeks. I patted them away with my shirt sleeve, grateful for the privacy of our seats.

34

I COULD NOT specifically recall stories or cowboy tales about Pemberton. Nor could I remember passing through it on my long trek up to the Cariboo years ago. Yet in my mind, it was a worn-out strip of shacks, overwhelmed with cow patties, rain, and mosquitoes. I was wrong on almost all accounts. As we rolled closer, rounding the bend from Mount Marriott, Lillooet Lake wove beneath the train bridges like blue milk. Towering mountains drove high up into a brilliant sapphire sky. Bright green pasture rolled out below a postcard-perfect town, dotted with pretty, painted, clapboard houses and rose gardens. As the train shushed and squealed into the station, the doctor returned to my side.

The beauty of the town did not entirely ease the embarrassment of being transported like a baby off the train by a grizzly-sized man. Without asking, he hefted me up into his arms and lumbered me down off the train steps. Katie had been given the task of lugging the doctor's satchel, which she straddled and dragged in the dirt as she waddled around with it. We moved through the train station, collecting gawks and snickers as we passed. The doctor seemed unperturbed. In fact, he beamed and his dark eyes twinkled. His clothes smelled of warm hay and cedar. *He's enjoying this*, I realized with annoyance. Everyone here thinks he's carrying home a second bride. This sense was confirmed when we stepped out the other side of the station and began dismounting the steps. A Native man outside fell right off his bench with laughter. The doctor beamed wider. *What will his wife say?* I cringed.

Heat radiated from my cheeks. I glared at the road ahead, resolved to salvage the last of my dignity. "This is silly," I said. "Put me down. I can walk."

"It's not much farther," he said, without missing a beat.

"I can walk. I'm sure I can walk. I'll just hold onto your elbow."

"Well, I could do that." He took in a big breath. "But I believe you'll feel quite awkward when you have to ask me to pick you back up. You can't make it on one leg. It defies the logistics of motion."

Good lord, he's sure of himself, I thought. I shut up and tried to perform a magic trick on myself. Namely, turning invisible.

Luckily, at least there were fewer onlookers on the street than in the station. A little girl about Katie's age pressed her nose between the white slats of a tall picket fence. Katie, now dragging the satchel off to one side, reflected a similar who-are-you stare back at her. An old prospector sitting on a fallen log watched with great fascination. Out of thoughtfulness for my humiliation, the doctor didn't look down at me. I turned away from the warmth of his breath on my cheek. He just strolled along as if carrying women through town was common. Same old song. Nothing new here.

A woman shaking a rug on her porch froze and gawked with consternation. *Probably a friend of his wife's*. I avoided her inquiring eyes. I couldn't remember the last time I'd seen a white woman. I thought about it a long while. Many months. The end of last summer, the O'Haras had passed by on their way to Cache Creek. Linda O'Hara had been lovely company. A brave woman. Heading all the way up to Cache Creek with a man she had married only two months before. In all likelihood, she hadn't seen another woman since me, either.

Pemberton was bigger than I expected. We walked past a couple of saloons, a butchery, a hardware store, and even a red-roofed cinema.

"That over there," he said, motioning with his chin to an ordinary white storefront, "is the grocery store." That marked the beginning and the end of his stint as the tour guide.

We arrived, at last, at a yard overgrown with wildflowers. The doctor turned up the pathway to the porch. White clap-boards ran up to a wood-shingled roof. A delicate cherry tree swung blossoms and red, feather-like leaves in the breeze. Troublingly, the home lacked a doctor's sign. But smoke rising from the chimney suggested that someone was cooking inside.

He hiked up the stairs with Katie thump-thumping the satch-el behind us. He swung open the door and set me down on a pale blue sofa. A sigh escaped me—as if I had done all the heavy lifting and not him. I smoothed my jeans and straightened my shirt, preparing to meet his wife, in what would surely be an awkward moment for us all. The doctor passed through the door to the kitchen and closed it behind him. Meanwhile, Katie flopped extravagantly belly first beside me, exclaiming about how far she traveled with the satchel.

The doctor burst back through the kitchen door, sailing right past me and into another room at the front of the house. A moment later, a small woman with a deep tan and pinned back hair zipped past us without so much as a glance in our direction. *Wife? Assistant?* I could hear the two of them talking in the front room, but couldn't discern the words. A moment later she reentered the room, with the doctor following behind.

"Eloise, this is Annabelle and—" He bent inquiringly to Katie, who lifted her face from the couch, revealing a scowl.

"Katie," I offered, touching her back warmly. Warmth is akin to politeness. And touch is one of a mother's many reminders.

"Annabelle, Katie, this is Eloise." The doctor motioned to his companion. He had a subtle, endearing manner about him, but she was tightly composed. Grady watched Eloise closely, gauging her reaction. For her part, she bore civility like a steel load. She had a straight nose that descended to a small, organized mouth attempting a smile. Her sleek black hair formed a snug bun at the nape of her neck. Her coffee-stain eyes were bright, but unreadable. She nodded at me. I stood to greet her, but the doctor motioned for me stay seated. With a blink, she turned and left for the kitchen, pushing the swinging door with sharp efficiency.

"Surely, we're a bit of a surprise for your wife," I consoled.

"Assistant," he corrected, eyes twinkling. "Assistant and housekeeper. But I'm afraid the observation still holds." He looked at the kitchen door. "She's also a friend," he added, voice tinged with apology. Whether he meant "friend" as in "friendship" or as in "mistress" wasn't my concern. I swept Katie's curls from her eyes.

As I lounged on the sofa like an Egyptian queen, Eloise decorated the mahogany table with a basket of bread and steaming bowls of beef and leek soup. She set down a pot of Red Rose and four pink teacups. Katie lifted herself from the couch and floated over to the table in a trance. She hovered, gawping from food to Eloise, wondering what magic tricks might dazzle next. The doctor—insisting I call him Grady—kindly brought me the washing bowl and towel, so I wouldn't have to hike to the washroom to scrub the road from my hands. He took my arm and wrapped his other about my waist, half carrying, half limping me to a seat. Luckily, I'd burned up all the blush in my cheeks, so I wasn't disturbed by the sensual heat of his hand.

The soup tasted of pure liberation. Steamy, rich broth filled nose and head before touching spoon, tongue, and belly. Patterns of crumbs fell from the crusty bread over the glistening broth. Although Eloise sat with a cool and aloof air, her food tasted like love. The steam from teacups and broth caught up in Katie's eyes and mine, too, dampening them with gratitude. The hungry are easy to please. By the time I finished, I felt revived anew, and whole again. I sat back and met the curious gazes of my companions.

"Well," I offered, "that was extraordinary." Katie stared at Eloise like she was an angel or apparition. Eloise's mouth curved into a tidy, satisfied smile.

More splendors awaited us because as soon as the dinner dispersed, a bath was drawn—a delicious warm bath all to myself. Since leaving the ranch, the only washing up had been over cold creeks or a tiny washbasin. But Grady asked Eloise to heat the water for "the trail-weary travelers," a task made easier with actual running water in the house. Katie went first. Then Eloise settled her into the bed in the front room.

As the light began seeping from a brilliant blue sky, I sank into a steaming tub of my own, wafts of white steam drifted up, like ghosts of the days past. Water lapped around my limbs like tiny bells. All the answers might be revealed through that exquisite music. *Peace. Rest.* The sun turned her lantern down to the smallest orange flame before I lifted myself up and rained down onto the bathroom mat. It was hard work not standing on my bent ankle. In truth, it throbbed with its own answers, the ones I didn't want to hear. But worry was a few yards off. Sometimes rabbits stand in the meadows only a few feet away from predators—foxes, coyotes, wolves. They give themselves moments of rest. Blinking slowly, chewing a nip of spring leaves. Danger is close, but this moment is for resting.

That night, I slept curled around Katie in the small bed. I dreamed that we slept in a cave, a warm and wide cave that Grady himself had dug out and prepared for us. He stood at the opening, both to keep us safe and because he didn't know how to approach. In that sleep, I opened my eyes and saw a bright red jewel—a garnet—on a necklace on Katie as she slept. And I covered it with my hand so no one would know its beauty. So deep was the sleep, so enchanting the dream, layers of weight lifted off me. Blankets of dread, fear, and doom.

In the morning, tall blue mountains fanned over the landscape and ignited the rising sun. Sparrows darted over wildflower fields. An orange cat trotted up the road. The quick, sturdy steps of Eloise through the house lent hope to my hungry belly. It was an entirely lovely stopping place. A respite before the journey began anew. I shook my head thinking how I tried to decline! I eased out of the bed without waking Katie and pivoted to the chair to dress. Inspecting my ankle, I was relieved that the purplish red swelling had lightened to red. Nonetheless, I shuffled like a wounded soldier to the bedroom door. Outside it, someone had left a walking cane perched against the wall.

A little later, as Katie and I relished Eloise's marmalade scones and tea, I asked the doctor how many days it might be before I could be back on the road.

He patted invisible crumbs on his mouth with a napkin. Tossing me a sideways look, he said, "Not days. Weeks."

"No," I uttered involuntarily. "I can't." I set the teacup down. "I have to be on my way. Back to Vancouver. I must go sooner. Surely there's a way."

Grady finished chewing, then turned to face me. "This is not optional," he said paternally. "You won't be able to walk on that ankle for three weeks at least. Probably four." He sipped his tea, letting his diagnosis steep. He continued, "You're welcome to stay here. I can set up the spare room upstairs for Katie and put the cot in there. You can't use it yourself because of the stairs. Or, if you prefer, Lucy Davis has a boarding house. But you'll have to pay there. Here it's free."

Eloise looked at me expectantly, like a poised cat. Katie examined me sideways, with suspicion. *Was I going to make her sleep in caves again after this?*

A fire smoldered inside me. I folded and refold the napkin. It wasn't Grady's fault, but I couldn't check the urge to blame him. What's more, the urge to run—to run and keep running—filled every cell of my body. Why? I didn't know.

And indeed, how could I let these strangers pamper and care for me for weeks? I could neither help nor afford to pay. What they were asking—that I lie around and let them cook for me, clean up after me, draw baths for me, doctor me—was inconceivable. *How could I allow such care? Impossible!*

So I cleverly countered with another impossibility. "Then I

will help. I will help out around the house. I will do whatever I can to earn my board."

"Impossible," he countered without hesitation. "You need to rest and be off your feet."

I retorted, "Then I will tend to the darning and sewing. I can certainly manage *that* while lying down."

"Eloise, do we have any sewing or darning needing done?"

"Certainly not," she huffed. "I don't let things pile up."

I would not give up. I could find a way to help. I just couldn't think of it yet. It would come to me. I glanced at Katie's hopeful face. She was as helpful as a kitten with a knitting ball. I could feel Grady studying me. I pretended not to care.

"You see," I urged, "it's just that it's quite impossible for me to stay. And to accept your generosity is altogether too much. It's not possible." I had survived so much on my own—Hugh's violence, the lewd driver reaching for me, cold fearful nights out in the open protecting Katie. But this—being served, cared for, waited upon—I couldn't bear it. Inexplicably, tears welled in my eyes.

He scratched his chin and nodded, saying simply, "It's the *only* thing possible."

35

A ND SO, I lost my second battle with him. That afternoon,
Grady clattered around upstairs in what sounded like a party
of creaking boards. When the room was ready for Katie, he took
her delicate princess hand in his and led her to inspect it. Of
course, I was forbidden to hike upstairs, but she reported that it
was "splendid"—a word she heard Grady use.

In the days that followed, the two spent many moments together. Grady loved to regale her with wild tales—probably half
true—of his adventures as a bush doctor. This is how I learned
that he treated as many animals as humans. Indeed, some of the
odder country folk in his tales seemed less tame than Chester. I
grew a little jealous of the closeness between the two. Katie began
trailing after him for stories whenever he was around. And he
genuinely relished her adoration. He treated her—not as a child—
but as a small, intelligent person who was unfamiliar with the
ways of humans.

He said at dinner, "Katie, if you eat your peas that loud, all I
can think about is your teeth. But I'd rather be thinking about my
food." She laughed, her opened mouth speckled with green.

As for me, I spent long hours reading, or watching the tapes-
try of raindrops on windows, glistening sunlight on the meadow
grass, and drag-net clouds scooping light off the land. I slept
enormously. Some of the warmest, deepest sleeps of my life.
Roosters, the scent of Eloise's baking, and Katie's squealing
giggles failed to stir me. Grady said my body was conserving

energy for healing. But the weariness went beyond tendon and bone, deep into the soul.

As grey dusk washed over one night, I considered how fate had led me to Grady's home. He was lovely, kind, and gentle, and utterly welcoming. But freedom was on the horizon. I was on my own now. No Hugh. No Harvey. No Mother even. *The way to be free is to grab freedom by the tail and cling on. Isn't it?* More important, I refused to be a burden to anyone. I looked forward to the time I would depend on no one. I craved solitude. As soon as I could, I would go my own way. *Vancouver grows closer every day*, I reminded myself.

While drinking tea in the living room or dining with everyone, I watched the mild manners of this bear-man, Grady. Something about his calmness and his size—or the combination of both—made him quite unlike other men I'd known. He even spoke differently. Men I'd known on the ranch seemed eager to insert their opinions. Even their silence often bore the weight of self-importance. But Grady reminded me of a chess player who lets the opponent make the first move. He stayed silent until the conversation started. He went wherever the player moved, with skill and subtlety, pretending to follow while being three steps ahead.

Eventually I began to wonder, where was his wife? An eligible and kindly doctor surely chose a lovely wife. Curiosity overtook the risk of rudeness. "Where is your wife?"

His face fell to his plate. His hand tightened slightly around a slice of bread. "No longer with us."

"Oh, I'm sorry." My teeth pressed down on my tongue. Had I learned that he was a widower days ago, I would have felt a lot more uneasy entering his home. But now, he seemed so safe, so trustworthy to me.

Eloise chimed in. "He wears the ring to honor her, but I've told him enough time has passed. Jeanine would want him to move on."

"We were only married three months," he added with a sigh.

"She was struck by a truck, you see. I—I wasn't there."

"You couldn't have saved her," Eloise reminded him.

"I know." More quietly, "Anyway, that was three years ago. I'll take the ring off one day." Silence ringed us as they honored her memory.

I tried to conjure the image of a woman who could match him. *Who is Jeanine?* But my imaginings didn't fit the shape of his heart. Probably he had changed. Her death had permanently altered the shape of his desire. Perhaps now he preferred vast expanses of solitude. Perhaps life gave him only one love token and he'd spent it. The neighbor of my childhood home was like that. All the dials were set to platonic. To the widows who lived nearby, the breezy high school girls, my own mother, he seemed pleasant. Friendly. If hidden fires burned in him, I couldn't identify them by studying his face. There was a man to be envied. Grady might be like that. The benevolent friend. Which would explain his relationship with Eloise.

That night as I lay in bed, I tried to untangle the riddle of his character. He was a studier of character, like me. In moments when I snuck a glance at him, he was watching me. Surely a helpful trait for a doctor. But I was used to being the only observer. I was disquieted imagining his mental notes about me. One time, I was cradling the cold cup of tea in my lap, staring out the window, dreaming of an imaginary room a hundred miles off. I turned away from the window and saw him peering at me over the top of the book he was supposedly reading. Feeling rather exposed, I hurried the teacup to my mouth.

Questioning what he thought of me, I did the first of the foolish things. One afternoon, Katie was searching for caterpillars outdoors, and Grady was upstairs in his office. I was lazing on my bed with the weight of a book on my chest. *What does Grady think about?* I tried to imagine. As if his thoughts were housed in a cabin, I pressed my face to the window, just the way I'd done with Harvey, the cowboys, the elderly Native man. I was becoming more adept at peering into another's soul. I could sneak about, gathering information, then tiptoe away. The elderly Native man was the only one who ever noticed.

And so I wondered, *What does Grady think about me?* But when I peered in—

—He turned and looked right at me.

I froze. My eyes refocused on the wallpaper before me. *Was I cracking up?*

No, I was sane.

He was seeing me thinking about him. Plain as day. Looking at me. Was I peering into his thoughts or was he peering into mine? His feelings rushed toward me. *He liked me. A lot.* And he didn't mind if I knew—as long as the news didn't make me run away. He feared overwhelming me. And there was something else, too. Something that held him back.

And yes, you do run, he seemed to say. *You run and you hide because you're afraid you might get exactly what you most want.* That was intolerable to him. He'd lost a wife. He wouldn't take a risk on an escape artist.

I pulled back into my own world. Wallpaper, heavy book, bluish window pane. Shallow breaths escaped me, as if even breathing might make me more visible. I felt pale. I'd been found out. Pulled in, pushed out. Questions and possibilities whirled. If I was losing my mind, why would it happen now? People shattered under stress all the time. They glued back the pieces and recovered. That could be me. But this notion—that two daydreamers could daydream together—that rewrote the world completely.

My hand flopped onto the book on my chest. Held upright before me, the charge of black patterns crossing the page looked meaningless. *How could mere letters on a page mean anything now? He liked me.* I waited for words to march across the page, revealing their order and purpose, but they were dead ants. *Why did he like me? He was no benevolent friend!* His feeling was deep. The churning of a powerful river that overthrows even large stones. Something powerful swelled inside me, too. The world spilled over with potential. My eyes squeezed tight and my heart thumped rapidly.

Dinner should have been punctuated with awkwardness, as if we'd happened upon each other naked. But he smiled gracefully, calmly passing serving dishes, and chewing with pleasure. He sensed my skittishness and worked to calm me. I glanced at my arm. His hand was not there. I must have imagined it resting reassuringly on mine. He turned away in moments, letting me watch him, study him. My body felt warm, as if I radiated beauty from an unknown jewel inside.

Excess curiosity is a flaw of mine. So later that night I did the second foolish thing. I peered in at his thoughts again, daring him to notice me. *Had he truly known my thoughts?* And there he was. We were like two people touching fingertips in the dark, listening to the sound of our own breathing. He expected me to bolt like a spooked foal the moment he came close to me. That's precisely what I was inclined to do. But he wasn't supposed to know. Truth be told, I wasn't sure why I felt frightened. Meanwhile he had probably already figured out the reason and what to do about it, too.

36

DAYS PASSED. MY ankle was a throbbing purpled nuisance if I stood too long, and a cold lump of flesh when I lay about. Katie made herself at home, blowing dandelion puffs and talking to passing cats, begging Eloise for berries, and Grady for stories. She visited me in my room from time to time, but generally delighted in having other company. She surprised me. At the ranch, she was underfoot, under my apron, or beside me on the bench, rarely out of view, except to play with Chester. *Had she grown up so much? Or was she now more at ease?* Apparently, she did not need me as much as I needed her.

I languished in boredom. Daydreams unfurl like nonstop picture shows when the body endures chores, but the reel gets stuck when the body is still and the mind bored. I wanted, I suppose, what I've always wanted. Distraction. *From what? What am I running from here? Guilt? Boredom? Worry?* My mind flitted over the question, uncommitted to an answer. I wanted to hide. I thought of the empty rooms at our house in London, the lonely kitchen sink on the ranch, and other places I hid. When I thought of the way Grady looked at me, the warmth of his fingers gently touching my ankle, the heat of his body near, I wanted to wrap the night's blanket around me, become invisible even to God.

I dissected him. Took him apart with tweezers and magnifying glass, searching for the source of my discomfort. His pausing glances. His square hands and long fingers. The way he told me staying was the only thing possible. His gentle, compelling, unbendable persuasion. Then I found it. He had a richness, an earthy darkness that lingered around me day and night. It wasn't Harvey's hot, flashing heat. Grady's feeling was steady and enduring. The warmth of the sun. Not a falling star. No one had ever had feelings for me like that. Perhaps it was a trap from which I could never be freed. Or else, *I'm afraid to truly be loved.* Embarrassed at my vanity, I tried to wipe all these thoughts away. But the truth stains. No amount of doubt or self-consciousness can erase it. You can live around it and pretend. You can snipe at it. *Foolishness!* Eventually, the only option is to accept.

But that is not what I did.

Over the next day, through meals and chit-chat and absent-minded mothering, I found myself daydreaming again. This time about the abandoned room in our old house in London. I was drawn back to that room again and again. Now, I craved its comforting privacy. Quiet, like a thick blanket wrapping around me. No one could reach me when I wrapped myself in that white emptiness. My fingers drew extravagant creatures in the dust on the floor. Moist fingertips against cool windowpanes. Dust motes swimming through light. He could not find me here. Loneliness was a familiar friend, my eternal mute companion, always waiting when everyone else was gone.

What did I look like when I daydreamed of that place? If he peered in on me now, perhaps he would see nothing. An empty cabin. Had I acted differently during the last few meals? When I pondered it, I didn't like what I found. Coldness. Unreachable. A pang of guilt moved through me. I hoped he wouldn't take it personally.

I'm only staying out of his way, I told myself. *I've pried into his inner thoughts too much already.* Besides, I'm probably imagining everything—these wordless exchanges, the heat of his feelings for me. Hugh was right to let me go. Marbles roll about in my head. And Harvey. He must have sensed it, too. So that settled it. Nothing more to worry about, except how not to bother anyone else ever again. I picked up the book that seemed to have been resting on my chest for three days and began to read in earnest.

After dinner, Grady asked to assess my swelling and rub a healing ointment on my ankle. I agreed. *He's just ordinary*, I reminded myself, not a man who could speak to me with only thoughts. And he wasn't in love with me. So it didn't matter what he did. And I felt only ordinary gratitude. I was just a little cuckoo in the head and no one needed reminding. *So I will be ordinary, too.* All this ordinariness fit like a too-tight sweater, but I wore it anyway.

Grady set a washbasin and tonic bottle on the floor next to the bed. *He'll say something regular like, you've been a little distant. I guess you're anxious to move on.* Even in the straitjacket world where I was a cuckoo, he surely would notice I'd been drifting. So this kind of comment would be expected. He set the chair close to the bed. I sat up, staring at the blur of my ankle, rehearsing how to answer. *Yes, I suppose I've been distracted by this silly ankle.* I lined my pockets with mundane little fibs.

He did not look at me or speak as he slowly lifted the foot and set the ankle in his hand. Cautiously, he turned the ankle this way and that. He was oddly quiet. Perhaps avoiding me. The silence was too thick.

"How is it looking?" I ventured.

"Fine." He addressed my ankle. "Swelling reduced. Interior rotation still loose." The mechanical words fell out of him, stiff and clinical.

"I'm not familiar with that medical term."

"It's fine. Won't need surgery. Healing as expected," he said flatly. He wiped a warm cloth over my foot and rubbed in an ointment from his tonic bottle. It smelled of camphor.

"Surgery! I hadn't even considered that."

"No need to now. It's uncommon, anyway."

Sensing that somehow I'd offended him, I thanked him again for his kind attention, his home, his time.

He sighed long and stared at my foot. Looking up at me, he pronounced tensely, "You're welcome, Annabelle. Of course." But his tone didn't make me feel welcome at all. He pushed the chair back, grabbed his supplies and exited the room without a goodbye.

My heart leapt like a fish. "Grady!" I called.

Footfalls paused then returned to the threshold of the room. He stood without a word.

I couldn't think of what to say. I shrank into the pillow. "I'm sorry."

"For what?" he asked. He wasn't sure he wanted to know.

"I'm sorry..." I tried on a few notions, "for taking up space in your house."

He stared at the doorframe with a carpenter's appraisal, like he was deciding whether to rip it out.

I tried again. "And I'm sorry I've been rather preoccupied for a few days." I pinched a flower on the quilt. "I've been rude. I don't know . . . I'm not sure what's wrong with me."

The stiffness of his face gave way to something softer. Sadder. He came back into the room and sat down on the bed. I shifted over before rolling into him. He placed his hand on my arm.

"Fear," he said.

"Pardon?"

"That's what's going on. You're frightened as a filly."

I stared down at the blankets. My throat swelled and heart pounded. He lingered, his gaze hovering just above the floorboards. Fear lived everywhere inside me, making tunnels in my chest, cooling my arms, tightening my face, blurring my vision. Fear wanted to call itself by another name. Propriety. Realism. Fear wanted to translate his boldness into danger. Unpredictability. And when those tricks weren't working, fear told me, *He doesn't really like you. He's confused. He wants the one thing all men want. He's a stranger.* Fear said, *He too will leave you.* Fear plucked words from my mouth so I couldn't speak.

But Grady squeezed my arm just a little, bringing me back.

He rose from the bed and—as though I were as delicate as a china doll—gently cupped the back of my head and pressed a warm kiss to my mouth. The heat of his breath lingered on my lips.

37

CHILDHOOD LOVE IS like sweet clover trembling in sunlight. First love is like lemon honey, tasted only once in a lifetime. A loving friendship is a solid oak tree. The French don't bother with the banality of the word *like*. You either love or you don't love. This feeling from Grady was a down comforter wrapping me with the scent of home. A home I never knew I had.

He was everywhere. That night when I lay listening to chirping crickets, he filled the room. His body had grown limitless and luminous. I brushed a strand of hair off my cheek, and his hand brushed it, too. *He cannot stop thinking about me.* I looked up at the stars, bright piercings in the blue-black night, and he followed my gaze. Something had shifted in him. The dam gate had been opened. His warmth washed over me, a ribboning river, swirling me under and over with delicious heat.

The breath caught in my chest. *Could I deny this?* It was not possible. Stones of doubt turned over and over in the rumbling current of his love, ground down to nothing. I was overwhelmed. He had feared overwhelming me, and he'd done it. There was nowhere to hide from his huge and engrossing devotion.

For the first time in a long time, perhaps the first time ever, I felt truly beautiful. I saw myself the way he saw me. Not a worn-down runaway, but some rare, undiscovered beauty. An exotic flower, growing deep in the shade of a jungle. A mesmerizing scent, a singular history. To be treasured in this way was very nearly unbearable. Very nearly, but *not quite.*

Now things would change. His kiss was written inside me like a signature, and I wore it with immense joy. There could be no going back to idle chit-chat over dinner—or so I thought.

Over breakfast the next morning, Grady exchanged intimate glances with me, but he also leaned away from me and avoided talking to me. Though I longed for him to spend time with me, he vanished upstairs to his office, still chewing the last bite of breakfast. At lunch, Eloise explained that he had gone out to do a house call. He didn't come home for dinner. I felt Eloise's intelligent eyes trained on my reaction. She witnessed my disappointment, much as I tried to mask it with enthusiastic eating.

That night, Katie stood holding Eloise's hand at the foot of the stairs, waiting for her kiss good night. Before I could bend down to give it to her, she exposed my secret.

"Why are you sad, Mummy?" She peered up with innocent curiosity.

"Katie," I admonished, "I'm not at all sad." My cheeks stretched into a reassuring smile. And I pressed a soft kiss on the top of her head.

She squinted at me as I pulled away. "Yes, you *are* sad," she diagnosed.

"No, no." I shook my head, but the tears were already springing to my eyes. I shook them away. "Not sad, just sleepy."

It's embarrassing when a three-and-a-half-year-old plainly sees adult lies. She turned and led Eloise up the stairs. I heard her say, "Mummy likes to pretend." I limped back to my room.

I stared up at the ceiling for answers. So, he had one taste, and that was enough. Or perhaps all he ever wanted was one kiss. Perhaps he *is* the benevolent friend after all. Or a sampler like Harvey. These answers were all wrong, and I knew it. Even as I lay in bed, feeling the pain of his absence, his warmth surrounded me. He felt he knew me—had always known me. There is a lake in the Kootenays that a casual swimmer can cross in fifteen minutes, but scientists have never been able to locate the bottom. I can imagine kicking my legs in that water, trying to sense the depth, an exhilarating and alarming sensation. Grady's feelings sent delicious goosebumps rippling over my skin.

Breakfast the next morning was dominated by Katie's chattering and punctuated by Grady's awkwardness. He spilled tea on his shirt, sending Eloise scrambling for baking soda. He smiled unconvincingly at me and left the table with crumbs still tumbling down his shirt.

"Off on more house rounds," he announced, rising to leave.

"You'll be home for lunch?" Eloise inquired.

"Not likely," he intoned with mock cheeriness.

She briskly wiped her mouth and rose to clear the table. I couldn't translate the tension between them, any more than I could trouble out why he was avoiding me. I passed the morning playing and chatting with Katie, but later that afternoon when she was distracted, I ventured through the swinging door to the kitchen. I wasn't entirely sure what to say to Eloise, but the words just came.

"I was wondering if you might have a job for a cripple."

"Not likely," she chuckled. She eyed me up and down, then added more sympathetically, "Well, perhaps. If you don't tell Grady I let you." She set me up with the chopping block and a basket of radishes to prepare for pickling. She hefted the canning pot onto the stove and set out her jars. The habit to drift off into daydream was strong. But I'd come here for answers I couldn't find by retreating into imagination.

So after some small talk about pickling techniques, I began, "I had a question for you about Grady."

"Oh?" She lowered a jar into the pot with tongs.

I paused. "You've known him a long time?"

"Yes," she said slowly, "longer than long. We grew up as siblings after his mother adopted me."

"Oh, goodness!" I replied. I stalled, waiting for courage.

"So, yes, I know everything about him." She knew exactly

what I was asking, but she wasn't going to help me there.

I shuffled in my chair. "It's that he keeps making excuses to leave, just when I thought we were getting closer." There. I'd done it now.

Her delicate mouth rose in a grin and she raised her eyebrows. Peering at the garden outside, she finally offered, "He's afraid you'll leave him. He doesn't trust you yet."

"Oh, but . . ." I stretched to make sense of it. "He's afraid I'll leave, so *he*'s leaving?"

"Don't look for sense inside the heart's organ." She leaned against the counter, with folded arms. Peering at me sideways. "He won't come round until you show him something real. Be honest with him. If you hide from him, you'll lose him."

I blinked in surprise. The thought of losing him sent panic rippling across my skin.

She continued, "Jeanine was very, very pretty and a sweet girl. 'Sunlit gossamer,' he called her." My teeth set together. "And she was charming and convivial. But something about her struck me as hollow. She went whatever way the breeze blows. His love roars like a river, but hers was light as cottonwood seed. He'll never admit it, but they were not a good match."

"Oh! It's heartbreak upon heartbreak, then." Sympathy poured into the spaces jealousy vacated.

"You resemble her a little," she assessed. "Not just your features, but your mannerisms. The first moment I laid eyes on you, I knew he would take to you."

"Oh?" I mumbled, distracting myself with the radishes.

"But just like her, seems the lightest breeze could pull you away."

"Oh." My cheeks heated up.

"I'm sure he senses that." She inspected the boiling jars and began pulling them out one at a time. "It's not commitment he's afraid of. It's his own deep devotion. The feeling that it'll never be matched."

I was embarrassed, ashamed, and grateful all at once. Eloise gave me much to contemplate. I took it out on the radishes. No radishes in history have been sliced to such precision. If I wanted him to come closer to me, I would have to prove that I would not drift away like dandelion puff. No easy feat. *Could I even prove it to myself?* My heart banged the walls of my chest.

38

A T DINNER THAT night, I did nothing. He ate and chatted casually to Eloise and Katie. I was sullen and contemplative, chewing in silence. *How does one go about proving durability and presence? And was I definitely sure I wanted to try?* After the meal, Eloise swept up the plates and launched into the kitchen. Grady tucked Katie into bed. I loomed on the sofa strategizing moodily. A while later, Grady descended the stairs. He was not tense, but he steered around me and kept his eyes elsewhere.

"Well," he said with a sigh. "I'll retire early tonight. Sleep well, Annabelle."

I opened my mouth to speak, but no words came out. Instead I found myself rising from the sofa, hobbling over to him, and resting a hand on his arm. "Goodnight, Grady," I whispered. Rising on tiptoe, I touched my lips to his cheek—a kiss. He smelled of pine and sunshine. I lingered for a moment in the scent, then turned toward my bedroom. It was a flash of brilliance. I'd struck him like lightning. I could feel his whole body tense with longing as I quietly shut the door behind me.

When my eyes opened to the morning light the next day, his mood was as clear to me as daylight. Desire pulled him toward me with the force of a whitewater river. He clung mightily to the edge, trying not to be pulled, trying to think of anything other than me. He tried to dwell on my flaws. He shuffled the papers at his desk, pretending to study patient notes. When he kissed me, his heart came alive. But when I kissed him, his body came alive.

The force of the two together was more than he could stand.

What's more, I saw specific flashes of his desire. Glimpses of the future. His breath on my neck. The scent of my hair in his nose. His hand over my heart pushing me back gently onto the bed. His thumb over the tip of my breast. His longing was pent up to bursting. He wanted me again and again and again. Shivers brushed over my skin.

Breakfast that morning was quick and curt, the heat between us palpable enough to bottle and sell to the lonely. We said hardly a word. Eloise stayed contained in her own private thoughts, likely full of premonition and knowing. Sleepy Katie dwelled on each bite of oatmeal like it was a separate creature requiring welcome.

Later that day, I went outside to sit on the steps in the sunshine. Katie squatted at the edge of the yard, popping the heads off dandelions. When Grady appeared on the threshold, satchel in hand, he stepped gingerly around me, as if he might be swept up into my current if he came too close. I rose to see him off.

"Have some house calls to make," he excused himself.

"Of course," I replied. As he started down the path, I added, "Fear."

"Pardon me?" He turned to look at me—meeting my eyes for the first time in days.

"It seems you're paying house calls to Fear," I suggested, with a hint of a smile.

In two strides he was in front of me, cupping my head and pulling my lips toward him. His kiss, hard and soft. Aching and tender. Wanting. When he pulled away, I gasped from the intensity of it. He held my gaze. And once again, it was I who was afraid—I who wanted to run and keep running, toward him and away. But I held his gaze, even as my eyes glistened with the profundity of the moment. I let him see the spill of my emotions.

He nodded once. "Hmm." He turned and walked out into the day.

In the corner of my eye, I could see Katie, wide-eyed and

gaping. *Please, please don't ask me anything.* And she didn't. Not that day.

The next morning, I snuck outside just after waking. I wanted to sit in the early morning light. Something about the clarity of dawn. Katie joined me and we played family with bits of stick. I needed distraction and an outlet for my joy and fear.

"You're this one." She showed me the slender, barkless one. "Because it's pretty. And I am this one." She held up a chunk of twig barely the length of her thumb. "Because it's little." The May sun pierced the mountain ridges. A cherry tree was bursting with sharp burgundy leaves. Blue dogwood flowers carpeted the ground beneath it. Dandelions and lupins dotted the yard. A giddy contentment glowed inside me. Maybe I could stop running after all. What was it Grady had said? *You're afraid you'll get exactly what you want most?* What I wanted most was him. His love. It was true that it frightened and overwhelmed me. But in the middle of all that danger was a safety I'd never known. All those daydreams, yet I never imagined I'd find a man like him. Our souls were twins.

What was Grady thinking right now? And like a touch on the shoulder, I knew. He was thinking about me dressed in white. I could feel him standing in his office in the window above us and watching.

Katie tilted her head and smiled. "Why do you look away when we're playing? Are you playing a thinking game?"

"Well, sort of." In the slanted light, her blue eyes were deep lakes. "I suppose it is a thinking game."

"I'm going to try it, too." She clutched the stick people in her hand and furrowed her brow, concentrating. She was quiet for so long, I wondered if she might fall asleep standing. *Daydreaming of lollipops and ponies, most likely.*

"Mummy," the words were wise and distant, "are you and Grady going to be married now? Like you used to be with Papa?"

"Um." I brushed the hair from my forehead. "Why would you ask such a question?"

"Because I asked Grady and he said, 'I hope so.'"

"Oh?" I froze, unable to look behind me to the house.

"He said you're perfect for him. He said he always knows how you're feeling even when he can't talk to you." She turned to stare at me, surely hoping my eyes would reveal what my mouth would not.

"I don't know." I blushed, heat filling my body.

She was staring harder, but I looked away. The wind lifted a veil of dust from the road, danced with it and laid it back down. A robin landed on the fence post and called for its mate.

"Would you like it if I did?" I dared.

"He *is* a very nice man," she clarified with great authority. "And Eloise's biscuits are even better than yours. But," she added with gravity, "he doesn't have a dog."

I smiled. Then, mustering my courage, I turned and looked up at his office window. Katie looked too and started waving at him.

"Perhaps," I ran my hands over my knees, "he'll get one."

"Yes, perhaps," she seconded. "A white one! And I can call him Pony!" I laughed. She lay the stick figures on a bed of grass.

So I hadn't gone mad after all. Insanity hadn't hauled me down its narrow tunnel for a swift meal. I wasn't mangled inside by some internal beast. I had found a daydreamer, someone so different, but so very much like me. Someone who found me even when I was so carefully hidden. Steam rose from the meadows. A barn owl sailed silently overhead on its way home. The world was immense and full of unexpected gifts. I closed my eyes in gratitude.

The door opened behind me. A knowing smile rose on Grady's face. His warm arm wrapped my shoulder. Morning sunlight shimmered across the world.

Will you stay, Annabelle? Will you promise now to stay?

Yes, I told him. *We'll stay.*

Acknowledgements

This book would not be possible without the lively storytelling of my grandmother, Barbara Buckley. Although she does not figure as a character within the novel, her accounts of cooking, laundry, conversation, weather, teaching, and cowboys in the Cariboo during the Depression era form the foundation of this book. Part of the research for this novel began as an interview with her for a CBC Radio documentary for North by Northwest with Sheryl MacKay. In the documentary, my grandmother described at length her challenges as an isolated, white woman, raising children on a ranch at Soda Creek with my grandfather. I am deeply grateful to her for entrusting me with her tales of the hard work, loneliness, and longing while she raised my mother and uncle.

This novel began as part of a research project at the University of British Columbia and was funded by a generous grant from the Social Sciences and Humanities Research Council (SSHRC). Laura Moss, Vin Nardizzi, and especially Laurie Ricou guided the initial excerpt of this work which aimed to examine the nature of Canadian love stories in fiction. I am also grateful for the generous support of my father, Michael Kuchta, during those lean years at graduate school.

A novel of this kind walks a fine line between historical fact and narrative fiction. My mother, Sheila Kuchta, patiently answered dozens of my odd inquiries and filled in many historical blanks. Rex Moon toured me around present-day Williams Lake painting a captivating picture of the town centre, cattle holding pens, cowboys, and other local characters. The kind owners at Spring Lake Ranch answered many questions and allowed me to interview the cowboys they employed. A big thank you to the cowboys for encouraging me to join them in some of their tasks. It's not every day that a writer witnesses the birth of twin calves, a mother cow charging a cowboy, or the rescue and bottle feeding of a starving calf!

The writing of this novel took place over many years and in many locations. A great many chapters of this book were written in the quiet, comfortable home offered to me by my friends and colleagues at Kushiro Public University, Japan. Additional chapters emerged while cat-sitting for my friend, Redwood, off-grid in California. And others came into being in Berlin where colleague, Stan Persky, loaned me an apartment suite. I also wrote under the shade of fir trees, next to the trickling sounds of BC hot springs, in a cabin at the edge of Lillooet Lake. As Laurie Ricou helped me discover, stories are told—not just by people—but by plants, animals, weather, and landscapes. I've done my best to listen and translate voices of the Fraser River by Soda Creek, Cariboo Mountains, black bears, moonlight, clouds, and chickadees.

Key individuals offered advice and suggestions in the writing of this book. I'm grateful to readers of my early chapters: Heidi Mackay and Petrice Brett, and also Delia Brett, who has offered a lifetime of artistic inspiration (and set the bar impossibly high for the rest of us). Alexandra Boyer was the first to read the book cover to cover and offered important suggestions and thoughtful encouragement. Additionally, my publisher, Leila Monaghan, offered keen insight on a multitude of issues, and undoubtedly shaped the writing into a stronger book.

I recognize that problems can arise when a white woman (me) writes about historical Indigenous experiences. The solution, however, is not to erase those experiences from historical novels altogether. Thus, I'm deeply grateful for the gentle guidance of Justin Wilson on this matter. I am also deeply grateful for

Rasunah Marsden, Elder of Mississaugas of Scugog Island First Nation, for providing feedback on the chapters addressing residential schools and English language use.

Stan Rushworth, Cherokee, elder, and lifelong mentor, taught me the most important lessons I've ever learned about how to be a writer—and how to be a human walking upon this living Earth. Leading by example, he showed me how to write from a deeper place, and how to live from there as well. I struggle to express my gratitude.

Finally, I extend wholehearted appreciation for my children, Maxwell and Celia, who never doubted that writing a novel was something I could and *should* do—despite the rather chaotic life I provided for them as a low-income, single parent. Their patience, love, and faith in me has been one of the most enduring forces in my life.

Estella Kuchta

Estella Kuchta is a writer, researcher, and postsecondary instructor in Vancouver, Canada. She has worked as an intern for CBC Radio, an editor for Susila Dharma International, and a research assistant for best-selling author Dr. Gabor Mate. Her creative writing and journalism projects have been published, aired, and broadcast in newspapers and literary magazines, and on radio and TV in Canada and the United States. She earned a BFA in Creative Writing and MA in Literature from the University of British Columbia where she won several awards for writing. For two years, she lived on an isolated mountaintop with no electricity while raising her infant son.

Elm Books

Elm Books is a small independent publisher based in Laramie, Wyoming. We focus on strikingly original novels, and fresh new short story anthologies including mystery, romance and science fiction collections, and diverse children's books. All our books can be found at elm-books.com and at major booksellers.

Novels

Figures on a Beach by Kirk VanDyke
Duchess of the Shallows by Neil McGarry and Daniel Ravipinto

Anthologies

Death Series Mysteries edited by Jess Faraday
Death on a Cold Night
Death and the Detective
Undeath and the Detective
Death and a Cup of Tea
Death in the Age of Steam
Death by Cupcake (Forthcoming)

Romance edited by M.M. Ardagna, Lily Callahan, and Jess Faraday
Christmas is for Bad Girls
Fae Love

Science Fiction edited by Leonie Skye
Dark Space
Strange Flight

Children's Books

Superbeetle by S. Michele Chen, illustrated by Leda Chung
The Illustrated Phonics Booklet by E. Jennifer Monaghan, illustrated by Virginia Cantarella
Jamal and the Latrodectus Temple by Lee Mullins, illustrated by Lottie Patterson (Forthcoming)

CPSIA information can be obtained
at www.ICGtesting.com
Printed in the USA
LVHW041923071120
671047LV00004B/510